Dear Little Black

Thanks for picking up this Little Black Dress book, one of the great new titles from our series of fun, page-turning romance novels. Lucky you — you're about to have a fantastic romantic read that we know you won't be able to put down!

Why don't you make your Little Black Dress experience even better by logging on to

### www.littleblackdressbooks.com

where you can:

- ♥ Enter our **monthly competitions** to win **gorgeous** prizes
- ♥ Get **hot-off-the-press** news about our latest titles
- ♥ Read **exclusive** preview chapters both from your **favourite** authors and from brilliant new writing talent
- ♥ Buy **up-and-coming** books online
- ♥ Sign up for an essential slice of romance via our **fortnightly email** newsletter

We love nothing more than to curl up and indulge in an addictive romance, and so we're delighted to welcome you into the Little Black Dress club!

With love from,

The *little black dress* team

Five interesting things about A. M. Goldsher:

1. If you laid all of A. M. Goldsher's CDs on the ground in one single row, it would run from the Tower of London to somewhere around Windsor Castle.

2. Favorite food: sushi. Favorite dessert: sushi. Favorite snack: sushi. Favorite position: sushi.

3. According to the author's mother, A. M. began reading aloud at the age of two. First book? *Valley of the Dolls*.

4. Goldsher hasn't paid for a haircut since 1995.

5. A former sportswriter, the author has seen far too many professional basketball players wearing not nearly enough clothes.

*Also by A. M. Goldsher*

The True Naomi Story

# Reality Check

## A. M. Goldsher

little
black
dress

First published in 2008
by LITTLE BLACK DRESS
An imprint of HEADLINE PUBLISHING GROUP

A LITTLE BLACK DRESS paperback

1

ISBN 978 0 7553 3994 5

Typeset in Transit511BT by Avon DataSet Ltd,
Bidford-on-Avon, Warwickshire

Printed and bound in Great Britain by
Clays Ltd, St Ives plc

Headline's policy is to use papers that are natural, renewable and
recyclable products and made from wood grown in sustainable forests.
The logging and manufacturing processes are expected to conform to the
environmental regulations of the country of origin.

HEADLINE PUBLISHING GROUP
An Hachette Livre UK Company
338 Euston Road
London NW1 3BH

www.littleblackdressbooks.com
www.headline.co.uk

# Cast of Characters,
## in order of appearance

**JENN BRADFORD** Singer/songwriter/pianist/sex kitten/ classy broad. Leader of the almost famous band Jenn Bradford & The JB's. Would be more than almost famous if she listened to her manager and focused less on performing esoteric jazz songs and more on writing accessible, hook-laden, anthemic rock tunes. Once scored the number ten spot on the list of *People* magazine's 50 Most Beautiful People. Owns over two hundred pairs of vintage André Courrèges go-go boots, twenty-plus of which she brings with her whenever The JB's hit the road. Used to live in an ostentatious mansion in Brooklyn, New York, but for reasons that will soon become evident, was forced to downsize before realizing her dream of being on *MTV Cribs*. No matter what the tabloids say, her boobs are real, and her fire-engine red hair is 100 per cent natural. Okay, 99 per cent. Okay, 98 per cent. Maybe 97 per cent. But The Girls, they're totally 100 per cent, honest-to-goodness genuine. So there.

**ZACH BINGHAM** Handsome, cynical, pale, under-nourished, underpaid freelance journalist whose work has been seen in the pages of *Spin*, *Rolling Stone*, *Paper* magazine, *Alternative Press*, *NME* and *Mojo*. Known to some as 'Indie Boy'. Known to others as 'Weenie Boy'. Wants to make babies with Jenn.

**MASUHARA JONES** a.k.a. **MASU** Jenn's half-Asian/half-African-American manager. Works too hard. Eats nothing but junk food, and always forgets to take her vitamins. Hates jazz. Very short, very cute, very tattooed, very pierced, sometimes violent, and has no edit button. Owns as many Puma sneakers as Jenn does Courrèges boots. Has a thing for tall, buffed black guys with dreadlocks that go down to their butts, even if they're commitmentphobic manchildren.

**T.J. STEWART** A tall, buffed black guy with dreadlocks that go down to his butt. Commitmentphobic manchild. The JB's current bassist, and the best string-plucker that Jenn's ever played with. Hooks up with Masu on a regular basis, but won't tell anybody about their dalliance or officially call Masu his girlfriend. Jenn loves having him around despite the fact that his first cousin is a three-timing chump.

**BILLIE HOLIDAY'S GHOST** Gardenia-wearing guardian of all that is musical. Has Jenn's back, big time.

**PORTER ELLIS** Jenn's stuffy new neighbor. Founder and

former CEO, COO and CFO of *Billionaire.com*. Hates rock music. Loves jazz. Likes classical. Despises country. Very white. Divorced four times, and is fed up with dating. Periodically considers taking a vow of chastity, or just chopping 'it' off altogether. Financially set for life – for several lives, as a matter of fact – and he's bored, bored, bored. Some would say he's boring, boring, boring. Others would say he has potential.

**KEVIN MCALLISTER** T.J.'s first cousin. The JB's drummer and periodic background singer. Despite the fact that he lays down lovely vocal harmonies, he can't sing lead, and should never be allowed near a microphone unaccompanied. Jenn's former long-term, live-in boyfriend. Their break-up was ugly. Really ugly. And yet she still uses him as her percussionist both in the studio and on the road. Welcome to Awkwardsville, population: two.

**NAOMI BRAVER** Former frontwoman of the platinum-selling, Grammy-winning, alterna-chick-pseudo-emo band known simply as Naomi. Jenn's former musical cohort and eternal BFF. Moved to California after her fourth album stopped selling to pursue a career in acting which, despite massive amounts of hard work, excellent professional representation and legitimate talent, is not going well. In a deeply committed relationship with Jenn's younger brother, Travis. Misses living with Jenn and living in Brooklyn, but her muse told her to go to the West Coast and tear up the silver screen, so what're you gonna do?

# SPIN MAGAZINE

## December, 2008

**Record Review**

### JENN BRADFORD & THE JB'S
### *REALITY CHECK*
### Éclat Records

### by Zach Bingham

Here are three things you need to know about the number three:

The third time's a charm.

If there are three coins in a fountain, they're probably all seeking happiness.

And after listening to Jenn Bradford's third record, *Reality Check*, three times, I was forced to accept the fact that it's one-third less interesting than its two predecessors.

You can't pin the blame for the album's tepidness on Bradford's voice which, over the past three years, has improved considerably. Her crooning on her self-titled debut was scratchy and tentative, but that worked in her favor, as it made the entire album feel overtly honest and unpretentiously organic. She came into her own vocally on her remarkable sophomore set, *Guess Who Came at Dinner*, a virtuoso performance in which Bradford flaunted pipes as potent as those of her former collaborator, Naomi Braver.

If you have to point the finger for the record's unevenness anywhere, point it at Bradford's compositions. The tunes on *Reality Check* can be broken up into three categories:

- The Rockin' Stuff
- The Folkie Stuff
- The Jazzy Stuff

*Continued on page 51*

**JENN BRADFORD** I almost didn't continue to page 51, but I *had* to, because I'm a musician, and us musicians are hardwired to continue to page 51, even when we know there's a pretty good chance that what we read there is gonna make us want to grab an axe and chop our pianos into firewood.

*Continued from page 47*

The rockin' stuff is Bradford's meat and potatoes. On the title track, for example, she taps into her inner Chrissie Hynde, and comes up with a new take on New Wave that, had she banged out twelve other cuts like this, would have made *Reality Check* three times as good. The folk-oriented material doesn't work as well as the harder-edged tunes, but it's still pleasant, most notably the acoustic-piano-driven ballad 'Water' and the sweet vocal/bass duo 'Build Me Up'.

And then there's the jazzy stuff.

You watch Jenn Bradford in concert, beating the crap out of her keyboard, red mane flying, body contorting into a myriad of pretzel-like positions, and you might think, 'Okay, this chick wants to be Tori Amos when she grows up'. You'd be wrong. Jenn Bradford wants to be Ella Fitzgerald. Jenn Bradford wants to be Sarah Vaughan. Jenn Bradford wants to be Billie Holiday.

Well, Jenn Bradford is Jenn Bradford, and she should stick to being Jenn Bradford. If she wants to be a jazz singer, be a jazz singer. If she wants to be a rock goddess, be a rock goddess.

Artistic conviction is totally sexy. Fence-straddling totally isn't.

*Continued on page 56*

**JENN BRADFORD** Enough is enough. Page 56 can bite me.

Zach Bingham and I met for the first time at the beginning of September 2007, and from day two, he was all about feeling up my bare legs and looking down my shirt. But not from day one. On day one, he was a perfect gentleman, a complete professional, the cute writer guy from *Spin* who came to the recording studio at my house in Brooklyn to interview me about my third album, *Reality Check*. And I have to admit, he did a great job. He gives good interview. He conversed rather than grilled. He didn't ask the usual canned questions like, 'Why aren't you and Naomi playing together any more?' or 'Who are your biggest influences?' or 'How are you gonna follow up *Guess Who Came at Dinner*?' or 'Are those real?'

No, Zach was smoother than that. Somebody told him I was a foodie – probably my manager, Masu Jones, and he asked me about the connection between eating and music. He asked me how I believed the piano fits into a three-piece pop/rock rhythm section. He asked me why I despise synthesizers and sampling so much. He asked me if the thirty-nine Beanie Babies on my mixing board traveled with me to other studios.

Zach, he was being an impartial, thoughtful journalist. Me, I was being a flirty-pinup girl.

Flirty-pinup used to sometimes be my default mode when I'd get around cute writer boys. Flirty-pinup combined with skimpy clothes. How lame is that? I mean, it was likely these guys would've written nice things about me whether I touched their forearms, or crossed my legs in the exact right position, or stared deep down into their eyes, or did any of the other stupid tricks that constitute superficial flirting. It's not like I needed to get these journalists on my side and try to influence what they wrote about me; I'm a classy broad, and nobody was out to get me. But Zach immediately saw through all my shit. The fifth question he asked me was, 'Is your sex-kitten image contrived, or do you do this Marilyn Monroe thing when you're offstage or away from the press?'

Busted.

For the rest of that day, Zach was treated to the anti-flirty Jenn Bradford which, it turned out, he liked. How did I know? Well, that first day he was dressed to *not* impress: a ratty White Stripes T-shirt, baggy, faded shorts that probably came straight from the Old Navy clearance bin – not that I have problems with Old Navy, I'm actually a big fan, I'm just drawing you a picture – and scuffed Teva flip-flops. When he came back the following day for part two of our little *mano a mano*, he was decked out in a well-worn, but slick vintage leather jacket, jeans with strategic holes situated just below the knees, a pair of clunky Steve Maddens, and a whole bunch of product in his hair. On day one, he looked *cool*. On day two, he looked *hot*. I think I looked pretty okay on day two also, what with my tight pink Stevie Wonder middy T-shirt, and my short blue denim skirt, and an old pair of multi-colored platform flip-flops. My flirty-pinup moves on day two were completely natural and completely unconscious.

We sat down on the red leather sofa in my studio. That afternoon, Zach was the one doing the eye-gazing and forearm touching, which was disconcerting, because he was making me tingle, and it had been a good eight months since I last tingled, because my boyfriend Kevin and I were in a bit of a, shall we say, slump, meaning that on the rare occasions we made love, there was a lot of going through the motions. But I was a true-blue partner, and wouldn't dream of straying from Kevin, no matter how snoozy things were.

That might not have been the case back in the day, and that's back in the day as in when I was in high school. Oh, I suppose just after high school, too.

This isn't to say I was an easy lay when I was in my teens, but I've always liked touching, and being touched. Actually, in my teens, I was a pretty tactile chick, even more so than I am now, and I liked having all five senses messed with: hearing Luther Vandross, touching my man's smooth back, tasting the perfect tuna tartare, smelling vanilla of any shape or size, seeing a young girl smile at me during one of my shows. But touch and sound were the two biggies. High school for me was all about music and boys, music and boys, music and boys.

I sometimes still can't believe that the city of Brooklyn and the state of New York gave me a diploma, because I *never* did homework. Literally. If I spent eight hours studying over those four years, I'd be surprised. I'm talking eight hours *total*. Between songwriting, and rehearsing, and staying out until four in the morning, and being imprisoned in my bedroom for staying out until four in the morning, who had time to study?

Actually, my eternal best friend Naomi Braver had

time. She was a study nerd. I did what I could to de-nerd her, but she didn't get cool until we actually graduated – her at the top of the class with honors, me at the bottom of the class with shame – and then moved into our infamous one-bedroom box in the East Village. I say 'infamous' because that's where we came up with most of the tunes that made her a rock star, and me a rock star by proximity. This was also around the time she finally started believing what I told her at least once a day – that she wasn't a skinny little runt, that she was a hottie, that she was a killer singer, and that one day, she and I would rule the world.

For a while, we did. Rule the world, that is. We paid our dues, gigging at a café in Manhattan called Beaned for a few years, then at a mid-sized club called Upper East, then our little group got signed by Éclat Records. The label head Mitch Busey made our band change its name from 'I.Q.' to 'Naomi' in order to capitalize on what Mitch thought was Naomi's potential star power, which I had no problem with . . . at first. It took me a good solid eight months before I got all petty, and stupid, and jealous about the whole thing. I'll tell you about my pettiness, and stupidity, and jealousy later. I think I have to work my way up to that.

So almost immediately after our first single 'And Then' came out and blew up, things got big. Big sales. Big concerts. Big money. Big catfights. A big blowout. A big reunion. A big second album. It was all big. At times too big for me, frankly, but at the same time, too confining. Confining artistically, that is. I loved hearing

Naomi sing my songs, but after our second album together ran its course, I split. It wasn't like a Beatles type of break-up. No lawsuits. No arguments. Just love. The day I dropped the bombshell – the day I said to her, 'It's time for me to leave the nest, honey' – we shared approximately 216 bottles of wine, and then cried and hugged for about nineteen straight hours. Or something like that.

The funny thing was that we were probably even closer with each other after we stopped playing together regularly. She produced my first album, I produced her third and played on the fourth, and we showed up in each other's videos. My records were selling well – not as well as Naomi's, but I would never in a million years think of Nay as competition, so that was totally cool – and I had a killer boyfriend, and all the Beanie Babies I could eat. Good times. Even though we were on separate musical paths, Nay couldn't have been happier for me. Hells, *I* couldn't have been happier for me.

But I digress. The first day with Zach was all talk. The second day, when I played him *Reality Check*, it was all listening and touching. High school revisited.

Zach was the first person outside of my inner circle who got to hear the record from start to finish. He sat through the whole thing without saying a word. He stared at the speakers the whole time, which gave me plenty of opportunity to stare at his neck. And his angular face. And his long fingers. But mostly his neck. And he kept listening to the record. Three times through. It was kinda tense. Or maybe *in*tense.

After what seemed like six hours, the music finally stopped. A good two minutes after 'The Ballad of Heat' closed the album, he put his hand on my knee – and remember I was wearing that denim skirt, so my knees were bare – and said, 'You must be so proud of this record, Jenn. It's probably what you've been working toward for your entire life. I would think that to you, this is career-making stuff.' He moved his hand an inch up on my thigh, then an inch down to my shin, then two inches up on my thigh, then two inches down on my shin, all very slowly, all very hotly. I was getting big-time squirmy, and was a millisecond away from thinking about maybe possibly considering doing *something* to him – remember, it'd been a long time since I tingled – when my cell vibrated. It was Naomi.

I backhanded Zach's hand off of my leg, pressed the talk button, and said hey. Naomi asked, 'Whatcha doin'?'

I said, 'I'm playing *Reality Check* for a nice young man from *Spin*.'

Zach said, 'I'm not that nice.' I covered the phone's mouthpiece and told him to zip it.

Naomi said, 'Does he like it?'

I got up, told Zach I'd be right back, then went into the hallway. 'I can't tell if he likes the record, but he *really* likes me.' She didn't say anything. Then I said, 'He's kind of a hottie. I bet you'd like him. He's totally your type.' Actually, she probably *wouldn't* like him, and he was totally *not* her type. Naomi isn't into underfed indie rock nerds. She's into underfed movie nerds e.g. the love of her life a.k.a. my brother Travis.

Naomi said, 'No. No. No no no no no.'

I said, 'No, what?'

She said, 'Didn't you decide you weren't gonna be all flirty-pinup around writers any more?' I told her I had no recollection of saying such a thing. She said, 'Four years ago? Glenn Whatshisface? *LA Weekly?* After our Roxy gig?'

Oh. That. Not one of this classy broad's classier moments. Horrible sex for me and Mr Whatshisface. Horrible concert review for Naomi. Naomi was right. I have a history. And not only with writers. No, I'm not gonna tell you how many guys I've slept with. I'm not embarrassed about it or anything, but I don't want everybody who picks up this book to think I'm a total slut. A *partial* slut, sure, but not a *total* one. Plus it's likely my parents will read this, and yes, they're well aware that I am, as they've put it 'liberated' – although I'm pretty sure that 'liberated' is my mother's nice way of saying 'slutty' – but I think a concrete number would freak them out.

Naomi and I blabbed for a couple more minutes, then after we hung up, I zipped up to my bedroom and grabbed an old, baggy black, hole-filled, paint-splattered Adidas hoodie that hung down past my knees. I figured the looser and uglier my clothes were, the less cute I'd be, and the less cute I was, the easier it would be to send Zach on his merry way, which was most definitely the prudent thing to do.

While I was gone, Zach had made himself at home. He'd taken off his leather jacket and his shoes, and was spread out on the couch, a mellow grin on his face, looking like he owned the joint. I said, 'Um, comfy?'

He straightened up. 'I don't know what it is about this place, but it's real easy to get comfy.'

Looking at him being all hip and happening, I admitted to myself that if I was Kevin-less, I likely would've gotten comfy with him. Even though those indie rock boys – those pale, gaunt, funky boys – generally weren't my first choice, Zach could've swayed me. Maybe it was because he had a brain. Maybe we just clicked. Maybe it was his neck.

But maybe it was a bad idea to even entertain that kind of thinking. No, *definitely* it was a bad idea. See, he was writing about my third album, and by the time you get to your third album, you shouldn't be doing *any* flirting with writers, whether or not you're spoken for. The first album, sure. The second album, maybe. But by the third one, you should act like a grown-up. At least a little bit.

I told him in a very professional sort of way that he could ask me three more questions, then I had to take a phone meeting. He caught my tone, sat up even straighter and kicked back into journalist mode. Like I said, he's a smarty pants. He asked his three more questions, then handed me his business card and said, 'Give me a buzz if you have something you'd like to add to the story,' then he left.

ZACH BINGHAM It's exactly like I say in the *Spin* article. The first time through *Reality Check*, I dig it a lot. Second time, I dig it less. After the third time, I decide I have zero desire to hear it ever again. I end up selling the copy that Éclat sent me at one of the used record stores on St

Mark's Place, along with another fifty promo CDs I have zero urge to keep. That's a regular thing for me, selling promo CDs on St Mark's. Hey, a guy's gotta eat.

I'd like to get it on the record that my two-and-a-half star review has nothing to do with Jenn not going for my totally lame, awkward, uninvited advances. I cringe at the thought that I caressed Jenn Bradford's leg on the second day I met her. Uncool and unprofessional. Not to mention embarrassing. Never behaved like that with an interview subject before. Haven't done it since. Wait, I take that back, there was one other time. I'm sure Jenn told you about it. She hasn't? Hunh. Well, I guarantee you'll find out about it later.

Even people who despise me and my writing – and there were plenty of them, even at that point, believe me, although it got worse later – will acknowledge that when it comes to criticism, constructive or otherwise, I'm a professional. Extra-musical factors do not impact my reviews or features, ever. For example, I gave one of Madonna's recent records two-and-a-half stars, which is the same thing I would have given it even if we'd hooked up. Not that Madonna would hook up with me, but you get what I'm saying.

Anyhow, the *Spin* with my review hits the stands about three months after my meeting with Jenn, and I assume that when she reads it, she'll hate me, and I don't consider contacting her, because why would she wanna talk to me after I trashed her record? I assume I'll never speak with Jenn Bradford again – which is unfortunate, because the fact of the matter is, after the interview, I developed a major thing for her, and word on the street is that she's single again. It's totally unoriginal of me to have a crush on Jenn Bradford, but whatever.

Luckily for me – and somewhat shockingly – I assumed wrong about her not contacting me. She calls me a couple days after the magazine comes out and says, 'Nice review, numb nuts. But shouldn't you have given the album three stars for symmetry's sake?'

Funny girl. Smart girl. You see why I want to make babies with her?

**JENN BRADFORD** I didn't think about Zach much until Masu sent me the issue of *Spin* with his article – an article which, by the way, didn't include a single quote from our two-day interview session. I'm just saying.

I called him immediately after I read his piece and yelled at him for about ten minutes. After I finally ran out of gas, he asked me to meet him for dinner that night. It wasn't a date. It was just dinner.

**ZACH BINGHAM** After she calls me 'numb nuts', she yells at me for about ten minutes, then she asks me out on a date. It's not just dinner. It's a date.

**JENN BRADFORD** For our dinner-that-wasn't-really-a-date – which, by the way, was the first time I'd been out with a boy since The Kevin Incident – I decided I should wear an outfit that said, *I might be interested in messing around with you someday even though I probably shouldn't, because us artist-types shouldn't mess around* *with you writer-types, especially coming right off of a yucky break-up, but if you play your cards right, and treat me the way I deserve to be treated, and stop writing crappy reviews of my records, maybe – just maybe – you'll get to kiss me, but only for, like, six seconds, and you won't be allowed to touch me anywhere between my neck and my knees until I give you the go-ahead, and that could be a while, because I've been hurt, so keep it in your pants, buddy.* That outfit, of course, was a solid black scoop-neck long-sleeved Armani T-shirt and seven-year-old low-riding faded Lucky jeans that showed off an itty bit of my nice black lace Barelythere thong.

ZACH BINGHAM She shows up at the restaurant thirty-five minutes late. I generally allow for a forty-five-minute cushion, so I'm ten minutes away from taking off, but when she floats through the door, I'm tremendously glad I waited.

Even though she's wearing kick-around clothes, she looks amazing. If she'd dressed up for real, I might've proposed on the spot. But I don't gush at her, no way. I'm sure everybody gushes at Jenn Bradford. I think that by not saying anything about her appearance, I'm being different than everybody else she goes out with. Then I think that by not saying anything about her appearance, I'm being the same as every guy she goes out with, because every guy she goes out with wants to be different, so they don't say anything about her appearance. Then I think I'm being an idiot, and I stand up and give her a kiss on the cheek.

**JENN BRADFORD** Zach didn't say anything about how I looked. Virtually every guy I've gone out with said something about how I look. That was . . . different.

As for Zach, his outfit was a snooze. Indie Boy 101. Thriftstore chic. But his sideburns were trimmed perfectly, and his neck looked nice, so it was all good.

**ZACH BINGHAM** I don't put together a game plan for our date – and possible impending relationship, fingers crossed – but I intuitively realize that if I'm gonna snare her, I do indeed have to be different. I can't fawn, or patronize, or gawk. I have to be chill. Totally one hundred per cent chill, unlike I was on the second day in her studio, when I felt up her leg and far too obviously stared at her chest. Man, that was most definitely *not* chill.

The cheek kiss I give her is dry and impersonal. I say angrily, 'You're late.'

She says, 'I know. I got stuck on the phone with my manager. She's having problems with one of the guys in the band who shall remain nameless—'

I ask, 'Is it Stewart? I've met your bass player. He's kind of a strange cat.'

She says, 'No comment. Anyhow, I'm really, really sorry.'

On the surface, I don't accept her apology. I don't tell her it was okay that she left me sitting there by myself for over half an hour. I don't tell her how good she looks. That's what anybody would've done. What I *do* do is say, 'Woman, next time we go out, be on time.'

**JENN BRADFORD** Zach. Can. Be. Such. A. Cocky. Son-of-a-bitch.

**ZACH BINGHAM** Dinner's sort of weird, and sort of strange, and sort of fun. She eats almost an entire basket of bread, then orders a ton of food, far more than I do. She gets a Caesar salad, a large bowl of pasta fagiole, and chicken parmesan with a side of pasta marinara, and three or four glasses of wine, and tiramisu. I ask her, 'Do you exercise like a madwoman, or do you have crazy metabolism?' I don't understand her answer, because she sometimes talks with her mouth full, which you wouldn't expect from somebody as classy as Jenn Bradford.

After some conversational stumbling around, we hit on the one topic that offers us a level playing field: music. Jenn talks about music and the music industry with sincere passion, and she clearly knows her stuff. And I know she knows her stuff because *I* know *my* stuff, and she's right with me every step of the way. You can tell she's not only listened to and absorbed all kinds of records in all kinds of genres, but she's done her home-work, she's read history books, she's pored over liner notes. I try to trip her up with a random trivia question about Liz Phair – What TV show theme song did La Liz cover? – and right away, Jenn says, '*Banana Splits*. Duh.'

**JENNIFER BRADFORD** He started trying to trip me up with music dork trivia. Didn't work. But how could he have possibly known that from the time I was, I dunno, nine-ish or something, I obsessively listened to the radio and watched MTV and VH-1, and incessantly read music books and magazines and liner notes, and spent all of my allowance money on CDs, and at least two nights a month, I'd climb out of my bedroom windows and take the train into Manhattan all by myself, then flirt my way into whatever club I could, no matter who was gigging, just so I could see what it was that enabled whatever band I was seeing to land a gig in the first place.

You know what? You should ask Zach if he was pissed off that he couldn't trip me with his dorkitude that night. I'll bet you a dollar he uses some sort of tennis metaphor.

**ZACH BINGHAM** I'm kind of irked that she volleys back all of my musical serves, so I decide to change the subject. Once our chat drifts away from music – once it stops being a semi-stilted chat between writer and subject and starts being an open dialogue between guy-and-girl-on-date – the conversation begins to move back and forth between depth and surface, surface and depth. We talk about our families – mine's semi-fucked up and constantly disappointed in me, where hers is semi-normal and supportive. Lucky her. We talk about goals – mine's to write books full-time for a living, specifically rock bios, and hers is either to gig regularly with a jazz trio or, so she claims, run for President. And then we briefly touch on past loves. Or at least I think it'll be brief. I think it'll only garner a sentence or three, but out of nowhere, Jenn gives me the full account of why she called it quits with McAllister. I listen politely and attentively, even though I'd already heard the salient points of what happened between them.

How did I find out about the McAllister thing? None of your damn business. I've gotta protect my sources.

*[And now we take you away from the restaurant, away from the dinner-that-wasn't-a-date, on a trip back through the tendrils of time, to the final week of September 2007, a mere six days after Zach first interviewed Jenn. Be sure to fasten your seatbelt because this, dear reader, is going to be a bumpy ride.]*

**JENN BRADFORD** First of all, none of the crap that was written in any of the music rags about our break-up was true. Kevin didn't fly to the Caribbean with Mariah Carey. He didn't whip it out in front of one of the Éclat Records interns at a label listening party at the Plaza Hotel. He didn't go down on one of my backup singers after a gig in Dallas. He didn't go down on one of my backup singers *during* a gig in Dallas. Until right now, until right this very second, right as I'm telling you this, nobody ever knew exactly what happened except me, and Naomi, and my brother Travis, and my manager Masu, and Zach. And Kevin. And those two little skanks, whose names I never caught.

Kevin and I started out great. We met during Naomi's first big tour. His band, The Hoohah Johnson Experience, was opening for us, and Naomi and I were having that massive, stupid fight that I briefly mentioned earlier, a fight that almost killed our partnership. In retrospect, I realize that if we hadn't kissed and made up, it would have killed me altogether. Naomi too, probably.

It's possible that I let myself fall in love with Kevin so quickly in order to keep myself from falling apart over Naomi. But at the time – and still even now – I felt like Kevin and I probably would've fallen in love eventually anyhow, so I went with it. Our relationship took a natural progression, or at least as natural as it could have been between two people who spent a good portion of their adult lives on the road, playing music: we met, we toured, we talked, we toured, we laughed, we toured, we vibed, we toured, we kissed, we toured, we did lots of foreplay-type stuff, we toured, we consummated, we toured, we declared love, we toured, we moved in together, we toured, we discussed marriage.

Kevin and I made a most excellent couple. Physically speaking, we were on the same plane. We weren't one of those couples where people say, 'What's this hot dude doing with that ugly girl?' or 'How did that greasy guy haul in this total catch?' Like we looked totally cute walking down the red carpet together both times we went to the Grammy Awards with Naomi. Stuff like that made both of us feel good. Sure, it's shallow, but you take your victories where you can get them. We had a good verbal and spiritual thing going on, too – we had similar senses of humor, we both talked really fast, and we always had something to say to each other, most of which was interesting. People liked us together which, in retrospect, I think was part of the reason that *we* liked us together. The fact that we needed that sort of validation should've raised a red flag, but love will make you ignore or disregard that kind of thing.

After three years together, things stopped being great. As time progressed, our relationship evolved from the dictionary definition of solid and fun to the dictionary definition of mediocre and uninspired. Nothing was awful, but a good portion of the magic had definitely faded. I chalked it up to the fact that we'd been together for a while – thirty-six-ish months, which is about thirty-two-ish months longer than I'd ever been committed to one guy, and thirty-five-ish months longer than Kevin had stuck with one girl. Naomi told me that her and my brother's relationship calmed down after a couple of years, but the way she described how she and my brother calmed down didn't sound like my and Kevin's calm-down. Naomi and Travis had edged into comfort, while Kevin and I had edged into staidness.

I have to shoulder probably more than fifty per cent of the blame. What with all the demands on my time – touring, recording, interviews, photo sessions, remixes, guest appearances, blah blah blah blah blah – I wasn't the most attentive girlfriend. But Kevin wasn't setting the boyfriend world on fire, either. Sometimes he was all about buying me flowers, and playing me Miles Davis records, and giving me long-ass backrubs, then the next day, he'd be rude and cold. Not exactly the recipe for a long-lasting relationship.

But we did love each other, and we're both stubborn as hell, so neither of us would admit that there was anything wrong. I was determined to make him The One. I didn't realize then that you shouldn't have to *make* somebody The One. He should just *be* The One.

The Kevin Incident went down on Monday night, 23 September 2007, a date which shall live in fucking infamy. Naomi was sharing a bill with Sheryl Crow at Madison Square Garden. They were playing in Jersey the next night, then Philly a couple days after that, then one more show back at the Garden. She invited me to come along with them for their East Coast swing, and as I wasn't doing anything in particular that week, I threw some clothes and my makeup bag into a suitcase, hopped a cab from Brooklyn to Manhattan, and met up with Nay.

During Naomi's set – which kicked Madison Square Garden's ass – Masu texted me that Norah Jones wanted to bring me into the studio with her that Friday to cut a duo version of 'A-Tisket, A-Tasket' for her Ella Fitzgerald tribute album. Even though I thought that Norah was just okay, I couldn't pass up the chance to be recorded singing some actual, honest-to-goodness jazz. People needed to know that I did that sort of thing, that I was more than a rocker chick.

After Naomi came offstage, I told her about Norah, and she was so psyched for me that she literally carried me out of the Garden – which I have to admit was impressive, because I outweigh her by a good twenty pounds – tossed me into a taxi and said, 'I'm so proud of you, honey. Go screw your boyfriend' – she knew about Kevin's and my dwindling sex life – 'then rest up for a few days, then blow Norah away.' I swear to God, up until, I dunno, three or four years ago, Naomi was the biggest prude. Even today, it still surprises me when she says stuff like, *Go screw your boyfriend*. But it also makes me proud, because that's the kind of thing I'd say. I love being a bad influence.

It was still early when I got home, just after eleven, and I knew Kevin would be awake, so I threw open the front door and yelled, 'Baby, Norah Jones, Ella Fitzgerald, blah blah blah blah blah.' Nothing. No response, which was a bummer. I wanted Kevin to be the first important person in my life to find out. Okay, he would've been the third person – Masu knew first, then Naomi – but had I not been hanging out with Nay, Kevin would've been number two.

But there was no Kevin around to celebrate with. No hugs, no kisses, no laughs. Just me, myself, and I.

*[Now, please enjoy this bit of digressive commentary from Jenn's blabbermouthed bass player and feisty manager.]*

**T.J. STEWART** Me and Kev grew up on the same block in New York, in the LI. What's the LI? That's Long Island, baby. Anyhow, Kev's and my bass-and-drum hook-up on stage is tight because we've been playing together forever. Same like Jenny-Jenn and Naomi, you dig? Plus Kev's my cousin, and it's easy to share a groove when you share blood.

I have *much* love for the dude, but I don't have *any* love for how he hangs with the honeys. With his boys, he's chill, twenty-four seven, three-six-five. With the girls, he's straight-up schizo. One day he's all like buying 'em flowers, playing Miles Davis records and giving 'em long-ass backrubs, then the next day, he's rude and cold. And the longer he was with Jenny-Jenn, the worse it got.

And that shit he pulled on her at the end? *Daaayyymmmnnn*. The Teej can be a skeez, but even The Teej wouldn't do nothin' that bad.

Who's The Teej? That's me, dude. *Everybody* calls me The Teej.

**MASUHARA JONES** Nobody calls him The Teej. At least, God knows I don't.

Whenever we hit the road with Jenn, T.J. comes up to me at least once a week and is like, 'Yo, Shorty' – he always calls me Shorty, which I pretend to hate, but I think is pretty sweet – 'tell peeps in your press releases to call me The Teej. Your boy's trying to create an image for himself.'

**JENN BRADFORD** Annnyway . . . I had no place to channel all my nervous energy. I had to do something to cool out, so I thought it would be a good idea to take a trip to my quiet place a.k.a. the tub. I decided a coconut-lime bubble bath accompanied by a flock of vanilla-scented candles was the way to go. I dragged my suitcase up the stairs and into the bedroom, and what do I walk in on?

Kevin. And some skanky chick. And some other skanky chick. My boyfriend, and two girls. All naked. All cuddling. Stains all over the sheets. No, check that – stains all over *my* bedsheets. My beautiful maroon 650-thread-count bedsheets that I'd bought at Bloomingdale's almost six years before – in my pre-Kevin days, I should note – and were finally worn and faded to perfection.

So what's the first thing that pops out of my mouth? *'You ruined my sheets!'* Not one of my brain's finer performances, but considering the situation, you can't expect your synapses to be firing on all cylinders.

But after that, I believe I handled things very well. I kept my voice down. I didn't throw anything. I didn't hit or slap anybody. I didn't brandish any weapons – at least right away. I calmly told the girls to please put on their clothes and get out – they were gone in, like, six seconds – then I pointed at Kevin and ordered him to stay the fuck put. He obeyed. I think my deadly quiet tone scared him into submission.

I grabbed a pair of scissors from my office, went over to Kevin's closet and proceeded to cut every single piece of clothing he owned into at least two pieces. And when I say everything, I mean everything: T-shirts, jeans, suits, shorts, Nikes, boxers, socks, *everything*. Whenever he made like he was about to get off the bed, I snipped the scissors in the direction of his tiny, frightened, shrinking pile of junk.

After I finished cutting everything – which took about thirty minutes, although it seemed more like two hours at the time, I suppose because catharsis sometimes moves in slow motion – I walked over to the bed, rested the tip of the scissors right over his heart, and whispered, 'If you're not out of here in two minutes, I promise I'll use these somewhere you don't want them used.' His junk shrunk some more.

He said, 'You cut up all my shit. I don't have anything to wear.'

I said, 'You seemed pretty comfortable being naked in front of those two skanks. Go be naked in front of Brooklyn.' So he grabbed his wallet and left, one hundred per cent bare assed.

After Kevin slammed the front door, any toughness I felt evaporated, and I cried like a hurricane for a million years.

When I finally stopped hyperventilating, I decided to stick with my original plan which, if you'll recall, was to take refuge in my quiet place, that being our oversized Jacuzzi. No, wait, I mean *my* oversized Jacuzzi. The second that Kevin McAllister nakedly left the house, he lost ownership of everything. Except his drum sets. I'd let him have those back – a decision with which my manager strenuously disagreed.

**MASUHARA JONES** Yeah, Jenn's right, I wanted her to burn every single piece of percussion in that house. She wouldn't do it. But she's a much nicer person than I am, plus I don't think she has it in her to destroy a musical instrument. Her priorities are all screwed up.

**JENN BRADFORD** Anyhow, I did the same thing I always did when I took a bath at home: got my wine, lit my candles, dumped in too much bubble bath. How was I able to coherently keep my routine right after walking in on what I walked in on? No clue. Habit, I guess. My mind wasn't working particularly well, but my body knew what I needed. And yes, the wine and candles did help. But just a little bit. A *very* little bit.

While I was drying myself, I noticed the framed picture of me and Kevin on the vanity that Naomi snapped during a barbecue in our backyard last year, and it dawned on me that I had to get the heck out of Dodge. I couldn't be in that house any more, period. *Couldn't.* Everything in the place reminded me of us. Like I couldn't look at the Picasso print in the hallway without picturing us wandering through the Art Institute in Chicago a couple years ago. Or I couldn't look at the loofah hanging in the shower without remembering the way we used to cover ourselves in fruit-scented shower gel – pineapple's my fave, his was peach – and slowly wipe each other down. And then there was all the random crap we bought together: the cereal bowls, the toothpaste holder, the fax machine, the bedside lamp, the welcome mat. Virtually everything in the house reminded me of couplehood.

So yeah, I had to move, as soon as was humanly possible, and I decided then and there I was gonna downsize my living quarters. What I had then was a bit too much house for a little red-haired, broken-hearted pianist who was crying too damn much. But to paraphrase James Brown, the original J.B., the thought of condo-hunting right then made me break out in a cold sweat, so I finished drying myself off, threw on some clothes, grabbed my previously-packed suitcase, called a taxi and told the driver to take me to Manhattan and drop me at 201 Park Avenue South in Union Square.

It took all of eighteen minutes for my super-fancy suite at the super-fancy W Hotel to become a not-so-fancy used Kleenex repository.

**MASUHARA JONES** Jenn was a wreck, but I wasn't gonna let her miss the recording session with Norah Jones, so that Friday morning, I took the R train over the W to grab her, and my girl was not looking good. Her nose was all pink, and her eyes were all bloodshot, and her makeup was a streaky disaster, and her hair was sticking up about five inches, and I was all like, 'Honey, you look like the love child of Amy Winehouse and Rudolph the Red-Nosed Reindeer.'

She ran to the bathroom and goes, 'Shit! You're right!' and came out ten minutes later looking a little more like the Jenn I know and love. Not perfect, but good enough to be seen in public. I go, 'You're gorgeous. You ready to sing?'

She was like, 'Hells, no.' She practically yelled it.

I go, 'But you will be. Won't you?'

She whispered, 'Hells, yeah.' I'd never heard her whisper *hells yeah* before. She always yells it. It's her catchphrase, but she said it then like she'd gotten hit in the stomach. I wanted to hug her, but her body language was all, *Don't touch me.*

So we get to the studio, and there's Norah, and she's all nice and sweet and pretty and professional and cool, and she runs up to Jenn, gives her a hug and goes, 'It's so great to meet you, and I'm honored to have you on my record, and I think you'll love the arrangement my musical director did, and I'm so sorry about what happened with you and your man.' I thought, *Damn, news travels quick in the music industry. Not even a week, and Norah Jones knows the deal.*

Jenn got all tense, then pulls away and was like, 'What do you mean, what happened with me and my man?'

Norah goes, 'Didn't he fly to the Caribbean with Mariah Carey?'

Jenn relaxed and smiled a little bit – no teeth, but it was at least something. She was like, 'Yeah, that's close enough.' Then she took a really deep and shaky breath. I thought she was gonna start crying again, but she just goes, 'What say we do some singing?'

Then Jenn and Norah go into the recording room, and they talk about the arrangement for a few minutes, then they run down the song with the rhythm section a couple times, then they roll tape, and three passes later, they get a perfect take. We were out of there in less than two hours.

JENN BRADFORD That session with Norah was the most fun I'd had in the studio since Naomi and I cut our first album at this place in Park Slope, which it so happens was right around the corner from where we both grew up. We were practically children then, me and Naomi, total nobodies, and we were so happy to be in that studio – in *any* studio, really. Nay was on fire, and she belted out her vocals like she was Janis Joplin or something. My brother Travis was playing some stellar bass, all while madly crushing on Naomi, which I've gotta say was pretty impressive. And our drummer Frank Craft was also so, so, so amazing.

Me? Well, it was heaven. It was the happiest I'd ever been before, and probably since. Hells, I was playing piano with my friends and family – how could I not have been ecstatic? Plus nobody was putting any pressure on us to do anything other than make kick-ass music. Come to think of it, if anybody was pressurizing our little group, it was me, because being in that studio was what my entire childhood had led up to, and I didn't want us to blow it. And we didn't.

I know I sound like I'm lusting after the past. Maybe I am. Yeah, I truly still love the entire process of music – composing, recording, mixing, et cetera. Thing is, now it's more of a grind, more like a job, more expectations, more money, blah blah blah blah blah. Don't get me wrong – there's nothing I like more than writing and laying down a killer track, but it's not the same as it was. Back in the day, my songs were coming from a completely organic, almost innocent place, and the older I've gotten, the harder it's been to tap into that part of myself. Whenever I write a tune, there's all this baggage involved, like, *Will this song work as a single?* or, *If it does work as a single, what kind of video can we make for it?* or, *What kind of budget will the label give me for the video?* It's hardly ever, *Great jam, I can't wait to play it for an audience.* Intellectually, I knew that that was an unhealthy and slightly depressing way to go about the business of making music, but I couldn't snap out of it.

I dunno, maybe when you get closer to thirty, and you're stuck in a high-visibility business that demands results on top of results on top of results, there's a part of you that gets cynical, and hard, and self-protective. It's that annoying loss of innocence, you know? So to all you musician-types reading this, here's a piece of advice: if you ever manage to land a record deal, enjoy the hell out of your first studio sessions, because trust me, it'll never be that much fun again.

Anyhow, Naomi and I cut almost forty songs during our maiden studio voyage, some of which we'd been rehearsing or performing since our sophomore year in high school. Now *that* was catharsis. A healthy catharsis. And the reason I say that is because that's what it was like with Norah – the best catharsis imaginable. Nailing 'A-Tisket, A-Tasket' made me feel almost human again, made me feel strong, like I could at least start attempting to get past The Kevin Incident.

Yeah, I know I shouldn't let something semi-superficial like a good recording session validate me, but I'm kind of a validation junkie. Sometimes it feels like I *always* need validation which, considering what I've accomplished in my professional life, is kinda pathetic. I've actually spent a fair amount of time trying to figure out why I crave acceptance so much, and the only concrete thing I've come up with is that when you're an artist and you're attractive – and I feel arrogant for referring to myself as attractive, but there it is – you're not always taken as seriously as you'd like or may even deserve. There's always that whole, *You got signed because you have big boobs* thing, and it drives me nuts when somebody insinuates something like that, because I worked my butt off – Naomi and I *both* worked our butts off – to make this happen. It means way way *way* more to me if a guy or girl comes up to me after a show, or on the street, or at the mall and says, 'Jenn, I love your voice', instead of 'Jenn, I love your ass'. Not that I don't sometimes appreciate a *nice ass* compliment from the right person – what woman doesn't? – but confirmation from a random somebody that I have some semblance of musical talent is a really good thing.

**MASUHARA JONES** After the Norah thing, Jenn went back to her hotel and I went home. My cell rang the second I got in the door. It was Jenn, and she sounded good. Really good. Right away, she started talking about how she was gonna start looking for a new place to live, which is how I knew she was getting back to normal. I asked her if all of Kevin's stuff was outta the house, and she told me he sent her a text saying he'd taken everything of his except for two of his older drum kits, which he'd be back for soon.

I was like, 'Burn 'em! Burn 'em *all*!' She wouldn't do it, then she asked me if I was becoming a pyromaniac. I was like, 'Ha, ha, ha.'

It's as I said – that girl's priorities are all messed up; it's all music, music, music. To her, instruments are like people. If a guy pulls the kind of shit on me that Kevin pulled on Jenn, I'm hitting him where it hurts.

Or kicking him where it hurts. That's the way I roll.

What do I mean, 'kicking him'? Okay, well, as Jenn's manager, I've gotta have her back, and sometimes that means throwing down. Like, I never told her this, but this one time in Memphis during the first tour after The Incident, I went to Kevin's hotel room after a show and kicked him in the nuts with my nut-kicking purple suede Pumas, then I was like, 'If you say anything to Jenn about this, I'll do it again . . . and next time with my steel-toed Puma boots.'

It was awesome.

Anyhow, I go to Jenn, 'Okay, fine, don't torch his shit, but you have to promise to make it so you'll never see his scummy face again. Set up a time for him to come by the house and get his stupid drums, and make sure you're not there. Me and T.J. will hang out and see he doesn't steal your plasma, or your laptop, or whatever.'

She was like, 'That's fine. Except for the seeing his scummy face part. I still want him in the band.'

I threw my cell against the wall, and it broke into a thousand pieces. But she'll probably tell you I totally hung up on her.

**JENN BRADFORD** Ooh, Masu was pissed. She totally hung up on me.

**MASUHARA JONES** So I cabbed it over to the W and let myself into her room – she'd given me a 'just in case' key – and found her in the bathtub, covered in bubbles, candles everywhere, looking as chill as I'd seen her in years. Not happy, necessarily. Just chill.

I was like, 'That dildo is not staying in the band. Seriously, Jenn, I won't be able to stop myself from messing him up. Badly.'

She goes, 'He's staying in. He's a brilliant drummer. Except for Frank Craft, I've never played with anybody as good. I'm a professional, and he's a professional . . .'

I was like, 'Yeah, a professional dildo.'

'. . . and *you're* a professional, and the band comes first.'

Like I said, music, music, music. I go, 'Why don't you call Frank?'

She goes, 'The tour starts in January, and Frank gigs so much that he won't have time to get the material down, and the band sounds great the way it is, and you know it, and Kevin's staying with us, and you're gonna deal with it, and that's it, end of story.'

Once Jenn Bradford makes up her mind about something, it's not changing, so I was like, 'Fine, but the first chance I get, I'm kicking him in the nuts.' Which, as you know, is exactly what I awesomely did.

*[Now we take you back to the restaurant, where Zach and Jenn are still enjoying their dinner-that-wasn't-a-date.]*

ZACH BINGHAM Jenn finishes telling me about the McAllister thing over dessert, a glass of port, and three espressos, filling in some details that I hadn't heard about, and I think, what the hell am I supposed to do with this? Do I track the man down and smack him around? Do I pitch the story to *Rolling Stone*?

None of the above. What I do is say, 'Jenn, if you ever dated me, I promise I'd never have a threesome in your bed. A foursome, absolutely, but a threesome? No way.'

**JENN BRADFORD** I never in a million years thought I'd be able to laugh about The Kevin Incident at any level. I thought that when it came to my pal Kev, the laughter had died, or was at the very least in the intensive care unit. But laugh I did. Well played, Mr Zachary Bingham. Well played indeed.

I laughed for a good long while. More catharsis.

**ZACH BINGHAM** After she cracks up at my crap joke, that's when I think it becomes a real date to her, so I suggest we go and do one of the things I like to do on real dates when I'm in Brooklyn, which is take a walk in Prospect Park. To me, Prospect is the best park in the five boroughs. It's like Central Park, except smaller, and without the ducks and the hippies.

She agrees, so I pay the check then lead her down one of those gorgeous brownstone-filled sidestreets, and we're moving along kind of slowly, and it's kind of cold, and we do that thing where you accidentally-on-purpose make body contact – you know, rub an arm against an arm, or bump a shoulder. At least *I'm* doing it accidentally-on-purpose. I dunno, she might be a little drunk.

**JENN BRADFORD** We got to Prospect Park, and the stars were out, and I had a nice little buzz on, and I was freezing my ass off, and I was waiting for him to hold my hand, or put an arm around my shoulders, or hug me to keep me warm, or *something*, but all he was doing was talking about music and brushing up against me. Finally I stopped walking, and I took his arms, put them around my waist, threw my arms around his neck, and looked him in the eye. I liked what I thought I saw there – kindness, and interest, and sincerity – and decided it was officially time to start chasing away the Kevin ghost, so I said, 'Hi there. My name is Jennifer. I'd like you to kiss me.'

**ZACH BINGHAM** So we make out in the park for a while – and I hadn't made out in a park since high school, so it's pretty damn cool – then we go back to her big-ass house, and she drags me into the studio where I interviewed her, and we have sex on her piano.

That was a first for me, messing around on a musical instrument. And the whole time I'm thinking, *I can't wait to do this again*.

**JENN BRADFORD** No way was I gonna mess around with Zach in a bed that I'd had sex with Kevin McAllister in, so we went into my studio and did it on the piano. And that was, like, the sixty-sixth time I've done it on the piano, and it is *so* not gonna happen again. I've had enough keyboard imprints on my ass to last a lifetime.

*[And now, dear reader, we're pleased to introduce you to Jenn's sort-of-guardian-angel, the protector of all that is musical, the spirit who's been watching over our piano-playing friend since birth, the lovely, the talented . . .]*

**BILLIE HOLIDAY'S GHOST** Ahh, I too have had some sex-related backside imprints in my time. I've made love *everywhere*, including on musical instruments of all shapes and sizes. We're talking on pianos, and on kick drums, and surrounded by an entire arsenal of saxophones, and even once on an acoustic bass. I have no idea how I was able to pull that one off, but I did, by golly, and my behind hurt for three weeks afterward, plus I had the imprint of a G-string on the small of my back for days, and I don't mean a G-string like the panties all the girls are wearing these days, but a G-string like the top string on the bass. So I sympathize with my stubborn little redheaded white girl, my spiritual progeny, a lady who, had we lived in the same era, would have been my partner-in-crime.

And I say 'lady', because that's what Jennifer Bradford is. A true lady.

Why am I so concerned with Jennifer's piano escapades, you ask? Well, I watch over 514 of the world's finest girl singers. I'm not their guardian angel, exactly. My power is quite limited. I can gently nudge my girls into what I believe to be the best direction possible for them to make the best music possible. It doesn't always work, but I keep trying. Why? Well, somebody has to make sure these ladies stay in line. We can't have an army of Billie Holidays out there, all drinking and drugging and screwing around, and not utilizing their talent properly. Female vocalists with that magical combination of talent, heart, and inner and outer beauty are few and far between, and I have to ensure that there's always good music for us to download here in the afterworld. After all, the Big Guy likes His iTunes.

Anyhow, I'm not supposed to play favorites, but I do, and Jennifer's always been my number one girl; I hoped the writer was a solid choice to be her first lover after Mr McAllister. It seemed to me that Mr Bingham would be hip. The cat had a big ol' brain in his skull, and it looked like some decent moral standards, too. On the downside, he was reminding me of the chorus from a song I often performed live, but unfortunately never got to record. It's called 'I Fall in Love Too Easily'. 'All of Me' I recorded twenty-plus times, and 'Billie's Blues' almost thirty, but 'I Fall in Love Too Easily', *zero*. In retrospect, I could've chosen some better fellas to produce my records, but I often wasn't in the soberest state of mind to make good decisions. I can't quote you the lyrics here – the copyright laws up here are stringent like you wouldn't believe – but track them down and you'll understand what I'm talking about.

Do you see what I'm saying? It was too simple, too quick. I wasn't comfortable with how Mr Bingham went from being a probing, nonbiased writer, to a sex-and-love-crazed man-on-the-make. The quicker he fell for Jennifer, the less likely it would be that their lovemaking would have any lasting depth, and one of the many things I wanted for my best girl was to enjoy as much deep, meaningful lovemaking as possible.

Why? That's obvious. It would've fulfilled her, and fulfillment almost always makes for better music. Pain often makes for good music too, but after Mr

McAllister's performance, I figured Jennifer had suffered enough pain to last her a lifetime.

I was a little upset to see the two of them jump into bed – or on to the piano, more accurately – on their date-that-wasn't-a-date. She could've kept it cool for a month or so, and everybody would've been fine. But on the other hand, I couldn't get *too* angry with my girl, because I can relate. Just like me, my Jennifer is a sensualist. Except without the incessant booze intake and the heroin addiction.

Now Mr Bingham wasn't in love with Jennifer at that point, but the potential certainly was there – she had that effect on men. I imagined it was only a matter of time before she owned his heart. Jennifer moved quite speedily that night, and when Jennifer moves speedily, well, she's a heart thief.

Still, I tried to keep an open mind. Like I said, I wasn't allowed to interfere that much – they have some pretty strict rules up here in the music afterworld – but I could hope for the best outcome, and I knew hoping would help. I hoped that Mr Bingham would be good for her. I hoped he could help take her to the next romantic plane in her life – or at least get her through this one as unscathed as possible. I hoped he could help heal her heart.

I hoped, I hoped, I hoped.

# The New York Times

## January 15, 2009

**Concert Review**

## THE REALITY OF EVOLUTION
### *Check Out Jenn Bradford's Quantum Leap*

## by Carole Anne Rudolph

Over the past two decades, there have been only a tiny handful of piano-pounding female singer/songwriters who have put together careers that have extended beyond a pair of albums and a single national tour: Tori Amos, Cat Power, Alicia Keys, Norah Jones, Diana Krall, and that's basically it. The emerging (emerged?) Jenn Bradford is about to embark on what will be her fifth major American solo tour, this one in support of her third album, *Reality Check*, a mixed bag of Pretenders-ish New Wave ditties, Billie Holiday-ish jaunty beboppers, Joni Mitchell-ish folk ballads, and Bruce Springsteen-ish anthems. So, does Ms Bradford get added to our list? Before her record release party at the Bowery Ballroom on Saturday, the jury was still out. Before the final note had even finished ringing, the verdict was in.

As *Reality Check* is a multiple personality disordered stylistic mishmash, one would expect Ms Bradford's performance to be uneven and jarring. The fact of the matter is her endearing musicality, personal aggressiveness, and innate charisma are all intense enough to make even her weakest compositions seem convincing.

Stage presence-wise, where Ms Amos is aggressive, and Chan Marshall (a.k.a. Cat Power) is a disaster-in-waiting, and Ms Keys is sultry, and Ms Jones is demure, and Ms Krall is glossy, Ms Bradford is an overtly sexual showperson, suggestively touching her keyboard, and dropping unprintable innuendos in between songs. She has a likeable, unforced sense of humor, a factor that sets her apart — and oftentimes above — her fellow keyboard-slingers.

So does Jenn Bradford join the collection of contemporary piano women who will withstand the test of time? As she herself might say, *Hells, yeah!*

**JENN BRADFORD** The first place I lived after I moved out of my parents' home was that tiny, crappy apartment in the East Village with Naomi. After the first Naomi album blew up, Nay and I rented a huge, uncrappy house in a lovely little section in Brooklyn called Windsor Terrace. Then I bought that ginormous house where I lived with Kevin, which seemed like the next logical step: parents' house, tiny apartment, rent a big house, own a bigger house. When I used to dream about real estate as a kid, that's exactly the progression I hoped for. What? Yeah, I thought about real estate when I was younger. I grew up in the Big Apple; real estate is in my blood. Like my fellow New Yorker Donald Trump says, *Location, location, location*.

Anyhow, Kevin and I made that house into an amazing place – classy, hip and decorated, like, *perfectly*. It was the first place I could really call my own, and I loved the hell out of it, but as I touched on before, after The Incident, there were times I could barely stand to be in there. When I'd look at the widescreen TV in the living room that Kevin had picked out, my brain would tell me, *Leave, leave*. When I'd look at my lovely back-yard with the Solaire infrared grill, my heart would tell me, *Stay, stay*. Whenever I talked to Masu about it, she'd tell me, *Get the fuck out, get the fuck out*.

It was all very confusing, and for me, confusion often leads to inertia, and in this case, to me changing my mind about selling the place. Instead, after I settled back in after my couple weeks at the W, I started doing what I could to make the house livable in again. Every piece of Kevin's personal property had been removed, recycled, or cere-moniously burnt – I gave Masu a pair of his drumsticks to torch, which finally got her off of her fire kick – but there were still reminders all over the damn place. Like did I want to dry myself with the bath towels or sleep on the bedsheets we'd once shared? Hells, no. Did I want to keep the various Victoria's Secret outfits I bought specifically for his enjoyment in my dresser? Absolutely not. Anything that was even the tiniest bit Kevin-ized I got rid of. I even had the place fumigated to eliminate any trace of his scent. Clean pad, fresh life, new start.

But even after the purge, the trace memories wouldn't go away, and at the beginning of February, a couple weeks after my record release party, I finally accepted that I could never be happy living there, so I decided to bail. My bi- or tri-weekly hang-outs and hook-ups with Zach also helped sway me, because he brought a part of me back to life, a part that was ready to move forward, a part that said, it's time to buy a new bed and put it in a room that has never seen or heard of Kevin McAllister.

I didn't want to spend weeks and weeks house-hunting, so I just grabbed the first place that I liked, which took a grand total of two phone calls, one realtor, and three hours. It was a big, but not too disgustingly big three-bedroom unit in a three-year-old condo building in the Redhook section of Brooklyn. Three bedrooms were perfect: I could use the small one to sleep in; the medium one to store all my clothes and CDs and books and shoes in; and I could soundproof the big one and turn it into a home studio.

Packing up my junk was a spiritual bummer and a logistical pain in the ass. I hadn't done an inventory in quite a while, and the sheer number of shirts and skirts and dresses and pants, and heels and flats and go-go boots, and CDs and books and electronics and musical equipment was kind of overwhelming. Way *way* too much stuff – and some of it had to go. The clothing purge wasn't nearly as difficult as I would've thought – how many black tank tops does one woman really need? – but the music purge was practically impossible. Oh, I got rid of a few CDs – I gave some obscure indie stuff to Zach, and some obscure hip-hop stuff to T.J. and some obscure R&B stuff to Masu – but I couldn't bring myself to lose a single keyboard, or microphone cable, or speaker cabinet. All of which meant there was a helluva lot of packing to be done.

Believe it or not, on moving day, I didn't cry. Much.

My movers seemed trustworthy enough, but they were still New York City movers, so I knew it would be wise to stay in their faces whenever they touched a piece of musical gear or stereo equipment, because when it comes to my electronics, I get a tad irrational. Like if my Fender Rhodes ended up with a single scratch on it, somebody might've gotten decked. I could tell the movers were getting pissed at me for following them so closely and giving them so many hairy eyeballs, so right before they started unloading everything at my new place, I went all flirty-pinup and gave each of them a lingering kiss on the cheek. Things went a lot smoother after that.

*[And now some pointed observations from Jenn's new across-the-hall neighbor, the suave, the debonair Mr Porter Ellis.]*

**PORTER ELLIS** When I saw those movers maneuvering that plethora of electric music-making material through my building's back door and into our freight elevator, I was less than thrilled about my incoming across-the-hall neighbor. I counted six speakers and a sub-woofer enclosed in bubble-wrap, all of which I recognized as exceedingly high-end, and all of which had the potential to be exceedingly loud. From what I could tell, the instruments were mostly keyboards, although I thought I saw a couple acoustic guitars and several drum-kit components. The one saving grace was that, at least as far as I could tell, there were no electric guitars. Small solace, but it was something.

I went into the hallway, pulled one of the movers aside and asked him, 'What do you know about this guy?'

He said, 'Not a guy, man. A girl.'

There were ten units in my building – five floors, two on each floor – and for some inexplicable reason, all of them were owned by men. The Oscar-winning actor – a man. The two traders – both men. The CEO of that multinational corporation – a man. The ex-White House staffer – a man. That obnoxious trust fund do-nothing – a man. Or a boy, I suppose. The former astronaut – a man. The best-selling author – a man. My former neighbor, the high-class mobster – a man. Me – a man. Right at the juncture, considering my marital history, I was not interested in having any female energy in or around my living quarters. Being in a building full of men felt safe for me.

And now, a woman. Or a girl, I suppose. I prayed she

wasn't anywhere near my type. I didn't need the headaches.

The mover told me that my new neighbor was a musician. *No kidding*, I thought. He then told me that he forgot her name, but he'd seen her on MTV a whole bunch, and she was pretty famous. I wouldn't have known who she was anyhow, because I never watched MTV. I didn't like rock music, or pop, or rap. I was a jazzman, with a sprinkle of classical thrown in for good measure.

After all her furniture, and boxes, and musical and stereo equipment – and I can't emphasize just how much equipment there was – was loaded in, this young, attractive woman with long red hair gave the head mover a check and a hug. Then she marched right up to me, stuck out her hand, and said, 'Jenn Bradford. Your new neighbor.' Very businesslike. That was a check in the plus column. I appreciate businesslike.

I said, 'Porter Ellis.' She matched my firm handshake. 'Welcome to the building.'

**JENN BRADFORD** Right off the bat, I decided he wasn't 'Porter', or 'Mr Ellis', or 'Hey, you'. He was 'Porter Ellis'. Full name. All the time. Whether he liked it or not.

**PORTER ELLIS** She wasn't my type. What a relief.

**JENN BRADFORD** It took me, like, six seconds to peg Porter Ellis as a normal, boring rich guy. Barely interested in me as a person, totally uninterested in me as a woman, but even if he was interested in me, he was out of my age bracket. I liked the boys, like, you know, Zach. Not sure if that was the best policy – Kevin was a boy, and look what happened there – but that's where I was at.

He was attractive, but not a head-turner, this Porter Ellis, and I was frankly glad he wasn't a cutie – or, worse yet, a *cool* cutie. See, Zach and I were still kind of tenuous, and a cool cutie might've derailed me a little bit, which wasn't fair to Zach, whose only crime thus far was pretentiousness. Like when he would start in about, I dunno, the merits of indigenous hip-hop grooves played live down the track versus rehashed funk samples layered with individual snare drum samples, I zoned out. Otherwise, Zach was perfectly swell.

I think from Zach's end, there was no tenuousness. He'd made it evident that he liked me a whole lot, and I'm sure he was telling his friends that we were going steady or something. I did like the guy, but I wasn't ready to let myself go. Masu kept telling me I should play the field for a while so I could see what was out there, and to figure out what I was, or *wasn't* looking for in a guy . . . or if I even wanted to be with a guy in the first place. But the thought of putting myself out there was exhausting, so I figured I'd have some fun with Indie Boy, and see if anything developed. But Masu did have a point, so I didn't entirely rule out anything or anybody.

That being the case, if Porter Ellis was a cool cutie and I saw him every day, and got to be friends with him, and he invited me over for a glass of wine, and the mood was right . . . well, suffice it to say that there was a part of me that was still pretty vulnerable, and who knows what might've happened. But fortunately none of that would be a problem, because normal and boring and rich weren't qualities I was looking for in a boy. Or, in Porter Ellis's case, a man.

Still, I thought it would be a good idea to make nice with him. It would be the neighborly thing to do.

**PORTER ELLIS** She looked over my shoulder and into my apartment and said, 'Nice to meet you, Porter Ellis. Cool crib. Can I check it out? I'm in serious need of some decorating ideas.' Then she bulled past me and into my, quote, *crib*.

If I may backtrack for a moment, I'd like to point out that when I was growing up, my family was happy when we managed to have a couch that didn't have any cigarette burns on the cushions. We were thrilled when the chairs at our kitchen table matched. So after I sold *Billionaire.com* to that international consortium of money men, I made certain that neither myself nor my parents and siblings would ever sit on anything less than perfection.

Hey, do you want to hear something interesting? I've never really told anybody this before, but hammering out the purchase agreement with all those billionaires was sheer torture. Aside from the fact that it was painful for me to let my website go – it was my baby, you see – I could barely stand to be in the same room with those gentlemen. They were cranky, and self-important, and obsessive. But after the papers were signed, I was a billionaire myself. Go figure.

At any rate, it had taken me years to get my living space *just so*. Finding the right furniture was the most frustrating issue, because I was looking for *special*, and *special* isn't always necessarily easy to come by in terms of living-room seating. My sofa and love chairs weren't a typical sofa and love chairs, but rather what is referred to as a, quote, *seating system*. They consist of a series of balls made from a synthetic compound that can be arranged and then rearranged into most any shape. It's incredibly expensive, and incredibly odd, and incredibly *special*, and the only place you can buy it retail is in Switzerland, and very few people in this country own a set.

Jenn slumped down on the sofa section of the seating system, then wiggled around for a bit, then lay down. She said, 'Ohmigod, this thing is a total freak show.' Then she sat up and said very dramatically, 'I must have one of my own. *Must.*'

**JENN BRADFORD** Yes, Porter Ellis seemed *way* too stuffy and *way* too cranky, but that couch? As T.J. would say, *Daaayyymmmnnn.* I would've hung out at his place just to watch DVDs and eat pizza on that thing, no matter how cranky he was.

**PORTER ELLIS** I walked over to my office and pulled my decorator's card from my Rolodex. When I returned to the main living area, Jenn was nowhere to be found. I called for her, and she called back, 'Over here!'

She'd found her way into my bedroom, and had made herself comfortable on my bed. She said, 'Porter Ellis, that couch is amazing, but this bed is the most comfortable piece of furniture in the history of comfortable furniture.'

I said, 'The mattress is Duxiana. The duvet cover is 1500-thread-count Egyptian cotton. It'd better darn well be comfortable.' I gave Jenn the business card. 'Call my decorator. She'll point you in the right direction.' I then filled her in on the technical aspects of the seating system, and the history of the Duxiana company. After a couple minutes, she began to look bored, so I stopped.

**JENN BRADFORD** I got the feeling Porter Ellis was trying to impress me with all his stuff. Wasn't working. It would take more than fancy furniture for a guy like Porter Ellis to impress me. Like Zach's furniture sucked – actually, his entire apartment sucked – but I still found him to be a pretty impressive guy. Or at least he was the most impressive post-Kevin guy I'd come across. Not exactly a ringing endorsement, but there it is.

Okay, I will admit Porter Ellis's couch was a *little* impressive, as was the huge jazz CD collection in his bedroom, but that was about it. And that, in so many words, was what I told him.

I might've come off as a bit of a snot, but something in this guy brought out the ballbuster in me.

**PORTER ELLIS** She made a couple cracks about my furniture and record collection being the most impressive things in the apartment, present company included. I was about to crack back – I don't like to play the insult game, but I will if necessary, and I'm quite good at it – but she flashed me a smile that almost knocked me over. She may have had a smart mouth, but it was a beautiful one.

Terrific smile notwithstanding, she was getting on my nerves, so I hustled her to the door and said, 'Okay, I have to get some work done. Nice meeting you. See you around the building.' Very dismissive.

She stopped in my doorway, turned around and asked, 'What kind of work do you do, exactly, Porter Ellis?'

At that juncture, the truthful answer to that was, not much. I'd made some hugely successful investments with the *Billionaire.com* sale, but hadn't quite figured out what to do with the profits. Most of the time when somebody asks me what I do for a living, I'll make a stupid joke like, 'Paperboy to the stars', or 'Bill Gates's boy Friday'. But for some reason, I told Jenn the truth. I think I was still a little dizzy from that smile of hers.

She nodded. 'Hunh.' She stepped out into the hallway and said, 'You should take some of that money and open a jazz club, Porter Ellis. This city needs another good one.'

That actually wasn't a bad idea.

ZACH BINGHAM I show up at Jenn's new building the day she moves in, and I want it to be a surprise, so I explain to the doorman who I am, and then I hook him up with ten bucks, and he tells me, 'Fifth floor', then buzzes me in. There's a waterfall in the lobby. Imported mosaic tiles on the wall. The elevator is glass and looks out over the East River. Fancy. I feel mildly embarrassed that I'm tracking slush all over the place.

I get out of the elevator, and Jenn's talking to this guy who's decked out *just so*, and his hair is *just so*, and his buffed arms are *just so*, and his salt-and-pepper hair is *just so*, and from what I can tell by looking over his shoulder, his apartment is *just so*. Jenn has her back to me, and the guy sees me. I put my finger on my lips, tiptoe up behind her, and give her a little smack on her butt.

She turns around, gives me a big smack on my head, then says, 'Zachary Bingham, you dick, you scared the shit out of me.'

I rub my head, which hurts like a bitch, and say, 'Surprise!'

**JENN BRADFORD** No, I didn't smack Zach on purpose. Why would you think that? I liked the guy. Plus I'm not a violent woman. You must have me confused with Masu.

Was I glad to see Zach? Hells, yeah. I'm a big fan of the unannounced drop-in, especially on a day like a moving day. It showed character, and thoughtfulness, and sweetness, and kindness, all of which I was in serious need of. It was a nice way to christen my home. Actually, the official christening of my new home – as well as my new bed – came later that afternoon, but that's beside the point.

Was I glad that he squeezed my butt in front of my new neighbor? Well, not so much. Public butt-squeezing is the kind of thing you do when you're a real, honest-to-goodness, trusting, awesome-sex-having couple, and Zach and I weren't quite there yet. I did like Zach – and I *really* liked his brains, and I really, *really* liked his neck – but there was something a bit *off* about him, something I couldn't put my finger on, something that kept me from entirely trusting him. I think it had to do with the fact that he was a hustler. I don't mean that in a bad way, necessarily. When you're a struggling freelance artist of any sort – writer, musician, painter, whatever – you *have* to hustle. Like before Naomi and I got our record deal, six days a week, we would wander Manhattan handing out flyers for our gigs, and sit in front of Naomi's computer for hours sending out mass Evites to shows, and mail out dozens of press kits. Zach, in effect, had to do that every day in his life, and part of that attitude carried over to the way he related to me and the world-at-large. On some level, it seemed to me like he was always hustling.

I even kind of wondered if he'd hustled me into the sack. Still do. Maybe that's why, deep down, I couldn't envision him being a *boyfriend*-boyfriend – not that I was looking for a *boyfriend*-boyfriend, mind you – but I felt like he would always be just some guy I was seeing, a sorta-boyfriend. Well, maybe not *always*, but at least for the foreseeable future.

But those were my issues, and it wasn't fair to project that on to poor Zach. He meant well, no question. Spend time with the guy away from his natural habitat – that being either an independent record store or any club where he's on the guest list – and you'd realize in, like, six seconds, that underneath all the pretentious proclamations, and the sarcastic asides, and the hipper-than-thou attitude, he was a tall, skinny teddy bear, a straight-up, no-frills sweetie who took great pleasure in making his friends feel good. I mean, the guy had no money, but he scraped enough together that he was able to buy me the entire Kurt Vonnegut library, because I once casually told him I hadn't read any of Vonnegut's stuff. And even though they weren't as diverse as Kevin's, the mix CDs he made for me were pretty damn good.

If or when he reads this, he'll probably be annoyed that I called him a teddy bear, because he'll think it'll lose him some serious cool points with his fellow indie boys.

**PORTER ELLIS** It's not fair, but my knee-jerk reaction to people with facial piercings and visible tattoos is usually negative. I almost always turn out to be wrong on my judgment – one of the guys who was part of the group that purchased *Billionaire.com* had a pierced lip, and he was perfectly professional and kind, the kindest member of the consortium, actually – but I still can't help it. Sometimes I feel like my father, shaking his fist at the, quote, *youth of America*, which is silly, because I'm only a couple years past being one of them myself.

Anyhow, Jenn's lanky boyfriend had facial piercings and visible tattoos. And my knee-jerk reaction? Negative.

ZACH BINGHAM This *just so* dude gives me the massive stink eye, so I do what I do in situations when somebody seems to have issues with me – I try to kill him with kindness.

I stick out my hand and introduce myself, all politely and professionally. He almost breaks my hand. I think to myself, great, he has a hard-on for Jenn, and he's gonna stalk her from across the hall.

PORTER ELLIS I think to myself, great, these two are gonna play their music all damn night, every damn night.

JENN BRADFORD I think to myself, great, an alpha-male dick-waving contest. I'd better keep these two yahoos separated.

*[Fortunately for Jenn, Ms Holiday's spirit followed her over to the new crib.]*

BILLIE HOLIDAY'S GHOST Jennifer's condo building was supposed to be a sedate, nurturing situation for her, a setting where she could concentrate on her music and her happiness, and I think she deserved someplace like that after what that awful drummer did to her, wouldn't you agree?

I must confess that I surely did not see Mr Porter Ellis coming, and I surely should have, because I'm one of the handful of people up here who have what is referred to as 'an all-seeing eye'. But sometimes I don't pay it close enough attention. I guess this was one of those times. When you have 500-odd divas to take care of, sometimes you get tired, and when you get tired, you miss things.

Mr Ellis made me nervous – yes, he did. Jennifer didn't need any grouchy, stuffed-shirt neighbors giving her negative vibes, especially one who didn't like all kinds of different music. As I mentioned, I'm not supposed to intervene directly with anything in the living world, but somebody who doesn't like all different kinds of music? I thought I might have to do something about that. Maybe I'd get Janis Joplin to float into his room one night and give him a wet dream. That'd shake him up but good.

That said, Mr Ellis did have *some* good qualities. For example, he has a lovely jazz collection – a collection that includes a dozen-plus CDs by a certain brooding female vocalist who liked to wear gardenias in her hair. That was proof positive that the man wasn't all bad.

Maybe he'd be okay to have around. Only time would tell.

# LA WEEKLY

## February 25, 2009

### Concert Preview

### The JB's ARE COMING, The JB's ARE COMING
*Sexpot Pianist Jenn Bradford Plans to Rock the Rox*

### by Erik Garcia

A handful of the country's snootier music scribes have made it known (time and again) that they feel Jenn Bradford's overt sexuality — and overt goofiness — have turned her into a cartoon of sorts, an alterna-emo rendering of Jessica Rabbit. What these snoots fail to realize and/or acknowledge, or have out and out ignored, is that Jenn has evolved into one of modern rock's most reliable, most thrilling female artists. On her latest outing, *Reality*

*Check*, for example, she glides from style to style seamlessly and naturally, something that Gwen Stefani or Pink couldn't make happen even if they exhumed John Hammond and had him produce their respective albums.

The chameleonic approach to her recent record was wholly by design, and wholly Jenn's conception. 'During pre-production [for *Reality Check*], my A&R guy, Mitch Busey, said to me, "Babe, pick one effing sound and stick with it",' Bradford laughed. (She laughs a lot, this Jenn Bradford.) 'I said, "Eff that, Mitch. This is the way I rock it. I'm a complex broad".'

Maybe so, but musically speaking, *Reality Check* isn't particularly complex. Taken individually, each tune is accessible and memorable, even the challenging jazz-oriented material. But as the album is admittedly all over the map, there's a chance that she'll alienate her devoted core audience, something which isn't overly concerning to Jenn. 'I think my people will stick with me. They're loyal. I mean, even though I've done some crappy concerts in LA, the Roxy is almost sold out for [Tuesday's] gig. My fans rule.'

Nine times out of ten, the Jenn Bradford concert experience is far different than the Jenn Bradford album experience, so it's almost always worth the effort and expense. During her live shows, she likes to take liberties with the material, adding an extra chorus here, an extended piano solo there. Maybe Jay-Z will show up and drop a verse or two. Maybe she'll do five minutes of stand-up.

Or maybe she'll go no-frills and play a bunch of cool Jenn Bradford tunes. All of which means you'd best get on the horn or the computer and book yourself some tix, like, yesterday.

*Jenn Bradford and The JB's perform Tuesday night at the Roxy Theater, 9009 W. Sunset. Doors at 8.30, show at 10.00. For tickets, call (310) 276-2222, or visit Ticketmaster.com.*

JENN BRADFORD Ah, touring across the United States. How do I love thee? Let me count the ways. Um, zero.

It wasn't always that way. I used to *love* touring. New cities, new people, new clubs, new food, new go-go boots – it was all about the newness, and newness is generally awesome. But by the time you've made your fifth trip to Detroit, or your sixth trip to Houston, or your seventh trip to Atlanta, you're big-time ready for some oldness.

Yeah, I was fed up with touring as an entity, but the gigs themselves? They usually made up for all the bullshit. Give me an attentive crowd, a nice piano, a good sound system, and my rhythm section, and I'm a happy girl.

Our first tour after *Reality Check* came out was of the cross-country variety, and it was scheduled to last three months. It started on the West Coast, which was a beautiful thing, because I was in desperate need of a little bit of sunshine and a lot of above-freezing temperatures. I was bummed that I had to leave my new condo – I'd just finally gotten settled in, f'r cryin' out loud – but I was psyched to perform our new material for actual living, breathing crowds. On the other hand, I was freaking a bit, because the album hadn't been getting the best reviews, and I was concerned that our audiences would just want to hear the *Guess Who Came at Dinner* stuff, while I wanted to move forward. Of course I'd happily play the hits, but mostly I wanted to show off those fresh-out-of-the-oven tunes. All I could do was put it all out there and hope for the best.

As for leaving Zach, well, that was a mixed blessing. No doubt I'd miss the guy – it's that whole honeymoon phase thing – but he was getting a little clingy and possessive, which I was not up for. I was up for casual-plus. Zach, well, he was up for *anything*.

And when I say *anything*, I mean *anything* – especially when it came to our sex life. Kevin wasn't the most adventurous lover. Zach was. He wasn't into S&M, or food fun, or anything like that – for him, it was that Donald Trump thing I mentioned before: *location, location, location*. Where I was perfectly happy to be messing around in my nice new bed, Zach was perfectly happy messing around anywhere *but* the new bed. On the floor, in the tub, on the kitchen table, under the kitchen table, against this wall, against that wall, on the deck, on the living-room love seat, on the studio sofa, behind the television. He begged me to do it outdoors – Prospect Park, specifically – and back in, say, my super-tactile high school days, I probably would've taken him up on it. Now, too many people had high quality cameras in their cell phones, and I did not need to see my pale, freckled tush posted on TMZ.com.

Yeah, I'd definitely miss Zach some, but a few months away from New York might be good in that it would be just enough time to see if I missed him *lots*. And who knows – he might decide while I was gone that he'd be better off without me anyhow.

**ZACH BINGHAM** She thought that I might think I'd be better off without her? All my girlfriends up to that point were children. Jenn Bradford was a woman. And once you go woman, you never go back. So no, I wouldn't ever have thought that.

**MASUHARA JONES** When our booking agent gave us our tour schedule, I was like, *What?* Check it out:

First stop, New York, then down to Philly, then back up to Delaware, then back down to Newark, then back up to Rhode Island, then back down to Pittsburgh, then we'd fly to Los Angeles, then drive down to San Diego, then up to Seattle, then back down to San Francisco, then back to Los Angeles. And that was just the first two weeks.

As if the routing wasn't bad enough, I had to see Kevin on a daily basis. Gross.

*[Kevin McAllister refused to be interviewed for this book until two weeks before press time, and only briefly at that. The author would like to thank a certain someone for convincing Kevin that it would be a good idea to participate in the project.]*

**KEVIN MCALLISTER** The only reason I'm talking to you is because Miss Masuhara Jones threatened to physically attack me if I don't, and being attacked by Miss Masuhara Jones once was more than enough. Her itty-bitty feet did some damage to this brother's junk. Okay, I suppose I'm also talking because it might not be a bad idea to get my side of the story out there. I'm sure Jenn has trashed me to you plenty already.

What's my story, you ask. What did she tell you? Really? Damn. Maybe I'll keep quiet about that particular portion of my life, and focus for now on that first post-break-up tour.

I don't know the real reason why Jenn wanted me to stay with the band. She's always said that it was because she dug playing with me, but at the time I thought it was more than that. See, Jenn's always trying to prove something, always looking for validation, and in this case, I think she wanted to show people she could keep her band together no matter what. Or maybe she wanted me around to keep an eye on me. Or to get back with me. Seriously, I don't know.

I kept doing the gig because I liked playing with her – the girl can sing, and play, and write, a true triple-threat – plus she hooked her sidemen up with some good coin.

**JENN BRADFORD** The only reason Kevin was still with The JB's – the *only* reason – was because the boy could play.

Okay, there was one other reason. It pains me to say that he looks cute on stage, and the more cuteness we

have on stage, the better. Now don't get the wrong idea –
he stopped looking cute to me when I dumped him. But
I'll acknowledge he's a hottie, and I thought it would be
nice to throw a bone to the female sector of my fan base.

ZACH BINGHAM For whatever reason, in general I'm not
the luckiest guy in the world. I'm a writer, after all, and
we writers usually have to make our own luck, but
sometimes, once in a rare while, I manage to get
sprinkled with fairy dust. The week after Jenn splits, out
of nowhere, Tinkerbell pays me a visit in the form of a
features editor from *Rolling Stone*.

This guy emails me that he likes the *Reality Check*
review I wrote for *Spin*, and would I want to do a full-
blown feature on Jenn, maybe even for the cover. My
first thought is to immediately recuse myself from the
situation, because I thought it might be impossible to
write an unbiased article about somebody who you're
sleeping with. But then I think, *Do I really need to write
an unbiased article?* I'm aware that Jenn thinks of us as
casual, but from my perspective, we're dating. She calls
me her sorta-boyfriend. That means she's my sorta-
girlfriend. And to me, even with the 'sorta' qualifier,
that's still dating.

Yeah, I acknowledge it's not what you would call the
most solid dating situation in the world. I'm not
delusional. But I am a dreamer.

At any rate, why shouldn't I bang out a 'rah-rah Jenn'
piece for *Rolling Stone*? That's one good way for a sorta-
boyfriend to become a *boyfriend*-boyfriend. Isn't it?

**JENN BRADFORD** When we landed at LAX, there was a text message waiting for me: ROLLING STONE WANTS TO DO A FEATURE ON YOU. I'M DOING IT. CALL ME ASAP. MANY HUGS, INDIE BOY.

Talk about a conflict of interest for him. Talk about an interesting conflict for me. Are writers allowed to do 8,000 words on somebody whose toes they've sucked? Apparently so. Was I happy about it? I wasn't sure. No matter how professional Zach was – and when he wanted to, he could be as professional as any music writer I'd ever dealt with – the article would be different than it would've been had we *not* shared several magical toe moments. Maybe the article would be better, maybe it'd be worse, but no matter what, it would definitely be *different*.

And then there was the question of how we would relate to each other on the road. Would we want to make things public, and hold hands on the bus, and make out behind a speaker column? Would we want to keep it on the down-low, and sneak away for a romantic dinner, and tiptoe in and out of each other's hotel rooms at three in the morning? There was also the possibility that in those close confines, we'd get completely sick of each other.

The most pertinent question though, was, *Why the hell don't I quit stressing, and let the whole thing play itself out, and see what happens?* It couldn't hurt. At least I hoped so. I didn't want another batch of hurt. I'd finally gotten rid of fifty-plus per cent of the last batch.

Masu agreed. She said, 'Just make sure he spells your name right. And be nice to him.' Always managing, that one.

I told her, 'I'm always nice to him. I like him.'

Masu said, 'Then what's the problem? Liking him is a good thing. Isn't it?'

I said, 'Sometimes. He's funny. But he's young. But he's cute. But he's pretentious. But he's super smart. But he's a hustler. But he's talented, and cool, and he has a nice neck.' That was the best explanation I could give her. I wasn't able to offer up any solid answers, because I didn't have any.

Masu said, 'You're right about him being cute. And I think you guys are cute together.'

Personally, I didn't think 'cute' was the right word for us. 'Inconsistent' might've been more apt. Sometimes we were awkward, sometimes we were sweet, sometimes we were distant, sometimes we were close. In retrospect, I realize our inconsistency came from me. See, I couldn't shut my brain off the way I used to. Before The Kevin Incident, I was pretty much all about five things, and five things only: music, friendship, love, sex and food, in that order. Now there was lots of white noise, and lots of pressure, and lots of nerves. If I wasn't thinking about The Kevin Incident, I was thinking about how *Reality Check* was selling, and if I wasn't thinking about *Reality Check*, I was thinking about touring, and if I wasn't thinking about touring, I was thinking about missing my old life with Naomi, and if I wasn't thinking about life with Naomi, I was thinking about blah blah blah blah blah.

But Masu had always done right by me, had always given me good career advice – and personal advice, for that matter – so I texted Zach and told him that if he wanted to, he could fly out to California and ride the bus with us for a week or so. We then BlackBerried back and forth for a few minutes. He made me laugh. I remembered his neck, and his stubbly kisses, and the sweet smell of his vanilla deodorant. I began to think the whole thing might be fun.

**ZACH BINGHAM** Two days later, I fly out to LA, and hop on their tour bus right after their gig at the Roxy – a show that seriously smoked, by the way – and Jenn's sitting in one of the captain's chairs, and nobody else from the band is around, and I give her a little hello kiss, and immediately: *weird vibe*.

**JENN BRADFORD** He gave me a little hello kiss on the mouth, which was very nice, and I went with it for a bit, but I sensed it had the potential to become *way* more than just a little hello kiss, so I pulled away and said, 'Whoa, calm down, boy.' I was glad to see him and all, but making out with a writer in front of my band wasn't classy, and as we all know by now, I'm nothing if not a classy broad.

**ZACH BINGHAM** The kiss starts out well, but devolves into something wholly impersonal. Zero warmth. Zero heat. That's cool, I think. Probably best. Journalistic integrity.

But man, do I want her. So does everybody else in the world, it seems. But I've had her. And I want her again. And again.

We separate, and Stewart jumps on the bus and immediately starts sucking up to me, which is the surest way to write yourself right out of my story. I mumble, and grumble, and give him attitude, and make it obvious that I don't want to talk to him, so he disappears into the back. McAllister comes on, and he tries to crush my fingers with an oh-so-macho handshake – just like that Porter Ellis dude – then he stomps off to the back. Masuhara gives me a full body hug that was far sexier than Jenn's tepid greeting, then bails. Then it's just me and Jenn again.

I say, 'So,' trying to sound all sexy and seductive. I look her up and down, and she's still beautiful, even dressed down in her post-show gear, which consists of a tight, faded black Ramones T-shirt, frayed, low-riding cargo shorts and bare feet. But she's clearly tired. I don't know if it stems from being on the road, or just having played a high-energy show, or what. I make another tentative move into her personal space.

She says, 'So.' Her 'so' isn't sexy and seductive like my 'so'. Her 'so' is *so* dull. In that one syllable, she conveys distance, and exhaustion, and professionalism. Impressive syllable, I think.

I take the hint, and slip completely out of lover mode and into writer mode. Pulling my notepad out of my back pocket I say, 'Feel like talking?'

She looks away, sighs and says, 'I feel like leaving.'

**KEVIN MCALLISTER** I'm not gonna deny that when the dude from *Rolling Stone* showed up on the tour bus, and right away started getting all touchy-feely with Jenn, I got kind of annoyed. After every gig, guys flock to her – actors, models and random good-looking dudes, you know, that sort of thing – and it never bothered me, both before and after our break-up. But there was something about the way she interacted with this skinny white boy that made me uncomfortable.

**JENN BRADFORD** I told Zach to sit tight, I needed to pee. Tour bus bathrooms are gross, especially when there are boys on the bus who refuse to lift up the seat when they do their thing, so I got in and out of the WC as quickly as I could, then headed to the back lounge for some think time.

I stared out the window. People were filing out of the Roxy, most of them couples, most of them holding hands, most of them smiling. I liked the smiling part, because that meant we'd put on a pretty decent show. The holding-hands part, well, I guess the best word to describe the way I felt about that was 'wistful'.

It dawned on me then that I'd made a boo-boo. I shouldn't have let Zach travel with us. Why? A couple of reasons.

First of all, from a purely logistical perspective, it's bad for band unity to welcome a lover into the circle. For example, I've always thought that Paul, George and Ringo got pissed off at John when he started bringing Yoko around *not* because they were jealous that she was stealing him away from them, but because when you're recording with your band, and that band has been together for a long time, you want as few people in the studio as possible. Having a stranger around – especially if it's a new boyfriend or girlfriend – will totally mess with the group's groove.

Now I realize once you reach a certain level of popularity, you're never completely alone as a unit. If you're on the road, the crew will always be there, and if you're in the studio, the producer and engineers will be there. But that's cool, because they're part of the team, plus you can walk away from them whenever you want to be alone, and nobody's feelings will get hurt. A journalist isn't part of the team, and never will be. When he's around, you always have to be on your toes. You have to make sure you don't say or do anything that'll look bad in print. I'm not passing judgment on Zach or his fellow writers. That's just the way it is.

Reason number two was the fact that Zach was there to do a job, and he took his job very seriously, and him doing a seriously good job meant that he'd be all up in our business. Having Zach sticking his tape recorder in everybody's face, all while trying to mack on me at the same time, had the potential to create some seriously soap operatic drama.

Plus there was that whole do-I-or-do-I-not-like-him-a-lot thing.

What I should've done for the purposes of the article was to set it up so Zach and I would go out to lunch, and talk for a couple of hours, and be in a public place the whole time, just like all my other interviews. But there we were, stuck on the bus together, me feeling awkward, him probably feeling hurt, and no way out for either of us.

I needed to figure some stuff out, so I thought it might be a good idea to pick Zach's brain before we raised anchor and shoved off to the next port – find out if he had any ideas how we could make this week as smooth as possible for everybody involved. So I trudged up to the front, and Zach and I stared at each other for a few seconds, and I opened my mouth, but before I could say anything coherent, I was interrupted by a familiar squeal.

*[And now a timely guest appearance by Grammy-winning, platinum-selling vocalist/actress Naomi Braver.]*

**NAOMI BRAVER** Okay, first of all, I've gotta tell you that the Roxy gig was the best gig I've ever seen Jenn do, even better than her first solo gig at Irving Plaza in New York, the one where I came up and did a song with her, the one after which we cried and hugged and hugged and cried for a bajillion hours.

I love Jenn. She's such a rock star. Even if she wasn't a rock star, she'd *still* be a rock star.

So I climbed on to her bus, and there's my redheaded rock star and this pierced-up indie boy, standing right in each other's personal space, and it looked to me like they had either just kissed, or were about to kiss, or were doing everything they could in order to stop themselves from kissing. I assumed this was the writer guy she'd messed around with a few months back, but I wasn't sure, because I hadn't heard anything about him in forever, and Jenn and I talk, or text, or IM, or email at least once a day, and she tells me everything, including stuff I don't want to know about. With me, Jenn never leaves a single thought unsaid. Sometimes it's fascinating, but sometimes it's gross. I'll spare you. Point being, if she hadn't mentioned him, it was because there wasn't anything worth mentioning. Or so I thought.

Her indie boy was cute, but if I saw him on the street, I wouldn't have pegged him as Jenn's type. Not that she has a specific type, but she definitely has a thing for black guys, and this particular indie boy was as far from black as you can get. He was so white, you could practically see through him. She also tends to gravitate toward guys with some semblance of muscle tone, and this guy was super scrawny. Pale and skinny. Kind of a pierced-up, tatted-up, boy version of me. Heh. Kidding.

**ZACH BINGHAM** Out of nowhere, Naomi Braver shows up. Yeah, she's an international superstar and she seems to be an interesting chick, and it would be great to get some quotes from her for my piece, but the only thing I'm thinking right at that moment is, *Take a hike, Naomi.*

I wanted Jenn for myself for a while. I'm selfish like that. So shoot me.

**JENN BRADFORD** I was so happy to see Naomi, I could've kissed her on the lips. With tongue, even. She said, 'I could come back later, if you want,' then she took a step toward the door. I practically tackled her and said, 'Nonononono. Stay – please stay. Please.'

I introduced her to Zach and explained why he was there, and then I came up with a brilliant idea. I asked Naomi, 'Feel like riding with us for a few days? We'll have you back in LA at the end of the week.' Having a rock goddess like Naomi around would make Zach's article that much better. Plus Naomi's my fave person in the whole world, and having her close by would rule. Plus her presence would guarantee that Zach and I would have less time alone together, and the less we were alone together, the less likely it would be that we'd start groping each other – or *not* groping each other and feeling awkward about the whole thing. Win/win/win.

The thing is, Naomi isn't what you would call the most spontaneous person in the world, so when I invited her to stay, she got all namby-pamby. She said, 'I dunno. I've got an acting class on Thursday, then an audition on Friday, and I've got a rehearsal on Sunday for that play I'm doing next month, then I'm gonna be an extra in this stupid low-budget movie on Monday during the day, and Travis was gonna make me dinner that night, and I lost five pounds because I'm so stressed out, so none of my pants fit, so I don't have a week's worth of clothes that I'm willing to be seen in public with.'

Zach said, 'Sounds like you've got a lot going on. Probably best if you stayed home.'

Naomi heard something in Zach's tone of voice she didn't like, and I know that because she shot him this look she'd been perfecting over the last couple of years, the kind of look that chops a guy's balls off with a rusty knife. It always cracked me up when she got tough with the boys, because back in the day, when she dealt with the opposite sex, she was a massive dork. And she'll agree with that.

So after a few seconds more of glaring, Naomi said, 'I'm coming. I'll borrow some jeans from Jenn. I'll buy a belt. Let's boogie.'

**ZACH BINGHAM** I've interviewed dozens of singers and actors and politicians and athletes – and I very rarely get starstruck. Even Jenn, who is probably the most beautiful woman I've ever written about – and I've written about Beyoncé and Keira Knightley and Jessica Alba and Halle Berry – didn't make me nervous.

But Naomi has a *thing*, and it's oddly intimidating, so when she starts giving me attitude, I shut up. I can't help it.

**JENN BRADFORD** I told Zach he could sleep in the front lounge of the bus, then gave him a tiny good night pat on the bicep and a tinier kiss on the neck – I couldn't resist – then I dragged Naomi into the bus's middle section. I lent her a pair of my pajamas, gave her a huge good night hug and crawled into my bunk.

Just to set the scene, I should mention that my bunk was located on the right front side of the cabin. I gave Naomi the bottom bunk on my side. Kevin had the bottom bunk on the left rear. That was as far apart as the two of us could sleep on the bus, which was still too close for my taste. But whenever I started to think about that too much, I'd tell myself over and over again, *He's a kick-ass drummer, he's a kick-ass drummer, he's a kick-ass drummer . . .*

**NAOMI BRAVER** I love flannel jammies. The only person I know who has a better flannel jammie collection than me is Jennifer Marie Bradford. The ones she lent me that night were red, and had cupcakes and candy bars and Hershey's Kisses all over them.

Here's a secret: I kept them. Here's another secret: I told her that I accidentally spilled bleach on them, so I had to throw them out. Now that's a completely ridiculous statement, because I've never bought a bottle of bleach in my life, and also because I'm so lazy with my laundry that I always throw my coloreds and whites into one machine.

Maybe don't put any of that in the book. It isn't the place to air my dirty laundry. Heh.

**JENN BRADFORD** Naomi looks way smooth and sexy on stage, but in the real world, she's a major klutz, so I wasn't particularly surprised when she fell out of her bunk, like, six seconds after the bus started moving.

**NAOMI BRAVER** Hey, it was better than that time in Europe when I fell out of a middle bunk, and I had a six-inch bruise on my ass that, according to my man Travis, is still visible in the right light. Maybe don't mention that in the book, either.

**JENN BRADFORD** I poked my head out from behind my bunk curtain and asked Naomi if she was all right. She lifted up and pointed to her elbow, which was a tiny bit scuffed, and said, 'I got a little ouchie. But I'm wide awake now. Let's you and me go in back and you can tell me what's up with Indie Boy.'

Despite my mental and physical exhaustion, I was pretty wide awake too, so we went into the back lounge. I put on a Billie Holiday CD and gave Naomi the scoop. The *full* scoop, including about my and Zach's piano tryst, and our bathtub tryst, and our glass elevator tryst – that was a good one, I have to admit – and our kitchen table tryst.

She said, 'Oh, for the love of God, stop.' Like I said, I gave her the *full* scoop, partly because I needed to share, and partly because it was nice to relive those semi-magical moments, and partly because it was fun to gross Naomi out. Then she asked, 'You think it's smart to have him travel with you?'

I said, 'I'm not sure. What do you think?'

She said, 'I'm not sure either. Maybe I should hang with him a bit. See if I can catch a vibe. I was kinda rude to him.'

I said, 'I noticed. Give him some time. He grows on you. Maybe you'll even bond with him.'

She said, 'I like bonding with your boyfriends. Except for that guy David Walsh. Remember him?' I did. I dated David Walsh when Nay and I were living in our East Village shoebox. Nice enough guy and a fine guitar player, but he wore bikini-brief underwear and would sometimes forget to put his pants on in the morning. Naomi told me time and again how tired she was of his package staring at her while she was trying to eat her Cheerios. David had a nice package, granted, but I could see her point.

Anyway, I told Naomi, 'Masu thinks it's a good idea he's here. She thinks a *Rolling Stone* cover would be awesome.' Naomi had had two big articles about herself in *Rolling Stone*, but neither of them made the front page.

She nodded and said, 'It *would* be awesome, but it seems to me that this week could get strange. You like him, but he *lurves* you. And Kevin's here. Yikes.' This is yet another reason I love Nay: she doesn't just get *me*, she gets *it*. Then she smiled and said, 'Okay, here's what we're gonna do. I'm gonna shadow you. I'll make sure you're not alone with him when you don't wanna be . . .'

I said all sarcastically, 'That is such an awesome idea.'

Then she said, '. . . and if you decide you want me to run interference for you, or if I need to get your attention, we'll say a secret password.'

I said all seriously, 'That is such a gay idea.'

She said, 'Yeah, gay in an awesome way.' Then she looked at the pajamas I'd lent her and said, 'If you want me to keep you from being alone together, the secret password is *cupcake*.'

I rolled my eyes and said, 'That's swell, Nay-Nay. What do I say if I *do* wanna be alone with him?'

She checked out her jammies again, and said, 'The password for that is *candy*. And don't call me Nay-Nay.'

No matter how much of a mega-star Naomi was, she'd always have my back.

And she'd always be a dork.

ZACH BINGHAM The next morning, McAllister wakes me up around eight o'clock by flicking my arm. Scares the shit out of me. It takes me a second to remember where I am. He says, 'S'up, man? Sleep okay?'

I say, 'I suppose.' I didn't, really. Jenn Bradford isn't U2, and can't afford a lavish tour bus, so the sofa-slash-bench I sleep on in the front of the bus has the thinnest of padding, and is only about six feet long. I'm six feet two inches, and have no padding of my own whatsoever. Which is not conducive to quality sleep.

He nods and says, 'Cool. Want some coffee?'

I say, 'Sure. Thanks.'

He puts some beans in a grinder, then puts the grounds into the coffee machine, then says, 'Cool. Ever seen the West Coast?'

I say, 'Nope. First time.'

He says, 'Cool. Looking forward?'

I say, 'For sure.'

He says, 'Cool. You doing Jenn?'

I have no idea how to field that one. On the one hand, I want to throw it right back in his face, to give him precise details of her body, and the way she moves, and how she smells. On the other hand, Jenn told me he's a bit unstable, and his right tricep probably weighs more than my entire upper body and my whole left leg combined, so I do the prudent thing, and ignore the question altogether and say, 'Do you have any non-dairy creamer?'

**JENN BRADFORD** Naomi shook me awake around eight fifteen and said, 'Bad news for you – your ex and your current are bonding by the coffee machine. And bad news for me – I want some coffee.'

I buried my face in my pillow and thought, *Wonderful, it's already starting.* I said, 'Do me a favor. When you get your coffee, make sure nobody's saying anything that shouldn't be said, or doing anything that shouldn't be done. You know what I mean?'

She pulled the pillow off of my face and said, 'Are you insane? I'm not going up there by myself. Cupcake, cupcake, cupcake. Or is it candy, candy, candy?' She then yanked my blanket off and said, 'Get your butt out of there.' Before she became a mega-star, Naomi Braver was a mellow and non-demanding, albeit neurotic girl. It was odd that she was bossing me around – I was usually the bossy one. But in general, I liked the ballsy, sane version of Naomi better than the tentative, kooky one.

**NAOMI BRAVER** The first thing I noticed when I saw Kevin in the light of day was that everything about him had changed: the way he stood, the way he talked, the way he breathed. When Jenn and I first met him, he was funny and romantic and self-deprecating and cute. Now he was angry and sad. However, I will acknowledge that he was still cute.

**ZACH BINGHAM** McAllister and I are staring at each other, and I feel like I'm in a cheesy Western, like he's gonna challenge me to pistols at fifty feet. I'm not intimidated. I realize he won't do anything right there on the bus. Frankly, the whole stare-down makes me feel stupid. I want to make a joke, but the dude is on hair-trigger, and I don't wanna take the chance of setting him off.

About two minutes into our cheeseball movie moment, Jenn and Naomi make a stumbling entrance, both barely awake. If *Rolling Stone* ever thought outside of the box and ran a picture of Jenn fresh out of bed, instead of something where she's all made up and stylized, they'd sell a zillion issues. Her hair is a disaster, and she has sleep creases on her cheek, but at the same time she's fresh and adorable and galactically gorgeous – and *real*.

**JENN BRADFORD** When I saw the way Kevin looked back and forth between me and Zach, all angry and sad, I felt a little sorry for the guy. But only a little. I shouldn't have felt at all sorry for him. Would you? I didn't think so.

Anyhow, neither of the boys was saying anything, and the tension between the two of them was intense, but Zach managed to give me a sweet smile nonetheless. Much of the time, Zach played like he was the cynical, oh-so-hip rock snob, but when he let his guard down – like when he smiled like that – I could see the boy had some depth that he himself probably wouldn't even admit to.

**NAOMI BRAVER** Zach gave Jenn some massive goo-goo eyes, even though she was sporting her I-just-woke-up-and-look-like-I-got-hit-by-a-truck look. The boy was smitten. But Jenn has that effect on a lot of guys. Personally, I think that having men falling in love with you twenty-four seven would get annoying after a while, but that's me.

**ZACH BINGHAM** For some reason, Jenn started saying 'cupcake' over and over again. Then she grabbed Naomi's sleeve and said, 'Or is it candy, candy, candy?'

Chick singers, man. Sometimes they're loveable, sometimes they're freakazoids.

**NAOMI BRAVER** Jenn dragged me back to the bunk area and said, 'This isn't gonna work. He so should *not* be here. It's weirdness. Much too much weirdness. Me and Zach, and me and Kevin, and Zach and Kevin – *oy*.'

I said, ' "Oy" sums it up quite well, sweetie. But Zach's here, and it would be a seriously bad idea to chuck him out of the bus. Remember what happened with Simon?'

**JENN BRADFORD** Of course I remember what happened with Seymour Simon, or as he preferred to be called, just 'Simon'. He produced the first Naomi record, then he traveled with us as a soundman on our summer tour, and it was only after we'd been stuck on a bus together for those two months that we realized the guy was a sleazebag, a walking soap opera.

He was also gorgeous – think Robert Redford, circa

1980. He seduced Naomi – he had a thing for female vocalists, and tried to bag all the girls whose records he produced, and generally succeeded – then he macked on me while he was still doing Naomi, and I went for it for, like, six seconds, and felt like a moron. While all this drama was going on, my brother Travis was lusting after Nay – which he'd been doing for his entire post-puberty life – and wanted Simon gone. Long story short, we threw Ass Boy – that was our affectionate nickname for him – off the bus somewhere in Iowa, and before twenty-four hours had even passed, the news was all over the Internet, and even though everybody knew we did the right thing, we still came off as total idiots.

NAOMI BRAVER I told Jenn, 'Listen, he's here, so you may as well make the best of it. Look at it this way: he's good-looking and he seems like he's got a brain, even if he is kind of a weenie boy. Just be nice. Don't give him attitude. Don't say anything that'll make you look lame in his article. Besides, it'll only be a week. You might even enjoy it. Also, you'll be so busy that you'll forget he's even here.'

She said, 'How? How'll I forget?'

I said, 'No clue. Just be nice and have fun.'

She said, 'I'll try.'

I said, 'Seriously, be nice and have fun.'

She said, 'Seriously, I'll try.'

I said, 'No, you won't.'

She said, 'Yeah, I will.' And to her credit, she did.

**MASUHARA JONES** Have you ever seen a family of ducks traveling together before? It's a straight line, with the mommy duck at the front, and however many baby ducks following right behind. That's the way we rolled the week Zach was with us.

Jenn led the pack. Zach was always right behind her. Naomi was always right behind him. I was always right behind Naomi . . .

**T.J. STEWART** I was always right behind Masuhara. Shorty be havin' a *foine* ass.

**MASUHARA JONES** . . . and Kevin was behind all of us, except he kept a little more distance. Usually when we hit the road, we were all loose and chill, and – except for when Kevin got in one of his moods – straight-up fun. But when the writer was there, well, not so much.

**ZACH BINGHAM** I'd never hung out with a mega-selling band on a major tour for more than a day, and if it wasn't for Jenn's presence – or lack thereof – I'd have left this one after forty-eight hours. It's tension city. Every time I look to the left, there's Naomi, acting at once sweet and distant. Whenever I look to the right, there's McAllister, passively/aggressively making it known that, given the opportunity, he'd take a shot at me.

But where's Jenn during all this?

I can't get her alone. She won't, or can't sit still. And she keeps turning to Naomi and saying 'cupcake' or 'candy' – and I still haven't figured out what that's about.

I try to talk to her one-on-one before soundchecks, and after soundchecks, and right before she goes to bed, and right after she wakes up, and during breakfast, lunch and dinner, and I get nothing, because she won't stay in one place for any significant amount of time. Jenn won't give me anything but surface. She's become the worst kind of interview subject – closed-off, unapproachable and, frankly, very boring.

My story's gonna suck, and I'm miserable.

And I want to kiss her.

And I can't.

And I want Naomi Braver to stop calling me 'Weenie Boy'.

**JENN BRADFORD** Three days later, we hit San Francisco – and I frigging *love* San Francisco. If I wasn't a dyed-in-the-wool East Coaster, I'd move there in a heartbeat. I figured while we were out there, I'd take Zach to my favorite high-tone, chi-chi eatery, Restaurant Gary Danko. What with how I'd been yo-yo-ing the poor guy, he deserved to be treated to a high-tone, chi-chi, five-course tasting menu.

In the cab on the way to the restaurant, I couldn't think of any good conversational starters, and he wasn't even trying, so we made some awkward small talk. At the table, he was only interested in discussing the menu and the wine list. After the waiter took our order, I said, 'Okay, Indie Boy. What's the problem?'

He gulped down his glass of Pellegrino, stifled a burp, then said, 'You honestly don't know?'

I had a theory – he was pissed that I wasn't being at all affectionate – but I wasn't one hundred per cent certain, so I said, 'No, I don't.'

He said, 'This whole week, you've made me look and feel like an idiot.'

Oh. Guess my theory was wrong. I asked, 'What're you talking about?'

He gave me a pissed off look. I'd never seen him look pissed off, and it wasn't pretty. Zach has an angular face which naturally falls into a smile. When it's frowning – well, anger isn't his good side. He said, 'Listen, if you agree to do an interview, you do the fucking interview. I've been literally chasing after you for six days now, and you haven't given me shit. Anybody that sees me following you from the bus to soundcheck, then from soundcheck to the catering hall, then from the catering hall to the dressing room, then from the dressing room to the stage is probably thinking, *Who's that dude stalking Jenn Bradford?*'

I said, 'Nobody's thinking that.'

He said, '*Everybody's* thinking that! It makes me come off as unprofessional and desperate. And frankly, it's not doing wonders for your image, either.'

I said, 'My image? What're you talking about?' I looked around the restaurant. Nobody was staring, but people were definitely giving us some sideways glances. 'And try to keep it quiet.'

He said, 'Some of the local beat writers have been asking me what the hell's going on with me and you. I tell them, and they ain't exactly impressed.'

I said, 'What're you telling them?'

He said, 'That you're ducking me. Don't worry, I haven't said anything about us—'

I said, 'Thank you. I appreciate that.'

He said, 'Don't thank me. I'm only keeping quiet because what's the point of saying anything about us? I'm more into you than you are into me. What's the point?'

I said, 'I'm into you.' And I meant it.

He said, 'But not as much as I'm into you. And that's fine, you've been through some shit, and you're gonna be on the road so much for the next year that I'll barely see you anyhow, so I've accepted that, and I'll take what I can get, because two minutes of Jenn Bradford is better than no minutes of Jenn Bradford.'

I thanked him. See, I told you he could be sweet.

He said, 'But I'm heading home tomorrow, and if I write my article based on what I've gotten from you this week, it's gonna suck, and I'm gonna look more like a dipshit than I already do. If you don't want me to touch you outside of New York City, then fine, but at least let me interview you for real. Okay?'

I took a taste of the first appetizer – some lovely glazed oysters with caviar and zucchini – and said, 'Okay.'

So he pulled out his miniature digital recorder, and we ate, and he asked me questions, and we drank, and he asked me more questions, and we drank some more, and we ate some more, and by the time we got back to the hotel after two in the morning we were both thoroughly full and tired and buzzed, and you know what happens with a sorta-couple when they're full, tired and buzzed at a San Francisco hotel after two in the morning.

Sex. Lots of sex. Lots of sex that involves harder-than-expected neck biting.

I was a vampire.

**ZACH BINGHAM** She's on fire. It's all very sweet and tender, albeit in a rugby scrum kind of way. I end up limping back to my room with a bruised thigh, a raw member and a bloody neck.

The whole thing makes me feel kinda lousy about what I'm planning to write. But only a little bit. I have my priorities. At this point, being a good writer is fulfilling and lasting. Being a sorta-boyfriend is frustrating and ephemeral.

You have to make choices. Then you have to live with them.

And my choice was made.

**JENN BRADFORD** I had a ton of promotional crap to do when we got back to LA, so my vampire attack was Zach's official send-off. I wouldn't be back in New York for over a month, which gave me plenty of time to re-evaluate our situation. It came to me that maybe the reason I treated the poor guy so inconsistently – and 'inconsistently' is putting it mildly – was that I believed being in another long-term relationship could lead to another ugly break-up, and another ugly break-up could lead to me being fucked up in the head worse than I was after Kevin, and I most definitely didn't need that, especially in light of the fact that I was almost starting to feel normal-ish again. Can you say 'trust issues'?

But I still couldn't decide whether or not I wanted to take me and Zach to another level, whether I should promote him from sorta-boyfriend to *boyfriend*-boyfriend. The only way to figure that out would be to make sure we got some quality time together when I got home from our upcoming European tour.

Which is exactly what I intended to do.

**BILLIE HOLIDAY'S GHOST** The rest of Jennifer's tour went the way that most big-time rock 'n' roll tours go these days: lots of driving, lots of fast food at dirty highway oases, lots of watching the same DVDs over and over again, lots of young men breaking wind without excusing themselves, lots of hurrying-up-and-waiting, some good reviews, some not-so-good reviews, some enthusiastic crowds, some not-so-enthusiastic crowds, some fun, some bull-puckey. Not exactly glamorous, but it's better than working at the post office.

I should mention that Jennifer called Mr Bingham four times after he went home to New York. He never called her back, and it saddened her. But Ms Braver decided to stick with Jennifer for the rest of that tour, which softened the blow.

You know, Jennifer Bradford is a lucky woman. If I had friends like hers, friends who looked out for me each and every step of the way, each and every single day, I might still be alive today. Then again, maybe not. The reality of my situation was that my friends could've looked out for me till the cows came home, and I probably still would've found a way to mess myself up. I loved good drinks, good powder and bad men *way* too much to live a long life.

But that wasn't the case with Jennifer. She's more or less sane, and she has wonderful friends and family, so she doesn't need to self-medicate on any kind of serious level. Drinkwise, a couple glasses of pinot noir, and she's good to go. Powder-wise, she doesn't even touch the stuff. As for bad men, well, she's had a few. But she's a tough broad – just ask her, she'll tell you – so a bad man or three won't bring her to her knees. A good man might though. If only there was one in the vicinity.

Even when it seems like Jennifer's gonna mess herself up, she *doesn't* mess herself up. She's a survivor. She's driven like few others I know. For example, Ms Braver was the one who became famous first, but she couldn't have done it without Jennifer prodding her, and prodding her, and prodding her some more. That's the way Jennifer works.

Not only that, but she's always productive, regardless of her emotional situation. While all that junk on the bus with Mr Bingham and Mr McAllister was going on, Jennifer wrote three songs, two of which I feel are among the best she's ever written. But I might not be the best judge, because those two are both jazz tunes that can only be played with a swingin' upright bassist and a subtle drummer. And for the record, that probably wouldn't work with The JB's, because while Mr Stewart is swingin', Mr McAllister is *not* subtle. Yes, the boy can play. But not subtly.

Another thing that I adore about Jennifer is how she can write and write and write, no matter what's going on in her life. Me, I didn't write too many top-notch ditties. For instance, 'Fine and Mellow' was good, and I'm quite proud of 'Strange Fruit', and I liked 'God Bless the Child' the first 5,000 times I sang it, but that's the best of the best. I couldn't write if I had too much drama going on in my life. Or if I was high. And my life was all about commotion and inebriation.

I guess this is one of the many reasons why I feel so close to Jennifer, why I watch after her more than anybody, because I know she'll persevere even if Mr McAllister insists on starting trouble, or if Ms Jones is unable to properly handle her tasks because she keeps thinking about the fact that Mr Stewart is a mediocre lover . . .

**T.J. STEWART** *Say what?!?*

**BILLIE HOLIDAY'S GHOST** . . . or if Mr Bingham writes a magazine article that maybe he shouldn't have written.

# Rolling Stone

## May 29, 2009

### ROAD RAGE
### *Jenn Bradford: In Serious Need of a Reality Check?*

### by Zach Bingham

This story is about Jenn Bradford. It's also about me. You see, I made myself part of this story. This article is a self-indulgent piece of journalistic poop. But that's surprising to nobody, because I'm a self-indulgent piece of poop journalist. Thank you very much.

That said, this particular article's poopiness isn't entirely my fault. I might've been able to come up with something less poop-like if I hadn't decided to write the truth. I could've made my week on the road with Jenn Bradford, and her band, and her former musical cohort Naomi Braver, sound all polished and sanitary. I could've written only about their stellar concerts, or the band's almost innocent joy about their slow-but-steady ascent, or the sincere kindness of their management team and road crew.

Maybe that would've been for the best.

Before I get to the meat of this poop, I should tell you right off the bat that the second I accepted this assignment, I broke Music Journalism Rule #2: Don't write an article about somebody you've had sex with. (Rule #1. F.Y.I., is: Don't mix up 'you're' and 'your', or else your editor will think you're a ditz and never hire you again.) In retrospect, I should have told my editor, 'I've been doinking Jenn. Get somebody else.'

But I didn't. Thus the poop.

One could theorize that Jennifer Marie Bradford was constructed in a laboratory by a scientist who wanted to create the perfect almost-rock-star. Check the checklist:

- Face that could stop (or start) wars
- Body that could stop the Earth from rotating on its axis
- Smoky, Billie Holiday-ish singing voice
- Excellent-but-not-*too*-excellent piano voice
- Ability to write poppy-but-not-*too*-poppy tunes

On a certain level, she's a robo-musician who can perform and compose non-stop, circumstances be damned. I saw her rock San Francisco working on practically zero sleep. She destroyed San Diego despite suffering through the worst sound system I've ever had the displeasure to encounter. And she spanked Los Angeles while being all but stalked by this dude who was trying desperately to get back in her pants. That dude, of course, was me. I'm not too proud to beg, baby. Never leave me. Never go.

'It's my job,' Jenn explains when asked how she manages to deliver quality music in the face of piled-high obstacles, either real or imagined. 'It's what I do. I'm unfit to do anything else. I've only had two jobs in my life – coffee slinger and musician. Who else would hire me, except maybe for a record label? My CV blows.'

I'd been sleeping with Jenn on and off for about three months prior to when I was assigned this story, which might explain why, from the second I joined Jenn's traveling circus on the West Coast, I was met with a wall of silence from the head JB.

The fact that Naomi Braver was guarding Jenn's chastity with her life was also a problem.

*Continued on page 99*

MASUHARA JONES Zach was right about one thing in that bullshit article of his – he *is* a pooper.

JENN BRADFORD Zach's swell little article didn't come out until a couple weeks after we'd returned from that quick springtime European tour. Remember how I told you I was pretty fed up with touring in the US? With Europe, it was just the opposite. London – awesome. Paris – awesome. Berlin – sucked, but Rome, Nice and Madrid more than made up for it.

The timing of the article couldn't have been worse. I was already in a shitty headspace, because before I could even do my laundry – which I had a ton of because, well, good luck dealing with an Austrian Laundromat – I read an email from the fine folks at Éclat Records saying that *Reality Check* wasn't, as they put it, 'meeting expect-ations', and that in a few days, I had to do a week of non-stop radio interviews and podcasts. They said that was the most cost-efficient way to promote, and the fact that they were thinking about cost-efficiency was a scary sign. Record labels only pump money into promoting a product that was selling. They don't throw good money after bad. It was heartbreaking to think that Éclat considered *Reality Check* done in only five months.

When it comes to sales figures, I've always been a bit spoiled. The first two Naomi albums went respectively platinum and double platinum. My first solo album sold about 300,000 copies, and *Guess Who Came at Dinner* went gold to the tune of 650,000. But poor *Reality Check* was having a tough time of it. We're talking under 100,000. Good numbers for a baby band. Heinous numbers for a veteran singer/songwriter like me.

If *Reality Check* died – if it stopped selling altogether – my career as I knew it would literally be over. Oh sure, I could keep releasing albums left and right, but it was unlikely that any major label would touch me, and an indie label wouldn't give me any significant budget for recording or touring, so I'd probably end up being on my own. *Jenn Bradford's new record available only at JennBradford.com.* That would be fine, I suppose, but I wouldn't be able to live anything near the lifestyle I'd become accustomed to, which wasn't even all that extravagant. I'd have to sell the condo, and probably much of my recording gear, and move into a tiny little apartment in Manhattan – or move out of New York City altogether. Yuck.

All of which meant I didn't have the time or energy to even think about why Zach refused to return my phone calls or emails. Frankly, I didn't even want to go there. Him blowing me off was a little too close to Kevin territory for my taste.

Besides, there was another guy I couldn't get out of my head. And not necessarily in a good way.

**PORTER ELLIS** After Jenn said that little sentence – 'You should open a jazz club, Porter Ells' – it was all I could think about. For the next twenty-four hours, it was like a static in my head: *open a jazz club . . . open a jazz club . . . open a jazz club.*

So I dived right on in. That's what I do. If I get a good notion, I make it happen. Fast.

I began laying the groundwork for the venue a mere week later. I got a realtor on the case, I called my designer, I interviewed architects and PR flacks, I tracked down booking agents, I hired a market research firm, and I bought approximately 400 new jazz CDs. You see, this had to be done right. The best New York jazz clubs thrive for decades. The worst go under in mere months. I wanted mine to be around for my children to run. I had one shot, and I had to make it my best.

I had the capital, I had the time, and I had the passion for the music. It was a brilliant idea. Frankly, I was annoyed I hadn't thought of it myself in the first place.

**JENN BRADFORD** A few days after I got back from Europe, I was totally exhausted, but totally starved, and totally bored of takeout, and hunger won out over exhaustion, so I dragged my ass out of bed and went shopping to refill my empty fridge and pantry. When I got home, all loaded up with grocery bags, who's holding the front door all gentlemanly-like for me? My snoozy, snooty across-the-hall neighbor. In the interest of improving neighborly relations, I gave him a smile and said, 'Porter Ellis! Porter Porter Ellis Ellis! Porter Porter Porter Ellis Ellis Ellis!'

He didn't smile back – it seemed that Porter Ellis wasn't much of a smiler – but he was nonetheless very polite. We small-talked pleasantly for a couple of minutes while we waited for our super-slow glass elevator to show up. As the doors opened, he said, 'I've been thinking about you, Jenn. Practically non-stop.'

*Great*, I thought, *my boring neighbor's gonna start stalking me*. When we got into the elevator, I scrunched over to one side, hugged a couple of grocery bags to my chest and said, very neutrally, 'Yeah?'

He said, 'Yes. Remember when you mentioned I should open a jazz club?'

I said, 'I suppose so.'

He smiled and nodded, and said, 'It's happening.'

I'm used to being hit on, and when I'm not interested in the hitter-onner, I do my best to not hurt anybody's feelings, but like I said, I was tired and hungry, a combination that often leads to irrational thoughts, stupid decisions, and a case of the foot-in-mouths, which explains why my first thought was that Porter Ellis was doing this club thing to woo me, the same smarmy way he showed off his apartment and his furniture that first day we met. I said, 'That's nice. But don't do it for my sake. Don't try and impress me. I won't be. Impressed, that is.'

Porter Ellis looked at me like, *What're you talking about?* Then he said, 'Excuse me?'

I said, 'Don't open your little club for my sake. I mean, I have a boyfriend already.' Actually, I only had a sorta-boyfriend who'd stopped returning my phone calls and emails, but Porter Ellis didn't need to know that. 'And just for future reference, doing something like that isn't a good way to get a girl to like you.'

Porter Ellis gave me another baffled look, and I realized that I'd screwed up. He said, 'Are you so arrogant as to believe that I'm making this enormous investment of time and money and energy and resources so I can impress *you* enough that you'd fall into bed with me? Are you *really* that deluded?' He stopped to glare at me, then continued: 'And I'd like to add that I've been married four times, and know how to get dates. I have no romantic interest in you whatsoever.' He said all this very calmly and quietly, which for some reason made me feel even shittier than I would've felt had he yelled his lungs out. He scrunched over to his side of the elevator, and gave me a look of death.

Somebody in that tiny – and getting tinier – elevator had an ego that was in serious need of a reality check. And it wasn't Porter Ellis.

**PORTER ELLIS** The nerve of that woman! I offer her a sincere compliment and a thank you, and she immediately assumes I want to have sex with her. How dare she? She didn't know me. She didn't know a thing about me. She didn't know that when it came to business, the only person I needed to impress was myself. She didn't know that before I make a business move – or a social move, for that matter – I take nothing for granted, and look at a situation from every angle to make sure I can anticipate any possible problems.

Nor did she know that I was on a hiatus from women. Had she known it, she might not have believed what she believed.

I should mention that I never raise my voice at anybody. Raising one's voice equals losing control, and I don't like to lose control of any situation, be it business or personal. I also don't hate people. It takes too much time and energy.

But I do ignore them. That's easy.

**JENN BRADFORD** Porter Ellis didn't say a word to me for the rest of the elevator ride up to the fifth floor. He just kept glaring. I put down my grocery bags and said, 'I'm so sorry for the misunderstanding, Porter Ellis. Let me know if there's anything I can do to help you with this club thing. I can hook you up with some great sound engineers, and I can get you tons of phone numbers for tons of musicians. This city needs another jazz joint, and I'm sure you'll do a great job with it, and I'm happy to do what I can.' I reached into my purse, grabbed one of my business cards and put it in the breast pocket of his shirt. 'Here's my number. Use it.'

Then I went and made another dumb mistake.

**PORTER ELLIS** She marched right up to me, put her arms around my neck, and jammed her thigh into my crotch. Then she had the gall to kiss me on the neck. It was only a tiny kiss – it was almost as if a warm, wet butterfly had landed on my shoulder – but it was highly inappropriate.

**JENN BRADFORD** Porter Ellis reached behind his neck, gently removed my hands, then exited the elevator and went into his apartment. The quiet way he closed the door was louder to me than a slam.

How many times have you heard somebody say, 'I've never been so embarrassed in all my life'? How many times have you said it yourself? Well, when I called Naomi that night and told her the story, and when I ended with, *I've never been so blah blah blah blah blah*, I damn well meant it.

She said, 'Are you sure about that? What about the time we had our little meltdown in front of 200,000 people at the Glastonbury Festival? Or the time at the Staples

Center in Los Angeles when you licked the piano so hard during our encore that you chipped a tooth and bled all over that amazing three-thousand-dollar Badgley Mischka dress? Or that time in high school when you got busted going down on William King in the men's room outside the auditorium? Or the time when I walked in on you in our first apartment doing something to David Walsh that was so gross, I can't even bring myself to repeat it.'

I said, 'You've been listening to *Jenn Bradford's Greatest Embarrassment Hits*. Thanks, Nay.'

She said, 'I'm just giving you some perspective, honey. Nobody knows about this thing with your neighbor but you, me and him. On the other hand, *everybody* knew about you and William King.'

I said, 'This isn't making me feel any better. Or any less stupid.'

She said, 'Don't feel stupid. No need. He's just some guy. Whatever.'

I was quiet for a few seconds, then said, 'I don't know what's wrong with me. I'm tired all the time. And when I'm with people, I wanna be alone, and when I'm alone, I wanna be with people. And then I go and molest my neighbor.' Naomi didn't answer, so I said, '*Hello?* Anybody home?'

She said, 'I'm thinking. I mean, this is totally what I went through after "And Then" hit big. Remember?'

I said, 'Not really.'

She said, 'Yeah, you probably don't, because that's when we weren't talking.'

I said, 'Oh. Right.' Nay and I went through a two- or

three-month period right before we cut our second album when I was ready to strangle her, and probably vice versa. Why? For a variety of stupid reasons, the two primary ones being that she *was* dating our producer and she *wasn't* dating my brother. There was also the issue of me thinking she had total disregard for my contribution to the band, and her thinking that I wanted her to publicly give me all the credit for our success. All of it seemed monumental at the time, but I wince when I think about how idiotic it all was. Add that on to the wincing I was doing about Porter Ellis, and, well, there was a whole lot of wincing going on. 'I never asked you how you got through that. I totally suck.'

She said, 'You don't totally suck. Only partially.'

I said, 'Thanks. You've been a great help, Nay-Nay.'

She said, 'Don't call me Nay-Nay. And I didn't do anything specific to get through it. I ate boxes and boxes of Oreos, and I went on a lot of walks, and I took two or three naps a day. I waited for it all to pass. I'm not the most proactive person in the world. You are.'

I said, 'So what do you think I should do?'

She said, 'Write your neighbor a note telling him you're sorry for being such a slutty bitchface. Write some songs. Lay low until you have to go on the road again. Be productive. You always are. And get some Oreos.'

I said, 'I'm more of a Cherry Garcia girl.' She laughed a little, then told me she had to go, and that she loved me, and to let it go, and to get some rest, and then she hung up.

I don't know, now that I'm talking about it out loud,

that thing with Porter Ellis – I guess it was more of my flirty-pinup shit. I have a nice brain, and I couldn't figure out why it always insisted on using my body to fix my problems. I suppose the thinking was, when in doubt, make out. Sad. It made me wonder if I'd be trying to kiss my way out of sticky situations for the rest of my life. Or at least until I got fat and old, and nobody would want to kiss me.

I winced for another hour or so, then I went to sleep and dreamed about being fat, and old, and unkissable, and making a living playing the entire *Guess Who Came at Dinner* album at a dinner theater in the Catskills. It wasn't pretty.

I resolved the next morning to start exercising. I had to nip that fat thing in the bud.

**PORTER ELLIS** The next morning, there was a note taped to my door. It was from Jenn. It was exactly one sentence long. It said, *I'm sorry for being such a slutty bitchface, Porter Ellis.* Crude, certainly, but it did make me smile. A little.

It took a while for that exchange in the elevator with Jenn to fully wash itself away. Oh, I suppose if I'm being honest with myself, it never fully washed away. Its memory never completely disappeared.

For the next few days, I almost wished I'd run into Jenn so I could tell her off again. She struck me as being quite wrapped up in herself, and I think it would've been good for her to have somebody point this out to her in no uncertain terms. I suspected that since she had experienced a modicum of celebrity, nobody ever talked back to her. On the other hand, I wouldn't have been devastated if I never saw her again. To me, closure is overrated.

I guess what hit me the hardest was that Jenn questioned the impetus for my club project. I've always considered myself to be an upright person with honest motives. In this case, all I wanted was a place where jazz lovers could go to hear jazz they loved. That's all. Period. End of discussion.

**JENN BRADFORD** For the next couple of weeks, I was a virtual hermit. I barely went outside. It was just me and my piano, my television and my computer, piles of CDs and DVDs, and a few dozen take-out menus. I was able to do all the interviews Éclat had lined up for me over the phone. Who needed to leave the house?

I may have been a slug, but at least I was productive. I wrote about two albums' worth of material, but I was in such a weird space that I didn't think any of it was any good . . .

**BILLIE HOLIDAY'S GHOST** Oh, it was all good all right. Very, very good.

**JENN BRADFORD** . . . but I still kept plowing ahead.

After a while, I started sleeping really badly. The only thing that helped me crash was super-loud music or obnoxious action movies.

**PORTER ELLIS** After the fourth night in a row of being woken up by either some random jazz/rock fusion CD, or some random big-budget film DVD being played at an unearthly decibel level by my pal on the other side of the hall, I slid a note under her door that said, *Could you please temper the volume of your media?* Once again, I felt like the old man shaking his fist at the youth of America, but it was wrong to blast music and movies from midnight to eight in the morning.

**JENN BRADFORD** After I got Porter Ellis's note, I bought myself a good pair of wireless headphones. Not my favorite way to enjoy my late-night sounds, but I figured it would be good for inter-building harmony.

**ZACH BINGHAM** My feature on Jenn is scheduled to hit the stands about three weeks after her band got back from Europe, and I'm totally ducking her calls and emails. I know she wants to know what's up with the article. Maybe she wants to know what's up with me – I hope that's the case – but I kind of doubt it.

The day I get my advance copy of the magazine, I make a surprise trip out to Redhook. It's the right thing to do, to drop the bomb on her face-to-face. The doorman remembers me; he calls Jenn and she buzzes me right in. And not only does she let me up, but she's waiting for me right in front of the elevator, where she runs into my arms and gives me the biggest hug she's ever given me. Some might construe it as a *boyfriend*-boyfriend hug. I didn't. That would be presumptuous.

We go into her apartment and do small talk for about five minutes, then once we're warmed up to each other, she says, 'I have to apologize again for being the way I was while you were with us. Don't take it personally. You didn't do anything wrong.'

I laugh a little, say, 'Forgiven', then pull out an advance copy of the soon-to-be-infamous issue of *Rolling Stone* from my briefcase. 'So here's the article.' I toss the magazine toward the coffee-table. The moment it lands, I wuss out. I decide I don't want to be there when she checks it out, so I pretend to look at my watch and say, 'I've gotta run. Don't hate me too much after you read it.'

She says, 'Hate you? I can't imagine ever hating you.'

**JENN BRADFORD** After I read the article, I hated him. A lot. Wouldn't you? I mean, how would you like it if somebody wrote eight pages in a national magazine documenting you at your worst? Icky.

The problem was that even though it was somewhat exaggerated, virtually everything Zach wrote was true, which made it even ickier.

**PORTER ELLIS** I was on the phone with my architect when I heard the screams. I'm sure the entire building heard the screams. I'm sure all of Redhook heard the screams. I was seriously considering calling 911, when a certain somebody knocked at my door.

**JENN BRADFORD** I tried calling everybody. Naomi wasn't picking up. Masu wasn't picking up. My brother wasn't picking up. I had to vent to somebody. And Porter Ellis was as good as it got which, when you think about it, was kind of sad. You see, things had been so hectic with me over the last three or four years that I'd lost touch with most every friend of mine who wasn't part of my professional life.

**PORTER ELLIS** I told my architect I'd call her back, then I answered the door. Jenn grabbed me by the wrist, dragged me into her apartment – I was amazed how such a slender woman could be so strong – slammed the door shut and shoved a magazine into my face. She started talking at me, but she was crying so hard that the only thing I could understand was, 'Read this.'

I read the article. It was mean-spirited, self-indulgent, badly written and embarrassing, and flat-out obnoxious. Her tears were more than justified.

I'm a fast reader, so I finished the article in about five minutes, but I pretended it took longer, which I felt would give her the opportunity to compose herself. After she got herself under control, I said, 'This is a man who clearly didn't get enough affection from his mother.'

Jenn sniffled and said, 'Apparently he didn't get enough affection from me, either.'

I asked her, 'When was this published?'

She said, 'Subscribers will have it tomorrow. It'll be in stores the week after. In eight days, the entire world will think I'm a slutty bitchface.'

There was a small part of me that indeed believed she *was* a bit of a slutty bitchface, but I didn't think it would be prudent to mention that, so I said, 'I'm sorry this happened to you. I'm sure it'll blow over.' I didn't want to get further involved, so I made my way toward the door. I wanted to call back my architect asap.

Jenn sniffled again and said, 'Why don't you sit down. I'll make you some tea.'

I opened her door and said, 'No, I really have to—'

She zipped past me, slammed her door shut, then started crying again. The only thing I could make out was, 'Sit your ass down, Porter Ellis.'

So I tiptoed over to the sofa and sat my ass down.

**JENN BRADFORD** Aside from Zach's oh-so-wonderful visit, I hadn't had any face-to-face human contact for almost a week, and unfortunately, right at that moment, it was Porter Ellis or a Beanie Baby named Puddles. It was a tough call, but I went the animate direction.

**PORTER ELLIS** Jenn recomposed herself and said, 'I'm making us tea. Earl Gray, lemon zinger, peppermint or ginger?'

She seemed so unstable that I was afraid making the wrong tea choice would set her off again, so I said, 'Surprise me.'

While she was in the kitchen, I took in her living space. It was a musician's space, no doubt about it. Or at least I thought so. See, ironically, I'd never been in a musician's home before. As much as I loved music, I'd never become friendly with any artists. It dawned on me that that was a bit odd.

Virtually everything in her apartment was about music: the prints on the wall, the CDs and music manuscript paper strewn on the floor, the multitude of keyboards, the stereo equipment, the two acoustic guitars in the corner, the random pieces of percussion on what at one point in time might have been a living-room table. This woman clearly lived, breathed and slept music. Maybe she wasn't all bad.

**JENN BRADFORD** When I came back into the living room with his tea, Porter Ellis was sitting Indian-style on the floor, thumbing through my manuscript paper. Normally I don't let anybody see any of my songs before I'm done writing them, but I was so messed up that I honestly didn't care. Plus I'd gone through Porter Ellis's stuff the first time I went into his place, so how mad could I really get?

I cleared my throat, which made him flinch. He stood up and said, 'I'm sorry. I shouldn't have been examining your work.'

I said, 'It's okay.' I handed him his tea and asked, 'What did you think?'

**PORTER ELLIS** I didn't know how to read music, and her lyrics were written in an indecipherable scrawl, and I had a feeling I wouldn't appreciate her style of songs anyhow. Which is exactly what I told her.

**JENN BRADFORD** I was so not in the mood for any negativity from Mr Porter Ellis. I thought he'd step up and help a girl, maybe say some soothing sweet-ish nothings, even if he didn't necessarily mean them. Yes, it's true, sometimes even the oh-so-tough Jenn Bradford needs soothing.

But he had nary a soothing thing to say. So screw him.

I yanked the paper out of his hands and said, 'Go. No tea for you.' I figured it would be better to be alone than deal with his veiled insults.

And then I started crying again. Seriously, if another guy pulls some shit on me, I'm buying stock in Kleenex.

**PORTER ELLIS** Jenn Bradford and Porter Ellis. Oil and water. We'd never be friends.

I went home and got back to work. After I finished up with my architect, I called my decorator and said, 'You know what might look nice behind the bar? A huge collage made of CDs and music notation paper.' She agreed, and promised to have me a sketch by the end of the week.

I almost wanted to knock on Jenn's door and tell her that her floor had given me the idea for some decorative art, because I thought it might cheer her up. Not that it was my job to cheer her up, but despite what you might think about me, I'm basically a decent person, and cheering people up is what basically decent people are supposed to do.

**JENN BRADFORD** After I threw Porter Ellis out, my cell came to life. I thought, *Please be Naomi, please be Naomi, please be Naomi.*

It wasn't. It was Zach. The balls on that boy.

ZACH BINGHAM I call her, and I say hey, and I don't apologize. I tell her I write what I feel, and she may not like it, but it's honest. I tell her that in a weird way, the article is a mash note of sorts. I tell her I bared my soul in front of the entire world. I tell her that few writers would attempt anything like that.

JENN BRADFORD A mash note? Puh-*leez*. It was something you'd find in a high school newspaper. A very well-written high school newspaper, granted, but a high school newspaper nonetheless.

While Zach kept trying to justify himself, I reread the article. The damn thing still upset me almost more than anything's upset me in my entire life, but I had to admit that Zach had some game. If it wasn't me he'd written about, and I read the thing objectively, I'd probably be impressed at how he was able to make himself come off at once as presumptuous, and egotistical, and super needy, and even a bit sympathetic. I suppose the worst thing somebody could say about me after reading the article was that I was a bit of a tease, and very wrapped up in myself.

I'll admit to having been a tease at moments, but I'm most definitely not wrapped up in myself. Just ask anybody who knows me.

PORTER ELLIS I didn't know Jenn very well at the time, but it seemed to me she was quite egocentric. So to answer your question, yes, from my perspective, Jenn *was* wrapped up in herself.

**NAOMI BRAVER** I dunno. I'm always too wrapped up in myself to notice. Heh.

**ZACH BINGHAM** Yeah, she was a bit wrapped up in herself. The good news about that for me was that it made for a better story. The bad news for me was that it made for a lousy sorta-girlfriend. Or at least an inconsistent one. Almost an imaginary one, even.

**KEVIN MCALLISTER** Man, Jenn had always been wrapped up in herself to some extent, and after *Reality Check* didn't sell, it got worse. I can't blame her, I suppose. I probably wouldn't have handled it much differently.

**MASUHARA JONES** Girlfriend's whole life was about touring, and composing, and being interviewed, and getting stuck in endless photo sessions, and everybody being all like, *Do this, Jenn*, and, *Do that, Jenn*. It's like, how could she *not* be wrapped up in herself?

**T.J. STEWART** I dunno if Jenny-Jenn was being all about Jenny-Jenn. All I know is the girl was the bomb, and had mad musical skills, and she paid me on time and the checks didn't bounce. Far as I was concerned, she could do anything she damn well pleased, long as the bread was straight and she said my name right at the gig.

**BILLIE HOLIDAY'S GHOST** Mr Stewart isn't usually on target with his odd Stewart-centric observations . . .

**T.J. STEWART** *Odd?! Stewart-centric?!* Yo, y'all are cold, woman. Ice cold.

**BILLIE HOLIDAY'S GHOST** . . . but in this instance, he was absolutely correct about one thing: Jennifer is the bomb.

I had a strong hunch Mr Bingham's magazine article was gonna be bad – his manner on the tour bus made it obvious to me – but I didn't know it would be *that* bad. The man made love to Jennifer on a piano, for God's sake, and just because she wouldn't let him do something similar again didn't give him the right to write so awfully about her in print. I believe Hunter S. Thompson's ghost is looking over Mr Bingham, so it's not a shock that he made such a grievous error in judgment. Hunter S. isn't what you would call the most responsible guide.

Jenn did spend a lot of time thinking about Jenn, but I considered that a by-product of her fame. I could relate, because I was wrapped up in myself for my entire life. And I was concerned for Jenn because look what being wrapped up got me: dead from cirrhosis at forty-four. Yes, I made music for years and years and years that transcended for years and years and years, but if I'd have gotten out of my own head, well, who knows what would've happened.

If you're an artist, you have to be somewhat of an egoist. If you can balance your ego with being a decent person, and being good to your friends, and treating everybody with fairness and kindness, you have a chance to be the heppest of the hep cats.

I want that for Jennifer very, very badly.

# BLENDER
## THE ULTIMATE MUSIC MAGAZINE

### July 14, 2009

### NEW YORK'S FORMER FINEST NOT LIVING UP TO EARLY PROMISE
*Jenn Bradford, Naomi Mired in Mid-Career Slumps*

### by Jimmy Redd

It wasn't so long ago that you couldn't turn on your favorite satellite radio station, or flip on your friendly neighborhood video channel without hearing (or seeing) 'And Then', the lovely mid-tempo ballad performed by Naomi and written by Jenn Bradford. Or when it seemed like every magazine you picked up – be it a music periodical, or a general pop culture rag – had a sexy little picture of Bradford. Those two photogenic, telegenic, stereogenic vocalists were everywhere.

Now, not so much. While Braver and Bradford haven't fallen entirely off the map, the respective careers of the Brooklyn-born twosome are in noticeable decline. Why is this worth mentioning, when there are thousands of other artists who haven't lived up to their potential? Because Braver and Bradford's career arcs haven't arced – it's been all upward. Until now.

After a series of noteworthy appearances on HBO's *Entourage*, Naomi Braver up and left her native New York, moved out to Hollywood, and then . . . nothing. Ever since the sinewy vocalist – whose four albums were all critical and retail successes – took a hiatus from singing and dived into the film and television pool, her profile, to say the least, has gotten significantly lower. Braver's small-screen credits have been mostly limited to third banana roles on basic cable series, and she has yet to appear in a single major theatrical film.

Yet Braver remains optimistic. 'You think this is bad? You should've been there some nights at that coffee place in the East Village, back when Jenn and I were gigging for three people and an espresso machine. I didn't expect this acting thing to blow up immediately.' But it's been over a year – are you frustrated? 'A little bit. But truthfully, I don't think I'm good enough yet. The singing thing came naturally. This, I have to work for, and I love it, so I'm willing to keep doing what has to be done.'

The situation is a bit different for Braver's former foil. While still a viable commodity within the music industry, the sales figures for Bradford's third album, *Reality Check*, have been trending downward for the past month — something that wouldn't be as much of a concern if her previous album, *Guess Who Came at Dinner*, hadn't performed so well in the marketplace for so long.

Unlike Braver, Bradford sounds somewhat resigned with her situation. 'It's not like I can set up a kissing booth at the county fair and give everybody a big ol' sloppy smooch if they buy a copy.'

In the opinion of an unnamed source at Bradford's label, Éclat Records, the blame for the album's disappointing numbers lies in the fact that *Reality Check* lacks a single tune with hit potential. 'The iTunes numbers back me up on this one,' said the source. 'There isn't one song that's broken out of the pack, sales-wise. On most of our better-performing albums, there's at least one tune that outsells the rest of the record's repertoire by a mile. On *Reality Check*, it's pretty much even across the boards.'

One could point at the infamous April *Rolling Stone* feature as a turning-point for Bradford. If you missed the piece — which seems impossible, because for a few weeks it appeared that everybody in the music industry was discussing it — *Stone* scribe Zach Bingham chronicled one week on the road with Bradford's band, a week during which he pined after his subject incessantly. The timing of the article coincided with the drop in numbers for *Reality Check*, but one might not have anything to do with the other, as the album had reached the six-months-on-the-shelves mark, a time when sales figures are expected to slump. (Bradford refused to comment on the article or its author – surprising, because she generally has a comment for *everything*.)

All of which begs the questions, can Braver and/or Bradford make respective comebacks within their chosen professions? Will they join forces once again and dominate the charts as they did four years ago? Or will the downward spiral continue until they are a pair of fond memories? As of right now, it's all very much up in the air, but these are two talented, perseverant women, and if they go down, it won't be without a fight.

MASUHARA JONES The downward spiral that everybody was talking about kicked in big-time during the summer college tour in the Midwest. We played at what seemed like every Big Ten university: University of Iowa, University of Michigan, Michigan State, University of Illinois, University of Yadda Yadda Yadda. This was a big part of Jenn's crowd, the college kids, so we were way psyched about what we thought were gonna be some big numbers. That was a critical tour, a make-or-break time for *Reality Check*.

We broke.

It was subtle at first. Like if you weren't paying close attention to the post-gig numbers, you wouldn't have any idea we were headed into the shitter. But it was happening. A few less tickets sold, a few less T-shirts sold, a few less Jenn Bradford action figures sold. Okay, we didn't really have Jenn Bradford action figures, but if we did, they would've been wasting away at the merch table right next to the unsold hoodies, posters, buttons, refrigerator magnets and playing cards.

Two weeks into the tour, it got worse, and I was like, *Where* is *everybody?* The University of Kentucky show was three-quarters filled, then the Indiana University show was about half-filled, and then at the University of Missouri show, there were only 221 paid customers in a place that held over 1,000. And the crowds were all quiet as hell. Jenn told me she was sometimes able to hear individual conversations from the stage. It was surreal, and depressing, and kinda creepy.

Éclat wasn't too thrilled about the whole thing. They weren't slitting their wrists or anything, but there were a lot of nervous emails, and I would write back shit like, GIVE US MORE PROMO $$$!!! ADVERTISE THE DAMN GIGS!!! Sometimes they would, sometimes they wouldn't. I didn't tell Jenn about Éclat's pestering, because she had enough on her mind, what with all the lousy press she'd been getting, and bitching about that dipshit Zach, and trying to make nice with Kevin, who was acting kind of weird, like one day all nice and talkative, and the next day, all withdrawn and cranky. At least he was drumming like a madman, though. As much as it pains me to admit it, I guess Jenn was right to keep him around. But I still wanted to bust him one in the chops.

Anyhow, you gotta give Jenn her props. My girl stayed cool the whole time.

**JENN BRADFORD** I was freaking the hell out. I kept it together outwardly, because if I lost it, I was sure that Masu would lose it, and she'd probably go off on T.J., then he'd get weird, then Kevin would get weird – or weirder, I guess – then the Earth would stop spinning, and our lives as we knew them would end, hallelujah. The only person who knew I was going nuts was Naomi, who I talked to on the phone every night for, like, six hours. My cell-phone bill was insane.

I was bummed out that I was bumming out, because up until that point, I'd never particularly cared about how many people came to a show. As long as we played well, and as long as one person clapped or danced, I was fine. But when the crowds thinned out, I was *so* not ready.

The *Guess Who Came at Dinner* tours two years before were amazing; we were selling out clubs that held 3,000 bodies. One album later, we were hemorrhaging money. Or I suppose *I* was hemorrhaging money. T.J., Kevin and the road crew were on salary, so even if we played for, like, six people, they still got the same $1,250 paycheck every Friday, and the same twenty-five dollars per diem. What's per diem? Well, for all you non-touring musicians out there, a per diem is a daily money stipend that a band member is allotted for food and random other personal expenses. Once in a while, I skip eating and use mine for makeup.

Anyhow, the tour bus had to be paid for, the hotels had to be paid for, the equipment repairs, like the amplifier T.J. rammed the neck of his bass through at that Indiana State gig, had to be paid for, and most of it came straight from my pocket. Don't cry for me – if I couldn't have afforded it, I would've played the gigs solo – but the situation most definitely sucked.

When we hit every city, I had to do an interview with the college newspaper's music writer. They were all very earnest and sweet, but everybody asked more or less the same three questions:

*Question number one:* What was the deal with Zach's article in *Rolling Stone*?

*Question number two:* Are you planning to stop doing all those boring jazz songs and go back to the rock 'n' alterna-soul?

*Question number three:* Since there weren't any hit singles on *Reality Check*, would you consider bagging the solo career and having a reunion with Naomi?

And then we got to Chicago, and things with Kevin started heating up again.

**KEVIN MCALLISTER** Hey, man, at first I was just an innocent bystander. She started it.

**JENN BRADFORD** The gig was at a club right near DePaul University, which held just over 1,500 bodies. I loved Chicago, and Chicago seemed to love me, and the energy was such that I always rocked it there, so when only 300 people showed up to the gig, well, that was the most concrete sign yet that *Reality Check* was on a slow road to purgatory. And it killed me, because I fucking *love* that album. You shouldn't play favorites with your children, but out of my three records, *Reality Check* was number one in my heart.

So I took the stage in a horrible headspace. All I wanted was to bull my way through the show, then track down a bottle of wine, a bathtub, a pair of flannel jammies, and a bed, in that order. And that is the sort of mindset that messes up gigs. Big time.

We played like ass. Check that: *I* played like ass. Kevin and The Teej were fine. But I was heinous. It was possibly my worst show ever, even worse than the time I chipped my tooth on the piano at the Staples Center. I let my band down, I let Masu down, but the worst part of it was, I let those 300 paying customers down. That killed me. But I gave them what I could. I just didn't have much to give.

We were staying only a few blocks from the University, so after we finished our encore – and I can't believe the teeny-tiny crowd wanted an encore, but they did – I grabbed Masu and told her I was outta there, then I found the nearest emergency exit and jogged back to the hotel. And here's a note to all you girls out there: it *is* possible to jog six blocks in go-go boots that have four-inch heels. All you have to do is practice, practice, practice.

By the time I got to my room, the hotel kitchen was closed, so I called the concierge and asked him if he could track me down a nice bottle of red, saying that money was no object. He said no problem, and he'd be there in thirty minutes. So I threw on a robe and drew a bath, and sure enough, thirty minutes later, *knock knock knock*.

I opened the door. No concierge, just Kevin McAllister. And it pains and embarrasses me to admit that my first thought was, damn, he's fine. It was awesome to see a friendly face, a face that for many years I'd been comfortable with, a face that at one time, I loved very much. He gave me this sad little smile and held his arms out, and I totally lost it. I pulled him into the room, slammed the door shut, threw him against the wall and kissed him so hard, so very hard. Then my throat got all lumped up, but I refused to cry, because I've been doing way too much of that lately. When I was certain the tears were at bay, I took Kevin's hand and put it inside my robe, on my tummy.

I love having my tummy touched. I melted a little bit.

We made out, and touched, and licked, and nibbled for about ten minutes, when, during a break in the action, I realized the who, the what, the when, and the where of the situation. I removed his hand from my stomach, squirmed out of his hug and said, 'Okay, bad idea. Really *really* bad idea. We gotta stop. I'm so so so sorry.' I expected an argument, and some name-calling, and possibly a thrown ice-bucket. But he just kept giving me that tiny smile, a smile that came more from his eyes than his mouth, a smile that caused some serious re-melting. I put my hand on his cheek and said, 'Kevin, what happened to us?'

Kevin was never the best apologizer in the world, and I was curious to see if he'd say he was sorry for The

Incident – which, I should note, he'd never done. He took my hand from his face, kissed it, and said, '*I* happened to us.' And that was his final word on the subject. Okay, not great, but better than nothing, I suppose. He kissed my hand again, and said, 'Listen, don't worry about the crowds and the sales. I mean, since when have you cared about numbers? Just play good shows, man. But even if you're not feeling it, like tonight, T.J. and I got your back. We'll rock the party right. Relax, baby.'

Ahhhh, he called me *baby*. I hadn't been called *baby* in a long time, because Zach wasn't one for terms of endearment. Why? I dunno, maybe he thought that being mushy would lose him cool points in the indie rock community. What he never figured out was that I liked being called *baby*, or *honey*, or *sweetie*, or *darling*, or, I dunno, *Goddess of All That Is Musical, Intellectual, and Sexual*. I fell into Kevin's arms, then after a minute or two, started kissing his neck, a neck that wasn't as nice as Zach's but was still pretty okay.

Kevin started playing with my hair – which I like even more than I like being called *baby* – and I was, like, six seconds away from ripping off the guy's red sleeveless T-shirt, when the who, the what, the when, and the where of the situation hit me again. I also remembered that kissing doesn't solve problems; for that matter, it sometimes creates them. You would've thought that I had learned something from that time I mauled Porter Ellis. Well, you'd be wrong.

Untangling myself from Kevin's arms, I then threw myself on the bed, hid my head under four pillows, then told Kevin thank you for the hugs and that he should go back to his room and get some sleep. I doubt he could hear what the hell I was saying, but I know he eventually got the gist, because when I woke up three hours later, he was gone.

In the interim, the concierge finally brought me my bottle of wine. I needed to drink about half of it before I could fall back asleep.

We were in Madison, Wisconsin the next night, at the University of Wisconsin, and it was the last show of the tour, thank God. Just like Chicago, the place was barely filled, and again I wasn't at my best, although far better than the previous night. And Kevin was right – he and T.J. indeed had my back, and rocked the party right.

Right before we were about to launch into the closing number, Kevin grabbed his vocal microphone and said, 'Jennifer Marie Bradford, last night was magical. I was touched, moved, everything-ed. You need me. And I need you. Without each other, there ain't nothin' we two can't do.' He removed the mike from the stand, stepped off the drum riser, and sauntered over to the piano. 'Jenn, I give you my word in front of this handful of wonderful people, no more threesomes.' Then he got on his knees and launched into a solo version of my favorite Earth, Wind & Fire love song, 'Reasons'.

**KEVIN MCALLISTER** What can I tell you, man? I was inspired. My little spoken intro was probably a sad way to kick it off, but I rocked EW&F, no doubt.

**T.J. STEWART** Kevin McAllister is one of the baddest-assed drum dudes ever, but the boy's singing is doo-doo. Straight. Up. Doo. Doo. He motioned me to play along with him, but I wasn't gonna be associated with that shit.

**JENN BRADFORD** I prayed that Simon Cowell would come out from backstage and say, 'Paula, Randy, here's a gun. Please shoot me and put me out of my misery.'

But Simon was nowhere to be found, which was unfortunate, because after Kevin finished butchering the song, he said, 'Now I'm gonna play a little composition I wrote for Jenn, called, "For Jenn". I sincerely hope you enjoy it.' Then he went back behind the drum set and performed the loudest three-minute solo in music history. It was a combination of John Bonham, Buddy Rich and a building demolition crew.

**KEVIN MCALLISTER** What can I tell you, man? I lost it a little bit. Shit happens. Stick love and/or lust into the equation and shit happens. But I still can't believe everybody was hating on my vocals. I used to sing harmonies on stage with The JB's and nobody was hating on me. If I could give you a taste of 'Reasons', you could make your own decision.

*[Kevin sang for the author. It was painful, so painful that said author asked the publisher for a bigger advance.]*

All right, so I can't sing lead vocals for shit. But you can't blame a brother for trying.

**JENN BRADFORD** *What do you do with that? What do you say to that? How do you deal with that?* I had no clue.

*[But guess who did have a clue. That's right, Ms Braver.]*

**NAOMI BRAVER** When she called me, I told her to fire him.

She said, 'When did you get so cold, Nay? The dude was trying to be nice.'

I said, 'I'm not saying you should announce it at a press conference or anything. Take him out for dinner and give him one of your patented *it's-not-you-it's-me* lectures.' Back in her pre-Kevin days, Jenn had an amazing talent for letting down guys so easily that they didn't even realize they'd been let down until months later. Granted, the lecture was usually accompanied by one of her Brazilian Tiger Fist thingies, which softened the blow, if you will. I then said, 'You'll drive each other nuts if you don't.'

Jenn said, 'I can't. I can't do it. I'd feel too guilty.'

I said, 'Has *he* ever sounded guilty about The Incident?'

Jenn said, 'Well, he apologized.'

I said, 'Was it a real apology, or one of those half-assed Kevin apologies?'

Jenn mumbled, 'Half-assed.'

I repeated, 'Fire him.'

She said, 'I don't have to make any decisions right now. I'll be home tomorrow, and we're not gonna be traveling for a while. I might set up some gigs for us in New York, which means no tour buses or hotels, so I'll only see him at the shows. I can totally put off making a final decision for months.'

I said, 'Ooh, okay, good call. Procrastination – I approve. Maybe he'll even quit the band between now and then. Maybe he'll decide it's too much hassle, too much drama and, I dunno, not enough bread or something.'

Jenn laughed and said, 'That'd make my life a helluva lot easier.' We BS-ed some more for a minute or three, but I had to cut it short so I could go and get some head-shots. I already had five different sets of them, but my manager wanted another one on file. Don't ask me why, because I don't know. As stupid as the music industry could be, the film and television industry was stupider.

Oh, I bet Jenn didn't remind you about what happened the day after Kevin's meltdown. One of the few fans that were in the house that night videoed the whole show on their cell phone, then the next day, they uploaded Kevin's performance on to YouTube. VH-1 picked up the story, which led to a small blurb in *People*, which led to a big blurb in *Entertainment Weekly*.

Jenn never once mentioned it. Once in a rare while, she could be tactful.

**MASUHARA JONES** A couple weeks after our college tour ended, Jenn took me for lunch to John's, my favorite pizza place in Greenwich Village, and told me about her idea of gigging only at small clubs in the New York City area. I was like, 'Are you out of your mind, girl? That's what newbie bands do. You're a stud. Studs get on tour buses, and they go to, like, Oklahoma, and then they go to Japan, and get sick per diems, and they have smoke machines and rear projection screens, and they hook up with random hotties who they'll never see again. And they get *paid*.'

Jenn goes, 'I'm not feeling very studly, Masu. I'm in the ozone. I need to connect with *somebody*, and you can't connect when the closest paying customer is, like, six miles away.'

We went back and forth for a while on it, and even though I didn't agree, I signed off on it, because it would make her happy, and if she wasn't happy, the shows might suck, and if the shows sucked, the record and merch sales would suck even worse than they did already. So I was like, 'You do what you gotta do, girl. But the money's gonna blow, and the other JBs aren't gonna be happy.'

Jenn shrugged, then goes, 'Whatever. If they quit, I'll fly solo. I've done it before.'

I figured Kevin would hang in. The guy was such a chump that he probably thought if he stuck around, Jenn would get back with him. All because of one kissing session. My girl must be a helluva kisser.

The funny thing is that Jenn would've been happy if the jerk-off stayed, because he made her feel safe on stage. I told her I dug where she was coming from – he was a sick drummer when he wasn't doing his impression of a demolition crew – and it was her gig, so I would support her decision no matter what. But I also told her he was a tool and a douchebag, and she should push him in front of an F Train.

**KEVIN MCALLISTER** When we were playing at all those colleges for all those sad crowds, Jenn was vulnerable, and I'd never seen her vulnerable, and it made me want to take care of her. I ain't gonna lie: right around then, I'd have gotten back with her. In a heartbeat. But I knew that was never gonna happen.

So I split The JB's. Too much hassle, too much drama. And now, not enough bread.

**MASUHARA JONES** When Kevin quit, he didn't even have the courtesy – or the stones – to call me. He texted. I understand why, I guess, but it still sucked.

The healthiest thing for Jenn to do at that point would've been to cut off all contact with him, to move forward, and yes, to actually find another drummer. But she didn't. Why? Well, sometimes she's an idiot. Which I told her.

But finding a new drummer wasn't really an issue at that point, because for this run of club shows, Jenn decided it would be cool to go drummerless anyhow. She was like, 'Everything in my life needs to be pared down, and getting on stage with only a bass player with me is about as pared down as you could get – at least without being totally alone. And I'm not ready for totally alone.'

I thought totally alone might not be a bad idea for her

– after Zach Bingham and Kevin McAllister, some solo Jenn-time might've helped her down the line – but I didn't say anything.

As for T.J., I figured he'd bail because of the huge salary cut, which would've bummed me out, because that boy was pretty sweet. A pretty sweet bass player, I mean. He would've been hard to replace. It would've blown.

**T.J. STEWART** The Teej was crazy down. And you can tell Lil' Miss Shorty Jones that the money was not an issue. I'd play with Jenny-Jenn for a buck-fiddy an hour.

**MASUHARA JONES** But T.J. stayed, and I was psyched. I'd gotten used to what him and I had on the road. It was cool, sneaking around with him, keeping it secret from the crew. It made the whole thing feel dangerous, and I was all about dangerous. I mean, check out my latest piercing. See? That's some dangerous shit, right? What? No, I can't wear any underwear until it fully heals. And no, you can't touch it.

Anyhow, with T.J., like I said, I was psyched that he was gonna hang in, but the bad part was that since we were staying in New York for a while, I guessed it would go back to being the same thing as before we left on tour, which was nothing. It seemed like he only wanted to be with me when it was convenient. When I'd say something like, 'Why don't we date when we're not on the road?' he'd say something like, 'A dude's gotta do what a dude's gotta do.' Whatever that meant.

But maybe that was for the best. Maybe it would've

been best to cut the whole thing off before it became a soap opera, like Jenn and Zach, or Jenn and Kevin, or Jenn and whatever dude she hooked up with next.

Love always becomes a soap opera. Sometimes I don't know why I even bother trying.

JENN BRADFORD Masu made all the arrangements. Starting at the end of August, T.J. and I would own the stage at Upper East for two weeks. There would be ten shows in all, and I viewed it as kind of an experiment. We structured the contract so that if the experiment succeeded, we had the option to play every Tuesday for basically as long as we wanted to.

Upper East was the first 'big' club that Naomi and I ever played at, way back when. Now it was the smallest club I'd ever played at as a solo artist. But if we ended up doing the Tuesday nights, it'd be a comfortable, familiar venue to call home base. Mixed feelings galore.

Since things were going so badly numbers-wise, I was a bit concerned the press would have a field day with the whole thing, which would further destroy the *Reality Check* sales figures. I'm sure the *Billboard* magazines of the world thought that Upper East was a step down. Masu thought I was nuts. The fine folks at Éclat Records were pissed because this wasn't going to help them sell any records outside of the New York area, and told me so in no uncertain terms.

Whenever I tried to explain my rationale, nobody understood the 'paring down' concept. Maybe I was explaining it badly. Maybe *I* didn't even get it.

ZACH BINGHAM Well, I understood what Jenn was doing, and I thought it was brilliant. The world would be a better place to live in if more major-label musicians went back to their roots and made themselves accessible to the general public.

You see, once you become so-called big-time, your perception of the world is altered. You're catered to. You're a commodity. People give you free shit, they do stuff for you. How can you *not* change? Now I believe that change is all fine and good, but all the catering affects your ability to relate to the world, and if you can't relate to the world, you can't write the kind of songs that made you successful in the first place. I'm not saying your music gets worse. It just becomes different, less organic, less all-embracing.

I think to myself, if Jenn gets in touch with the people, she'll get in touch with herself, and if she gets in touch with herself, I'll be able to give her next record more than two-and-a-half stars.

JENN BRADFORD Zach reopened the lines of communication via email. I received his first note two days after we got back from the college tour, which meant he knew my schedule, which meant he was paying attention. I wasn't sure how I felt about that.

Shockingly, he made it clear in that first note that he wanted me back, that he wouldn't go down without a fight and would do everything necessary to worm his way back into my heart – and/or my pants. And to his credit, he was using his best asset – his noggin.

Two or three times a week, I'd get a long email from him. He'd tell me his feelings about some book he'd read, or some new band he'd discovered, or some old flick he'd watched on *Turner Classic Movies*. His emails were always eloquent and funny. And smart. The guy was a brainiac, no question. He wrote that he didn't need any full-blown responses from me, just acknowledgment that I'd read and received his notes. Sometimes I gave it to him, sometimes not. I mean, I had to make sure he was a little on edge, right? Like everyone else, I have read *The Rules*.

He ended each email with an offer to take me out for a meal, no strings attached. There were times I was close to giving in – *really* close. But I told him I didn't want to see him face-to-face yet, and I told him I didn't want him doing any pop-ins at my building, and I told him that I had warned all the doormen not to accept bribes from him. I almost caved a couple times, but something told me I needed some more Jenn time.

**BILLIE HOLIDAY'S GHOST** That 'something' would be me.

**JENN BRADFORD** Zach emailed me that he'd be at the Upper East on opening night, and I guess I knew that that was coming. I mean, the guy's an excellent journalist, and this was a big gig, and good journalists do things like show up at opening nights for big gigs. I also knew I wouldn't want to deal with him at the club. It was the first time I would've seen him since he dumped his 'Road Rage' article in my lap four months before, and I had no idea how I'd react. I didn't want to take a chance that I'd get all emotional and wacky either before, during, or after such an important show.

I knew I'd need a buffer, somebody to keep him distracted and off of my butt. Naomi would've been perfect, but she was stuck in Cali doing a cameo in *Curb Your Enthusiasm*.

But all wasn't lost. There was one person who I thought might be able to do the job.

**PORTER ELLIS** My interior designer was brilliant. As good a job as she did with my apartment, she was twice as good with her layout for my pending jazz club. It was a relatively smallish space – maybe 2,000 square feet – but she was going to utilize every inch of it to perfection. When completed, the room would be rectangular, long and skinny. She planned to put the stage against the small wall on the north side. The bar – which was so long, I'd probably need three bartenders – would take up about two-thirds of the west wall. The seating area would be on a slight incline, which meant nobody would have to crane their neck to see the stage from any single spot in the club.

I had a feeling that the collage behind the bar would look amazing. You remember which one I'm talking about, right? The thing with the CDs and the music manuscript paper that was inspired by Jenn's disaster of an apartment. We also decided to throw a few instruments on to it for good measure – a trumpet and a saxophone here, some drumsticks and a cymbal there.

This second Tuesday in August, my designer and I were having a meeting at my apartment. It was an important one, because we were going to break ground the following week, and any last-minute suggestions had to be implemented immediately. I was so focused in on my designer's drawings that I didn't even hear the knock.

But my designer did. She elbowed me and said, 'Yoo hoo, Porter. You there? Somebody was banging on your door. They slid something under it.'

Misdelivered mail was an annoying regularity at my building, so I guessed it was the doorman giving me some random piece of advertising. Wrong. It was a manila envelope from my exasperating across-the-hall neighbor. Inside, there were three CDs by her, a flyer advertising a show at this club called the Upper East, and a note:

*Porter Ellis, O Neighbor o' Mine*

*I would consider it an honor if you came by tonight. I'll leave your name at the door, along with a plus-one.*
*And if you make it over, I promise I'll be nice. Or at least sort of nice.*

*xox,*
*Jenn*

My designer looked at the flyer and the CDs, then at me, then at the note, then she yelled, *'Jenn Bradford lives here? And you didn't tell me? I love her!* My fiancé thinks I look a little bit like her. And she signed it with an ex-oh-ex? Is there something you'd like to share with me, Porter? And can I be your plus-one?'

I said, 'There's nothing to share. And not only can you be my plus-one, but you can be me. Use my name. Take your fiancé. Enjoy.'

She said, 'No. No way. You have to go. She invited you, personally. If Jenn Frigging Bradford personally invites you to hear her play – and gives you an ex-oh-ex, even – you go. I'm not taking no for an answer. It says on the flyer the show starts at eight thirty, so I'll meet you in front of Upper East at eight. If you're not there, I'm not letting you see my final draft of the plans. Now let's get back to work.'

After she left, I examined the booklets from Jenn's CDs. Her record label had hired some exceptional photographers, and I say that because all the pictures of Jenn somehow captured her natural energy. I wasn't necessarily enamored of her particular energy – she ran a bit too hot for me – but I had to admit that she was a vibrant woman, and the fact that you could tell that by merely looking at her record covers was, from an aesthetic and artistic perspective, admirable.

I decided that if I was going to the show that night, I might as well prepare myself for what I'd be hearing, so I picked one of the discs at random and threw it into my CD player. It was the one called *Guess Who Came at Dinner*. Cute.

**JENN BRADFORD** While I was paying the pizza guy, I heard some music coming from Porter Ellis's place. 'Under You'. Track six from *Dinner*.

I hope he liked it. Or at least tolerated it.

**PORTER ELLIS** I had to see what all the shouting was about, so I listened to the entire record, from the first note to the last. And it was awful. Complete pop pap. Insipid lyrics being passed off as risqué. One song drifted boringly into the next, with barely a discernible change in key or tempo. I wondered, *How could this woman have become a star?* Is it really only just about being pretty? Or am I just too old to get it?

Then, out of curiosity – or maybe masochism – I put on *Reality Check*. Certainly not as terrible as the other one, but I had a strong feeling I wouldn't be listening to it again anytime soon.

I will say this though: the woman can sing. If you can fight your way through all the electronic flotsam and jetsam, you can tell that she has a voice that would fit quite well in a nice, mellow jazz quartet. And I decided that if she ever asked for my opinion, I'd tell her just that.

**JENN BRADFORD** Musically speaking, I felt great about everything, and part of the credit for that should go to my fine bassist. T.J. took it upon himself to rewrite and rearrange his parts for our duo gigs, which may not sound like a big deal, but the guy spent hours on it, and we rehearsed our asses off, and he didn't have to do any of it, and he's a maniac, but I love him.

**T.J. STEWART** Despite what you may have heard, The Teej ain't always 'bout The Teej. Sometimes The Teej is about the music, and if Jenny-Jenn needs me, I'll be there.

Also, Masu said that if I didn't come correct for these shows, she'd bust me in the nutsack with her nut-kicking purple suede Pumas. And just ask Kevin's balls what damage those damn things can do.

**ZACH BINGHAM** Jenn's supposed to hit at eight thirty, and I want to get a decent seat – not right next to the stage, but not at the back of the place – so I show up at eight o'clock, and from halfway down the block, I see Jenn, leaning against the doorjamb, her flaming hair flying in the breeze. I want to run up and give her a big hug, but it had been a while, and I'm not sure how she'll react, and I don't want to embarrass her in front of the long line, so I walk up and offer her a wave and a simple hello.

She looks at me and says, 'Do I know you?'

I know I won't be getting a warm and fuzzy hug and kiss from her, but I don't expect her to harsh on me so badly. Then I peer at her face and realize it isn't Jenn. At first I think that this woman could be Jenn's sister – she has the same red hair, cobalt eyes, swollen lips and lush body. More or less. Okay, maybe she doesn't look that much like her, but I have Jenn on the brain, and the brain will go where the brain will go.

She looks at her watch, then to the right, then to her watch again, then to the left. My flirting skills have lain dormant for a while, and I think, *Throw it down, Bingham. Jenn might not have you, so get back in the game.* I say to her, 'Your man's late, eh?' Super-duper opening line. My game is seriously rusty.

She looks over my shoulder and says, 'No. He's just on time.'

I turn, and there's Jenn's cranky, yuppified neighbor, all decked out *just so*, overdressed for the Upper East, in my opinion. He kisses Jenn's pseudo-Doppelgänger on the cheek, then squints at me, and says, 'I know you, don't I?'

I say, 'Yeah, man. Friend of Jenn's.'

**PORTER ELLIS** It was that journalist. After that article he wrote back in the spring, I can't believe he has the gall to show up at Jenn's show. How perverse. Then again, Jenn seems to be pretty perverse herself, so maybe she invited him. Maybe they even got back together. Whatever the case is, it's unbelievable, simply unbelievable.

Even though I had no vested interest in Jenn Bradford's career or emotional state, I wanted to tell the man off, to let him know that his sort of journalism is of the lowest and yellowest variety, and that he should have some integrity about his work and his subjects. But I knew that would likely lead to what could become a heated discussion, and I didn't want to start a scene in front of my designer – or in front of the entire Lower West Side, for that matter – so I simply offered him my hand and said, 'I'm sorry, I forgot your name.'

He looked at my hand for a brief moment, then gave me a shake. 'Zach Bingham.'

**ZACH BINGHAM** He says, 'Porter Ellis.' Unlike the last time we shook, he doesn't try to break my fingers.

He then introduces me to the Jenn semi-lookalike, who apparently works for him as a designer. My guess is that since Jenn would never go out with this guy, he went out and bought himself a mirror image.

I say to the designer, 'Did anyone ever tell you that you look like—'

She interrupts me. 'Yeah. I've heard it three times already tonight.'

I'm tempted to ask if I can join them, if only to bust the guy's balls, but I don't, because listening to Jenn's show is more important to me than getting involved in a pissing contest with Mr Just So. I'm about to wander off, when he says . . .

**PORTER ELLIS** 'Why don't you join us?'

I didn't really want to sit with the man. He was arrogant and talentless, and he lacked heart, and was very, very young. But I had a gut feeling that Jenn didn't want to deal with him, so I thought it would be a nice, neighborly thing to do to keep him occupied and away from her.

He refused. I insisted. He refused again. Then my designer, with whom I've worked on various projects over the last several years, and who knows my thought process as well as anybody, caught on and said, 'Come on. It'll be fun. The more the merrier.' Then she grabbed Zach's elbow with both hands and all but yanked him into the club and over to our seats.

**ZACH BINGHAM** I let myself get yanked. If Jenn won't touch me, her almost-twin will have to do.

**JENN BRADFORD** I stuck my nose out of the dressing room to check out the crowd. It was sold out. And right in the middle of the place, there's a table with Porter Ellis and Zach, and this chick who looks very familiar, blabbing away like they're old pals.

**ZACH BINGHAM** All he does is talk about himself. I'm dying for the show to start. I look at my watch. Still ten minutes. I think, *This'll be the longest ten minutes in my life.*

**PORTER ELLIS** Zach Bingham was so insipid and shallow, and he couldn't – or wouldn't – discuss anything other than Zach Bingham. Like I said, I don't hate people. I just ignore them.

And the minute the show started, that's exactly what I did.

**JENN BRADFORD** T.J. and I took the stage, and as he was doing his last second equipment check, I scanned the audience. I could tell even from that distance that Porter Ellis and Zach were getting along great, and they'd be enjoying each other's company so much that I wouldn't have to worry about Indie Boy getting me all flustered after the gig.

Zach was looking pretty cute. He had pissed me off so much with that article, and with his unreturned phone calls, that I had forgotten how damn hot he can be. He had a few days' worth of stubble going, which works big-time for him, and his hair was in perfect shape, while his shirt was unbuttoned enough so that his neck looked excellent.

I've gotta say that Porter Ellis looked excellent too, all dolled up in what was obviously a high-end shirt/tie combo. I had to admit, the guy cleaned up nicely. I'd never thought of him as attractive, but he was. Maybe it was because he was smiling. Yes, that's right, *Porter Ellis was smiling!* I guess there's a first time for everything.

Before I counted off the first song, I took a quick Jenn inventory. I was wearing a slinky little black dress I picked up at Zara, and my favorite red Courrèges boots, the ones with the five-inch stilettos. Yes, the heels made it difficult to stomp on the piano pedals, but sometimes we musicians have to make some tough choices, and in that particular instance, heels trumped pedals. The other good news was that I had just the right level of nervousness. Too little, and I get cocky and make mistakes. Too much, and I feel like barfing.

I tinkled a fast run up and down the keyboard, then shook my hair out of my face, which elicited an exaggerated wolf whistle from the back of the room. I said, 'You wanna come up here and do something else with those lips, big boy?'

Everybody cracked up, and I counted off the first tune, and the rest of the evening was a pleasant, sweet, warm blur.

**ZACH BINGHAM** She rocks it. It's better than the Roxy gig. Damn.

**PORTER ELLIS** I didn't like Jenn Bradford's music, but the woman had undeniable talent and presence. The stage lights made her hair glow like a dusk sunset. She smiled, she engaged, she cajoled. Her performance made me understand how somebody like my designer or Zach Bingham could fall in love with her music.

**MASUHARA JONES** I showed up late, right in time for the encore. I knew Jenn would be cool about me catching only the end of the gig. Matter of fact, she'd be happy to see me at all, because she thought I wasn't even gonna be there. She knew I had a date with this mad cute PR guy I met a few months back, and since she thinks everybody in the world should be having sex on a regular basis, she told me that she wouldn't want a stupid concert to stand in the way of me getting laid.

As it turned out, I didn't get laid. The dude was a snooze. Jenn's gig would've been way more fun.

So yeah, after the show, Jenn was cool, but T.J. was pissed. He was like, 'Yo, woman, we *killed*. Where the fuck were you?'

I looked him right in the eye – which was hard, because he's about ten feet taller than me – and I go, 'Hey, you're the one who always says, *A dude's gotta do what a dude's gotta do*. You get to do your do, I get to do my do.'

He was like, 'Whatever, yo,' then he stomped away,

then he stomped back and said, 'Yo, you know . . .' then he kinda sputtered for a second, then stomped away again. Then he turned around and yelled loud enough for the entire block to hear: 'Call me tomorrow, Shorty, or else we be havin' words!'

T.J. Stewart can be such a drama queen.

Making things more dramatic, I turned around, and what three-timing dickwad is standing right behind me?

**KEVIN MCALLISTER** What can I tell you? I was in the neighborhood.

I got there for the second half of the last song, and from what I heard, Jenn and The Teej sounded good. Damn good. But something was missing. I'm not saying that that something was me, but . . .

The music sounded empty. Jenn sounded lost. At least, that's the way I heard it.

**JENN BRADFORD** The whole night, I kept thinking of the phrase *addition by subtraction*. Sure, I missed having Kevin playing next to me. I guess if I have to come up with a metaphor for gigging with Kevin, it would be something like him reminding me of an old pair of shoes that look cool, and match all of your favorite outfits, and they're really comfortable – except for the fact that there's a tiny little nail sticking up from the bottom that, according to your local shoe repairman, can't be fixed without destroying your sole.

Kevin not being there added an entire new dimension to our sound. One less musician, but one more dimension. It was because I felt freer than I'd felt since Naomi and I were just a duo. My songs breathed more. There was elbow room. And it didn't hurt that T.J., as they say in the jazz world, played like a motherfucker.

After the show, I plopped down on the edge of the stage and chatted up whoever wanted to be chatted up, and signed every last autograph. I'd forgotten how much fun it could be to be at one with an audience, to interact, not to be hustled away in order to get on the bus so we could drive for ten hours, then do it all again.

Once the club all but emptied out, Masu walked over and said, 'You have a surprise guest.' She sounded pissed.

I hadn't told her Zach was coming. Ever since the article, she had it out for the guy, and had she known he was planning on being at the show, she might've made a pre-emptive strike to keep him away, like setting his apartment on fire or something. I said, 'He's not as awful as you think. He's trying to make amends. I might give him another chance.'

Masu yelled, *'Are you, like, out of your fucking mind?'* The few people who were still at the club – Porter Ellis, Zach, a handful of servers and their mates – turned to stare at her. The club got deathly quiet, then she repeated in a whisper, 'Are you, like, out of your fucking mind? You'd give Mr Threesome another chance?'

I said, 'No. I'm talking about Zach, dummy.' Then I looked around the room and said, 'Kevin's here?'

MASUHARA JONES I looked around and was like, 'Um, well, he *was* here.'

**ZACH BINGHAM** Jenn's signing autographs and talking to Masuhara, and Masuhara's yelling, and I'm talking to Porter and his woman, and all of a sudden, this guy sprints out of the club. He shoves people out of the way, he knocks over chairs, he breaks glasses. I could swear it was McAllister, but I could be wrong.

**KEVIN MCALLISTER** Masuhara was wearing those purple Pumas, and I was outta there on the quick, man. I wanted to congratulate Jenn, maybe even ask her out for some coffee, but one Masu ball mash was enough.

**PORTER ELLIS** I was ready to head home right after the last note was played, but my designer insisted that I introduce her to Jenn, so we waited around until the autograph hounds disappeared, which meant a few more interminable minutes with Zach. For some reason, he leeched on to me and wouldn't leave, that smarmy hack.

**ZACH BINGHAM** I don't know anybody else in the place, and I don't want to look like a Jenn stalker yet again, so I'm stuck pretending to converse with Porter, that pretentious jerk-off.

**PORTER ELLIS** That no-talent poseur.

**ZACH BINGHAM** That bourgeois snob.

**PORTER ELLIS** That duplicitous miscreant.

**ZACH BINGHAM** That hipster wannabe.

**PORTER ELLIS** That malnourished sycophant.

**JENN BRADFORD** Masu wandered off, and the next thing I know, Zach and Porter Ellis are going at it. Okay, they weren't *going at it* going at it, but they were having a macho-guy staredown, and it looked like they might go at it for real, and there was that poor girl with them who looked like she was gonna die of embarrassment. But eventually, the poor girl took Porter Ellis's elbow and dragged him over to the stage.

I'll admit it, I was happy to see my neighbor. I knew he wasn't a fan of my music, but the fact that he was there meant that he'd sort of forgiven me for my hallway maul-fest, and that was a good thing, because I hate it when somebody's pissed at me, especially if he lives within spitting distance. What can I tell you, I like being liked. If somebody didn't like me, I felt like I'd screwed something up. As it so happened, in this case, I *had* screwed something up, which legitimized my feelings, I suppose.

I jumped into his arms, gave him a huge hug and said, 'Porter Ellis! Porter Porter Ellis Ellis! Porter Porter Porter Ellis Ellis Ellis!' I'm sure he was thinking, *Jenn, you should get some new material.* I tugged on his tie, which turned out to be Hugo Boss, my favorite men's designer, and said, 'You look very handsome this evening. Did you enjoy the show?'

The guy almost smiled. 'Thank you for inviting me.'

He pointed to his girl and said, 'Jenn, this is—'

Then the girl, whose name I never got, proceeded to tell me how much she loved me, and how lucky Porter Ellis was to have me right across the hall, and how she was at Porter Ellis's apartment all the time, and maybe I could come by his place when she was there, and we could order some Thai food from that place in Carroll Gardens, and blah blah blah blah blah. Porter Ellis gave her an indulgent grin, filled with what looked to me like love. Or at least *like*. How about that? Porter Ellis had a crush. I was surprised, because I felt like he sent out a vibe of complete asexuality. I have a pretty good sex-o-meter, but even I can be wrong about that once in a while.

The funny thing was, I realized then that the girl looked a lot like me. Weird.

Oh, and I don't know if you were paying attention, but Porter Ellis never told me whether or not he liked the show.

**PORTER ELLIS** I didn't like the show, and even though I promised myself that if Jenn asked my opinion of her music, I'd give it to her in no uncertain terms, I couldn't bring myself to say anything negative, not when she was so patently pleased with her performance. Plus I figured my designer was giving Jenn enough compliments for the both of us.

**ZACH BINGHAM** Finally Porter's girl shuts up, and the two of them split. I think about making some sort of passive/aggressive move, like 'accidentally' tripping him up on his way out, but I play it cool and take the high road, which means ignoring his bougie ass.

**JENN BRADFORD** Masu was gone, and Porter Ellis was gone, and T.J. was gone, and anybody who wanted to chat me up was gone – everybody, that is, except for Zach, who was giving me the best teddy bear look he could muster.

He said, 'Well, I made it.'

I said, 'Yep. Sure did.'

We just stared at each other for a minute, then, in one of the cheesiest movie moments in my entire life, he put his hand on my neck and pulled me into a kiss.

My initial reaction was to shove him on to his ass. Pretty presumptuous that he'd assume I'd let him kiss me, wouldn't you say? But my second reaction, which came immediately after my initial reaction, was to kiss him right on back. It was probably a good thing Kevin had taken off. A Bingham/McAllister boxing match wouldn't have been good for anybody.

We cut off our smooch after what seemed like a good long while, then we went outside and hailed a cab back to his place. He was very sweet, and very apologetic, and he groveled, but not in a gross way, and he made me some tea, and we made out for almost an hour, and then we had mediocre sex twice on his living-room floor – apparently we'd forgotten each other's moves, likes and dislikes in only four months – and then later did it again on his futon, which was almost as hard as the floor.

My inclination was to leave after our bout on the futon, to go home and sleep in my comfy bed with my many comfy pillows, and crank up the air conditioning so it would be cold enough that I could put on a pair of flannels.

But I didn't.

Why? We had some sort of connection, Zach and I, and even though I couldn't put my finger on what it was exactly, it was undeniable. Obviously there was the physical attraction, and the mutual love for music, but beyond that, well, I wasn't sure. He could be selfish and petty, but he had a good heart most of the time; yet our connection had to be more than that, something on some level that I wasn't in touch with.

If I were forced to give an answer, I would guess it had to do with the fact that we worked on a similar intellectual plane. Kevin wasn't a dummy by any stretch of the imagination, but Zach had a bit more on the ball than my ex. Also, there was that whole challenge issue. I could usually pin down what somebody's about after one date. I'd known Zach for almost a year, and I didn't have a complete read on the guy. Who doesn't like an enigma?

I suppose the real question was, did I want to keep him in my life so I could figure out whether he merited consideration for something more?

As his rock hard bachelor-ish futon destroyed my back, I thought, *Why not?* What do I have to lose, aside from another piece of my heart?

**BILLIE HOLIDAY'S GHOST** Interesting night for my Jennifer, wouldn't you say? I mean, what a crowd: one former lover, one current lover and one confused neighbor, not to mention one horny manager and one clueless bass player.

A dramatic scenario certainly, but I've had it much worse. Hell, I did a show in Paris in '51 where there were six cats in the audience I'd fooled around with, not to mention that I'd previously slept with the pianist, and was currently sleeping with the drummer, both of whom you've probably heard of, and neither of whose names I'm gonna tell you. Now *that* was dramatic.

In any event, Jenn put on one helluva fine show. I could tell it got her creative juices boiling. I had a hunch that she was gonna come up with something big at some point in the next few weeks.

And I was right.

And unless you were living under a rock that year, you'll figure out exactly what it was.

# NEW YORK PRESS
## NEW YORK'S FREE WEEKLY NEWSPAPER

## September 10, 2009

### Concert Review

### SIZE, AS THEY SAY (OVER AND OVER AGAIN), MATTERS
*Jenn Bradford @ Upper East, September 6, 2009*

### by Lauren McIntyre

I've always respected what Jenn Bradford has been trying to accomplish over the past few years in terms of melding alternative, emo, R&B and blatant sexuality, a mixture that few could manage to pull off. Based on what I've heard from her previously, both live and in the studio, I wouldn't put her in the upper echelon of female singer/songwriters, but after her performance at the Upper East, I have to give the lady many, many props.

Backed only by her bassist from The JB's, T.J. Stewart, Jenn roared through a 90-minute set comprised of 15 songs culled from her three solo albums, as well as her two biggest hits from the Naomi era ('And Then' and 'Problem Identified', both of which you've probably heard several hundred thousand times by now, and both of which were thankfully rearranged here and thus given an injection of new life), plus a medley of the Nat King Cole tunes: 'Unforgettable', 'Route 66' and 'Straighten Up and Fly Right'.

As she's an undeniably talented and charismatic artist, this sort of pared-down setting would have worked perfectly well even at a club ten times the size of Upper East, but when you're in close enough proximity to see a glam sex bomb like Bradford sweating over her art, you can see she's more earthbound and vulnerable than you'd assumed, and thus she becomes more appealing. Plus it's big fun to see her bash the piano all up close and personal. Also impressive was her ability to successfully utilize her piano's pedals while wearing go-go boots topped (or bottomed) off with five-inch stilettos.

Jenn Bradford will be performing at Upper East every Tuesday for the next twelve weeks. If you want to find out how much size matters, get tickets, like, yesterday.

**PORTER ELLIS** For almost the rest of the year, all the way up through November, it seemed that every Tuesday night – or Wednesday morning, I suppose – I was awoken by one of two things: Jenn and Zach drunkenly and loudly staggering their way from the elevator to *her* front door, or Jenn drunkenly and loudly pounding on *my* front door.

Here's a typical scenario: it was just past two o'clock this one night – or morning, depending on how you look at it – and Jenn banged on my door loudly enough that I was surprised neither of us received a phone call from either the upstairs or downstairs neighbors ... or even from our neighbors across the street. My initial, sleep-fuzzy thought was that there was a fire in the building, and the alarm system had gone on the fritz, and the night security man was alerting everybody personally. An illogical thought – why would the doorman take our tortoise-like elevator from floor to floor if the building was burning? – but it was after two in the morning, and I'm generally not at my best at that hour, so what can I tell you.

I jumped out of bed, threw open the door, and was so out of sorts that I didn't even realize all I was wearing was my boxers. And there's Jenn, all dolled up for her concert in a lovely dress and what I considered to be some oddly chosen knee-high boots. And there's me, all undressed for my night's sleep, sporting a semi-erection, which stemmed from a need to urinate rather than procreate.

We stared at each other for a few seconds, then she looked directly at my crotch and said, 'Not bad, Porter

Ellis. And he doesn't look like he's at full mast. Very stirring.' She then placed her hand on my stomach, gave me a kiss on the cheek, pushed me out of the way, marched right into my apartment, headed toward the kitchen, opened up the refrigerator, then called over her shoulder, 'D'you have anything salty in here to eat? Or maybe some leftover pizza? I need grease. Grease, and Advil, and about a gallon of water.' By that point in our neighborly relationship, I'd figured out her modus operandi, so I was resigned to the fact that the only way I'd get her out of my apartment would be by the use of force. Unfortunately, I'm not a particularly forceful man in those sorts of situations – not that those sorts of situations arise on a regular basis – so I went into the bedroom, grabbed a robe and prepared myself for thirty or so minutes of babysitting my tipsy neighbor.

Coincidentally enough, I'd made some pizza that evening. I've always liked to cook, and after years of experimentation, I'd just about perfected a homemade herbed pizza dough; that night, I had loaded it up with caramelized onions, fontina cheese and goat cheese. I'm sure Jenn was looking for something on the greasier and drippier side, but at least it was something. She snatched the pizza from the fridge and was about to stick it in the microwave, when I stopped her and said, 'Let me put it in the oven. It'll heat up better that way.'

She said, 'Porter Ellis, you're too good to me.' Then she gave me another hug and kiss. But this time the kiss was on the mouth. There was a hint of tongue. I tasted wine.

I could've taken her to bed, I suppose. But I didn't. You see, I'd only been officially divorced for eight months – we'd been separated for twice that long – and wasn't eager to get into any sort of relationship, even a casual one, and especially one with somebody who I'd be stuck seeing every day. It would be so awkward if it didn't work out, which it most certainly wouldn't, because at the end of the day, the only thing Jenn Bradford and I had in common was a mutual love for jazz.

I slipped out of her embrace and walked her over to my seating system. She gave me a pout and said, 'Don't you think I'm pretty?' Then she slowly ran her hands up her legs and lifted her dress to the middle of her thigh. Then she leaned over and flaunted her breasts.

**JENN BRADFORD** I was *sooo* trashed that night. I don't remember a thing. What did Porter Ellis tell you about it? Really? God, I can be such a loser-kissing bandit.

**PORTER ELLIS** Jenn was unquestionably exciting, but I wasn't excited. Let me rephrase that: I wouldn't *allow* myself to be excited. I told her, 'I think it would be best if you got some sleep.' I held out my hand. 'Let me escort you to your apartment.'

She smoothed her dress back into place, pouted again, then yelled, 'I'm not leaving without that pizza, Porter Ellis!'

I said, 'Of course you aren't.' I went to the kitchen, removed her pizza from the oven, then wrapped it in a few paper towels. 'Here you go. Now let's get you home.'

'I'll get myself home, thank you very much, Mr Porter Won't-Kiss-Me-For-Real Ellis. Smell ya later.'

**JENN BRADFORD** I'm not kidding, it's a blank from when Masu put me into the taxi to when I woke up in my pretty black Nicole Miller number, crashed out half on the bed and half on the floor, with a piece of pizza sliming up my sheets. No, seriously, it *is* a blank. I swear on my Stevie Wonder CDs that I don't remember kissing Porter Ellis that night. I'm not saying it's not possible. I just don't remember.

Oh, shut up, you.

**PORTER ELLIS** For the next few days, it seemed like Jenn was playing her music louder than usual. Much louder.

**JENN BRADFORD** He's right. I was.

**PORTER ELLIS** I figured it was her revenge for me shunning her advances.

**JENN BRADFORD** He figured *what*? You're kidding. Oy. No, that was the week I wrote 'Addition by Subtraction'. And that one needed to be played *loud*. But you know that already.

**PORTER ELLIS** The following Tuesday night – or Wednesday morning – she and Zach made a racket, first in the hallway, then in her apartment. Then there was more loud music. She'll deny it, but I'm sure she was purposely trying to annoy me.

**JENN BRADFORD** I was playing Zach the song, that's all. And like I said, it needed to be played loud. And if Porter Ellis had complained to me – which he didn't – I would've gotten him some earplugs, because that's what good neighbors do. Right?

**ZACH BINGHAM** We get back to her place after the sixth or seventh Tuesday at Upper East, and Jenn drags me into her instrument room and fires up her Fender Rhodes, a vintage electronic keyboard that I've always loved the sound of. I'd never seen her play anything other than an acoustic piano up to that point, and she's made it clear that she's not a fan of playing instruments that need to be plugged in, so this is kind of a big deal.

She scrunches down in front of the Rhodes and says, 'Pop quiz. D'you wanna do me, or d'you want to hear me play this new awesome song?'

I say, 'Do you.' Good shows get her insane, and when she's insane, she's sexier than usual – if that's possible – so I figure I'll take advantage.

She makes a loud game-show buzzer noise, then says, 'Wrong answer, Weenie Boy.' She points to the floor. 'Sit.' I should point out that I like being called Indie Boy way better than Weenie Boy, and I don't particularly like being called Indie Boy. But she's whipped me so badly by this point that I'll generally do anything she tells me to, so I sit, even though all I want to do is have sex, then crash, then wake up around eight and be home by nine so I can finish my article about The Shins that has to be turned in by Friday. Then she launches into the tune, and I forget all about The Shins.

By now, anybody reading this book has heard 'Addition by Subtraction' ad infinitum, so I won't bother giving you some long-winded musicological dissection. But I will tell you that I knew immediately that this song would blow her up. I knew immediately that there was a possibility it would make her bigger than Alicia Keys, bigger than Tori Amos, bigger than Alanis Morrisette.

Bigger than Naomi, even.

**JENN BRADFORD** I was pretty certain it was a good song, but it's impossible to be one hundred per cent objective about your own material. And Zach, despite all his pretension and bluster, and questionable journalistic decisions, knows his music – and his opinion was not to be taken lightly.

When I finished playing him 'Addition by Subtraction', he was speechless. Zach Bingham was *never* speechless, so I knew I was on to something.

**ZACH BINGHAM** What made the song so impressive was its combination of commerciality and complexity. I'm not comparing Jenn Bradford to The Beatles by any stretch of the imagination, but in terms of crafting something that's accessible without sacrificing artistic vision, 'Addition by Subtraction' is very Beatle-esque. I tell her,

'Jenn, if you can write a whole album like this, you can retire.'

She says, 'You think? Are you sure? I mean, I like it, but it's hard to tell.'

This is the first time I see her questioning her music, which I find odd, because this is patently the best music she's ever made – and that's even taking *Guess Who Came at Dinner* into consideration. I tell her more or less what I told you about the Beatles thing, then I tell her to keep going in this direction even though this direction might not be her ultimate goal, which I think is more jazz-oriented, and thus less crowd-grabbing. I tell her that the rock game is a young woman's game, and that jazz isn't going anywhere, and she'll have time to experiment and stretch stylistically for her entire life, and that while she has some momentum, she should try and sell as many records and reach as wide an audience as possible. Use all the weapons at her disposal while she still has them. Then, when she has the audience in her back pocket, they'll buy any of her records, regardless of the style. They won't care if it's a Jenn Bradford *rock* record, or a Jenn Bradford *jazz* record, or a Jenn Bradford *hoedown* record. All they'll care is that it's a *Jenn Bradford* record. Us industry-types call that 'branding'. Marketing-speak at its finest.

Jenn turns off the Rhodes then just stares at me with an intensity I hadn't ever seen from her since the first time she played me *Reality Check*. After a minute or so, she breaks into one of those patented Jenn Bradford smiles – the kind of smile you'd take a bullet for – and says, 'I hear you, Weenie Boy. Points taken. Thank you for your input *and* your patience.' She stands up and slowly unbuttons her shirt, holding my gaze the entire time. She says, 'Now, my friend, it's business time.'

**PORTER ELLIS** I didn't truly fall back asleep after Jenn and Zach's banging entrance. I gave up trying around six thirty. It was a glorious day, so I decided to go for a power walk by the river.

While I was waiting by the elevator, I was treated to the sound of their lovemaking.

It was exasperating.

Was I jealous? Good God, no. Wait, let me rephrase that: I wasn't jealous over Jenn. I admit that I was a little jealous about not having somebody to make love with. My body – my *entire* body, from my brain to my feet – was telling me that it was time to consider putting an end to my self-imposed celibacy.

But here's the caveat: anything I had would have to be casual. Very casual. No more marriages. Enough was enough.

**JENN BRADFORD** After Zach and I finished messing around, I felt like starting the process of committing 'Addition by Subtraction' to tape. His pep talk inspired me, as did our lovemaking; you see, we'd finally gotten our love groove back. It took a few weeks of practice, but it was worth it.

I told Zach to take a hike, which didn't seem to upset him all that much. His not being upset made me an itty-bit upset, but all that melted away when I pressed the multitude of 'on' buttons in my recording room. I spent the next forty-eight straight hours working on a solo demo version of 'Addition by Subtraction', only breaking for food, sleep and peeing.

I finished the tune, but it wasn't *finished*-finished. I thought that before I debuted the tune for the fine folks at Éclat Records, I should flesh it out a bit, so I called T.J. He showed up an hour later, and I played him the song – and I'm pretty sure he liked it.

**T.J. STEWART** Yo, that tune was sick, man. *Sick.* Made me decide I would gig with Jenny-Jenn until she didn't want to gig with me no more.

**JENN BRADFORD** One take, The Teej played it in. He figured out the chord progression after listening to it a total of three times, then laid down the perfect bass line in one take. Wow. I almost called Masu and told her to come over and give him a blow job as a thank you gift from me.

T.J. and I listened silently and happily to the track about seventeen times, then he said to me, 'Something's missing, yo.'

I thought it sounded pretty damn good, so I said, 'What're you talking about? What's missing?'

He gave me a look and said, 'You know.'

I said, 'No, I don't.'

He said, 'Yeah, you do.'

I said, 'No, I *don't.*'

He said, 'Yeah, you do. Think about it.'

I thought about it. Then I got it.

**KEVIN MCALLISTER** The first thing she said to me was, 'I need you, Kevin. I need you *now*.'

The call came out of nowhere, man. Totally unexpected. I thought Jenn Bradford was done with me. I wouldn't have blamed her. I mean, at that point, the clip of me singing 'Reasons' to her was all over the Internet. It couldn't have helped her dwindling record sales.

I said, all sexy-like, 'Oh, I know you need me, baby. I knew you'd come around.'

She said, 'Not funny.' Then she laughed a little and said, 'Okay, maybe it was kinda funny. Now shut up, pack your drums and get your ass over here. *Now*.' I was with Jenn Bradford for four years, and I knew that tone of voice. It meant she'd come up with some badass music, and I couldn't miss out on that. Plus in a perverse way, I've always dug it when Jenn orders me around, so I packed my drums and got my ass over there.

Can't deny that I was looking forward to seeing the girl. And playing the music.

**PORTER ELLIS** After my walk, a shower and one of my famous mushroom, spinach and cheese omelets, I heard a whole bunch of banging and crashing out in the hall that sounded suspiciously familiar. Was it possible Jenn was moving out? Was it possible there would be no more loud music and late-night pop-ins? Was it? Was it?

It wasn't. Nobody was moving out. Somebody was

coming in. A drummer hauling a huge kit. I thought, *Great, as if the piano and the bass weren't loud enough.*

I should point out that even though I've been complaining to you about it seemingly non-stop, I have no problem with loud music in and of itself. I mean, I was in the process of building a music club, for God's sake, and it would be impossible to be there night after night if I couldn't tolerate high volumes. It only bothered me when it was somebody else's loud music. Me, when I need to turn things up, I wear headphones. I'm polite that way.

At any rate, I wasn't in the mood for The Jenn Bradford Show right then, so I decided to go into Manhattan and see how things were progressing with the club. And suffice it to say they weren't.

I'd initially wanted to open the doors in January, and the way construction was crawling along, I was looking at autumn, maybe late summer at best. The building's infrastructure wasn't anywhere near complete, which meant the interior decorators – as well as the company that was installing the high-end, just-out-of-the-laboratory sound system – were on hold. Plus, since I didn't have an official opening date, I couldn't book any acts, nor could I spearhead any kind of marketing campaign. And I hadn't even come up with a name for the place yet. But I remained calm and optimistic, even though it appeared my first venture into the arts was going miserably. I was a believer. Always have been. Probably always will be.

After that frustrating little visit, I didn't feel like going home, so I wandered over to Barnes & Noble in Union Square, and bought myself an 800-page Miles Davis biography, then went into the first tasty-looking, quiet-sounding restaurant I came across. I asked for a corner table, and hunkered down for a couple hours of fine lunching and fine reading, hoping that by the time I got home, Jenn and her little drummer boy would be done making their racket.

**JENN BRADFORD** I gave Kevin a hug, and it was pretty damn nice. No weird sexual tension. No anger. No duplicity. Just a hug between professional acquaintances who, at some point along the lines, might become actual friends. I could've kept the Cold War going – forever, really – but what was the point? The Kevin Incident was what it was, and Kevin was who he was, and The Incident wasn't gonna disappear, and Kevin wasn't gonna change, and I didn't have enough energy or focus to hold a serious grudge against him, so I figured I'd move on. I could be Kevin McAllister's buddy. Or at least I could try.

I noticed during our hug that he'd lost weight. While he was setting up his drums, I said, 'Hey skinny, wanna order some lunch? Sushi? Chinese? Your call.'

He said, 'Nah, man, I'm not hungry. What do you mean skinny?'

I said, 'I dunno. You don't seem quite as buff as usual, I guess.'

He looked down at his chest. 'You think? I haven't been lifting as much, but I've been eating just fine. I feel like I've *gained* weight.'

I said, 'Are you getting enough sleep?'

He said, 'I never get enough sleep.'

I said, 'What've you been doing?'

He said, 'What do you care?' He wasn't being mean or snappy. He was legitimately curious.

I said, 'I care.' I really did. We were together for a million years, and in a million years, your lives do a whole lot of intertwining, and those twines would never entirely disappear, no matter how hard you pull.

He said, 'I guess I should tell you that I've been seeing somebody.'

I felt a little pang. Maybe being buddies would be more difficult than I thought. I said, 'Just one somebody?' I was joking, of course.

He said, 'No comment. Let's do this.'

I played Kevin the tune about ten times, and it took him, I think, eight passes to nail his drum part. Even though he heard it a grand total of eighteen times – and played it a zillion times in concert after – it never dawned on our Mr McAllister that the lyrics of 'Addition by Subtraction' were about him. Matter of fact, it never dawned on either him *or* his bass-playing cousin.

I sometimes still can't figure out what's wrong with that gene pool. Inbreeding, maybe?

I spent the rest of the day and all of the next day mixing down the track. It didn't sound as polished as it eventually would when I recorded it at a real studio with a real engineer, but I knew it was strong enough to play for the head of my label, Mitch Busey, so I dropped him an email saying I was coming to the office tomorrow with a surprise that would make him cream. Now I normally don't say stuff like 'cream' – what classy broad does? – but Mitch likes it when I'm vulgar, and if a bit of vulgarity keeps my label head happy, who am I to argue?

That night, I emailed an MP3 of 'Addition by Subtraction' to Masu, and a few minutes later she called me, and said, 'Girl, that's the awesomest shit you've ever done, and you've done some awesome shit. I'm coming by first thing tomorrow, we'll do breakfast, then we'll lay it on Mitch.' The next morning, we hopped a cab to 53rd Street and Seventh Avenue. Mitch was waiting for us in front of his office building. He said, 'Babe' – he calls everybody 'Babe' – 'when I read that email, I got a hard-on the size of my thumb, which is a huge hard-on for me, because I'm usually the size of a toothpick.' He looked at Masu, then said, 'Babe, you don't even have to sing to get *me* thumb-sized. I just gotta look at you.'

See? I told you he likes vulgarity. I said, 'Thanks for sharing. Let's go hear this thing.'

After Masu and I got comfy on the couch in his corner office, my manager launched into a long-winded speech to Mitch about how this was the greatest song I'd ever written, and how it would put me on the map like I'd never been mapped before, and how it would get me Grammys and multiple platinum records, and how being my manager was the proudest thing she'd ever done in her life, and it was all very embarrassing and very wonderful.

**MASUHARA JONES** Yeah, I'm her manager, but I'm also her biggest fan. To me, musically speaking, the girl can do no wrong. I mean, if she recorded a song that consisted of three minutes of herself farting, I'd love it.

**BILLIE HOLIDAY'S GHOST** We have superb access to satellite radio up here, so I was able to hear 'Addition by Subtraction' whenever I wanted to, and I wanted to hear it a lot. I never got sick of it, and that's saying something, because I'm still sick of 'Strange Fruit', which is a song that many critics have called a classic. But what do the critics know?

I've always done what I could to keep Jennifer on the straight and narrow, but she's a tough nut. She usually does whatever she damn well pleases, even if it is obviously the wrong thing to do. Like kissing Mr McAllister that night in Wisconsin – that was obviously the wrong thing to do. I can't be too rough on her for that little mistake though. I once let the legendary saxophonist Lester Young feel me up while we were both playing a gig with the legendary orchestra leader Count Basie – right in the middle of the set! It was during the Count's piano feature, and we were standing in the stage wings, and this cat Lester was looking good, and playing good, and he snuck up behind me, and . . . well, that's all you need to know.

So you see what I'm talking about? Once in a while you get carried away. Like I mentioned before, my Jennifer is a sensualist. So am I. And that's what we do, whether we mean to or not. And I apologize for both of us to all the boys we've driven out of their minds because of it.

Anyhow, with Jennifer, sometimes I'll make it very obvious which direction she should take, and usually she pays heed, but sometimes she ignores me. I'm glad she takes chances – if she didn't, she wouldn't be making so much beautiful music for so many people – but sometimes she makes me crazy, and I'm crazy enough to start with. Right then, Jennifer was at a crossroads. Musically, romantically, spiritually, you name it, the girl had to make some choices. And I wanted to help. But she didn't let me. And look what happened.

Those damn redheaded white girls are too stubborn for their own good.

JENN BRADFORD Mitch flipped. He's a blabbermouth, so I won't bother to try and recount exactly what he said, but the gist of it was that he loved the tune just the way it was; he didn't think I needed to re-record it as long as he could get it properly remastered, and he wanted it on the streets in one month. He also wanted us to shoot the sexiest video ever, and he loved me so much that if he wasn't married, he would run away with me – but only if I could accept his toothpick-like penile status.

Obviously Mitch Busey is a freak, but he's a freak who can get things done. 'Addition by Subtraction' was available for downloading on iTunes three weeks later, then three weeks after that, it was available in stores, then two weeks after that, I shot the video, then two weeks after that, the video premiered.

Then, like, six seconds later, things changed.

# Billboard

## November 1, 2009

### NEW RELEASES – SINGLE REVIEWS
'Addition by Subtraction'
**JENN BRADFORD & THE JB's**

### Label: Éclat Records

A straight-up rocker from an artist who rarely straight-up rocks, this stand-alone single makes one pine for the forthcoming album from the fiery redhead – an album that, according to an Éclat spokesman, isn't even in the works. Her disappointing previous outing of last year, *Reality Check*, ran the gamut from New Wave to neo-jazz, but 'Addition by Subtraction' is firmly in the rock 'n' roll tradition, albeit with a funky Brooklyn edge tempered by a hearty dose of populist sensibilities. Think Janis Joplin meets James Brown, with a sprinkle of Paul

McCartney thrown in for good measure. Supported by what the Éclat spokesman claims will be 'the most blatantly sexualized music video in our label's history', look for 'Addition by Subtraction' to make a notable mark at both on- and off-line retail.

*Will Halliday*

MASUHARA JONES Jenn wrote up a treatment for the 'Addition by Subtraction' video, and after I read it, I was like, 'Honey, this thing is gonna make you either the world's biggest star or the world's biggest slut.'

She goes, 'It's just The Girls. What's the big deal?'

I looked at her boobs, then I looked at my boobs, then I go, 'Trust me, honey, The Girls are a big deal.'

NAOMI BRAVER I picked Jenn up at LAX. When she got to the car, she gave me a huge hug, then looked up at the sky and yelled, 'New York winters suck! Los Angeles winters rule!' Then she practically threw a piece of paper at me, and said, 'Read this.'

I said, 'Now?'

She said, 'Yeah. Now.'

I said, 'But I'm sitting in a No Standing zone.'

She said, 'Read it.'

I said, 'I'm gonna get a ticket.'

She said, 'I'll pay it. Read it.'

So I read it. Then I read it again. Then again. And even though it kinda grossed me out, I kept it, because I knew it would be worth something some day, and I might need to sell it on eBay after I retired from showbusiness, broke and hungry, which at that point was looking more and more like it was gonna be the case, because Hollywood had shown no love for yours truly. Anyhow, here it is. Yeah, you can borrow it to scan for your book, just make sure I get it back:

---

### 'ADDITION BY SUBTRACTION' VIDEO TREATMENT
#### by Jenn

| SONG SECTION | SHOT |
|---|---|
| Intro: | Me sitting at a piano, fully clothed, on a huge stage in an empty auditorium. |
| Verse 1: | Smash cut to me at the same piano, except without my boots. |
| Pre Chorus 1: | Same as above, except without my blouse. No pixilation. |
| Chorus 1: | Same as above, except without my pants. No pixilation. |
| Verse 2: | Same as above, except without my bra. Heavily pixilated boobs. |
| Pre chorus 2: | Same as above, except without my panties. Heavily pixilated boobs and 'thang'. |
| Chorus 2: | Smash cut to me naked at a crowded library. Nobody notices I'm naked. Lighten pixilation. |
| Bridge: | Same as above, except at a grocery store. Lighten pixilation. |
| Chorus 3: | Same as above, except I'm walking down Melrose. Lighten pixilation. |
| Out chorus: | Same as above, except I'm standing in the middle of an enormous crowd. Lightest pixilation possible. |
| Final shot: | A single frame of me completely naked that you can only see if you pause it at the exact right second on your DVR. |

NAOMI BRAVER Full frontal nudity? Yikes. Me, I'm embarrassed to show my belly button in public, something my record label used to make me do with far too much regularity for my comfort.

I know Jenn's always been proud of her body – and justifiably so, it's deadly – but this struck me as exploiting it, something I never thought she'd do. *I* always thought that *she* always thought the music would be enough. Sure, she was always somewhat sexed up on stage, but that made sense because she was also always somewhat sexed up *off* stage. All the low-cut tops – and bottoms – and the go-go boots she wore at her gigs, and on her videos, and during her photo shoots made sense, because that's the kind of stuff you always found in her closet, even when we were in high school. But sitting bare-assed in a library? That felt way wrong and contrived.

Which is exactly what I told her.

JENN BRADFORD I said, 'But I'll be pixilated. Plus in the scene in the library, I think I'll have myself reading some D.H. Lawrence. That'll class it up. Remember, I'm a classy broad.'

Naomi gave me a Naomi look, one of those looks that don't need any verbal elaboration. I guess I understood where she was coming from. I mean, she was like my sister, and nobody wants to see their sister in her birthday suit, especially on basic cable. And yeah, the video was over the top, but Zach had made a good point about using what weapons I've got while I still have them. I really took that to heart.

My body was in decent shape, but only because I'm one of those lucky people who can eat whatever they want and never gain weight – or if I did gain weight, it generally ended up in the right places. It's been that way my entire life. I've never had to exercise, so I've become an incredibly lazy person; therefore, once my metabolism grinds to a halt – and I know it will – I don't see myself hitting the gym on any kind of regular basis. So at some point, my body will be gross.

I also pointed out to Naomi that everybody agreed 'Addition by Subtraction' was the best pop song I'd ever written – better than 'And Then', even – and I wasn't sure I'd ever be able to come up with something that good again, so I thought, why not go all out and get those sales figures popping, which might make up for *Reality Check*. Then I said, 'Plus, stripping goes with the concept of the song. "Addition by Subtraction". Get it?'

She said, 'No, Jenn, I don't get it. It's far too subtle for my teeny-tiny brain to comprehend. Thanks for explaining.'

Ooh, Naomi was *pissed*.

**NAOMI BRAVER** Oh, by the way, I did get a parking ticket while we were sitting in the car, which Jenn still owes me fifty bucks for.

**JENN BRADFORD** I asked her, 'So are you gonna stay mad at me?'

She said, 'I'm not mad. Just disappointed.' Ouch. I'd have rather had her be mad. Mad would have drifted away. Disappointment would hang around for a while. Then she said, 'But if you want your moneymaker to make you some money, go for it.'

I said, 'It's not about money.' And it wasn't. I realize that in retrospect, it was about validation. You're probably saying, *enough with the validation*, already. I wish it were that easy. Isn't it fun being inside my brain?

Validation. It used to drive me. Especially after Kevin. There, I said it.

Nay and I were both quiet for a few minutes, which was strange, because usually if you stick the two of us alone in a room together, it's hard getting a word in edgewise. And if you stick the two of us in a room together after we haven't seen each other for a few months, well, forget it. But here we were, sitting practically motionless in traffic on the 101, not saying a damn thing.

Finally, I asked her, 'Will you come to the shoot tomorrow?'

She was silent for so long that I thought she wasn't gonna answer. Eventually she said, 'Of course. But I am *so* not gonna be your fluffer.'

I said, 'I'm not gonna need a fluffer.' Then, after a pause, I said, 'Honey, do you know exactly what a fluffer is?'

NAOMI BRAVER Yes, I know what a fluffer is. I think. It has something to do with boners, doesn't it? Heh.

Sometimes during video or movie shoots where there's some nudity, the set is closed to everybody other than essential crew people. That was most definitely not the case with 'Addition by Subtraction'. Jenn was perfectly okay with letting it all hang out – or, I guess, letting *most* of it hang out – in a roomful of strangers. And the guys on the crew were all over her, asking for autographs, begging Jenn to pose for pictures with them, snapping shots of her with their cell phones. And I bet that none of them even had a single one of her albums. They just wanted to be documented standing next to the hot, almost-naked chick who they thought was going to be *really* famous.

No, she wasn't naked when they were all taking pictures of her, she had a robe on, so settle down there, my friend.

Now I will say one thing about Jenn: she's a natural in front of the camera, way more natural than I am. She was so on fire that day that the director only needed one or two takes for the master shots, then a few minutes of coverage shots, then it was on to the next set-up – which made most of the male crew members happy, because each new set-up meant one less item of clothing on Ms Bradford.

**JENN BRADFORD** Okay, I'm gonna tell you something totally gross now. Up until right this very second, Naomi and Zach are the only people I've ever told about this. Oh, wait a sec, I think I might've told Porter Ellis about it when I was in one of my two-in-the-morning drunken stupors. See, for some reason, when I was in one of those two-in-the-morning drunken stupors, nothing was more fun than banging on Porter Ellis's door, flopping down on his seating system, and talking at him until I was tired enough to sleep. Plus he always seemed very put out by my unannounced arrivals, and when I was in a drunken stupor, nothing seemed more fun than putting him out.

**PORTER ELLIS** Believe it or not, sometimes I enjoyed those middle-of-the-night sneak attacks. Jenn was a decent storyteller, and she taught me more than I ever wanted to know about the music industry. And she made me laugh every so often. And she sometimes brought over some nice cheese, or a fancy jam, or a well-chosen bottle of wine.

But most of the time, I wanted her gone so I could go back to sleep.

**JENN BRADFORD** Another reason I liked dropping by was because Porter Ellis was a good listener. Or at least he pretended to be. Maybe he never talked back to me because it was always past two in the morning and he was tired, or maybe because I got on his nerves but he was too decent to throw me out, or maybe because I bored him and he didn't want to prolong the conversation, but for whatever reason, he never felt the need to contribute. And it was nice having some male energy paying close attention to what I was saying – or pretending to pay close attention to what I was saying – because the only other men I regularly spoke with, like Zach, T.J. and Mitch Busey, were blabbermouths, and often not particularly attentive ones at that. It's sometimes nice when a guy shuts the hell up for a while.

But I digress. Again. So here's the something gross.

The West Hollywood Library closed at eight o'clock, so the film crew couldn't set up until eight thirty, and we didn't start shooting until just after ten. It was supposed to look like I was completely naked for this section of the video, but I didn't want to be completely naked around a bunch of dusty books, so I put on a sheer, skin-colored leotard, which worked great. You couldn't tell I had anything on unless you were within two feet of me, and the closest the camera would get for that particular scene was five feet. Perfect.

Once I was all semi-clothed and fully made-up, I headed over to the table where I'd be situated, which was covered with books by Anais Nin and Henry Miller, who I decided were way cooler than D.H. Lawrence. I sat down and started thumbing through *Delta of Venus*. I hadn't read any Anais since high school, and back then, I thought she was all about sex. Now, I realized, she was only partly about sex, and mostly about love.

I was really getting into the book, when one of the grips came over to do the blocking. He put his hands on my shoulders and faced me at the exact angle to get the perfect shot, then he adjusted my seat, then he ducked under the table and put a chalk mark on the floor where my feet were supposed to be, then he stood up, put his hand back on my shoulder and said, 'You're all set to go, Jenn.' I'd been reading the whole time. I looked up from the book to thank the grip, and came face-to-face – or should I say face-to-crotch – with a massive lump in his jeans. It was huge, and frankly a bit frightening. He said, 'Can I get you anything?'

I turned away and said, 'Yeah. If it's not a hassle, could you go and tell somebody to grab me a Coke or something?'

He said, 'Oh, I'll get it for you. No problem.'

I said quickly, 'No, that's okay, I'm sure you're very busy.' I pointed at a random spot across the room. 'Have that guy over there bring it.'

He looked toward where I was pointing and said, 'Which guy?'

I buried my face back in the book and gestured randomly over my shoulder. 'That guy.' Then the grip stomped off. Or he stomped off as much as his, um, *condition* would allow. I suspect a massive lump like that would make it difficult for anybody to stomp properly.

A minute later, somebody reached over my shoulder and plunked a can of Coke on the table. He said, 'Here you go, Jenn.'

I turned around to thank him, and *boom*, another zucchini. This one was worse, because the guy was wearing loose-fitting khaki shorts. Welcome to Tent City.

I said, 'Jesus Christ, get that thing out of here!'

The guy said, 'What thing?'

I pointed to his pants, which were jittering. He looked down at himself and said, 'Oh, shit.' He grabbed one of the books from the table – it was *Tropic of Cancer*, ironically – and held it in front of his jumping lump. He backed away and said, 'Fuck, I'm so sorry,' then he gingerly tiptoed off. Before he'd even taken three steps, he turned around and said, 'Hey, if it's not a problem, could I get a picture with you?'

I pointed at *Tropic of Cancer*. 'Read chapter six. Then we'll talk.'

**NAOMI BRAVER** The next day was the money shot, when Jenn was gonna be naked in the middle of a huge crowd on one of the busiest streets in Los Angeles. That morning, while we were shoving down our bowls of Honey Nut Cheerios in my kitchen, she was all Little Miss Bravado. She said, 'This is gonna be awesome. Who needs to be at some stupid nude beach to be nude? Give me Beverly Hills, and I'm good to go.' But by the time we were halfway to the set, she wasn't quite as psyched. She said, 'Who's the dumbass that came up with this idea?'

I said, 'Um, you.'

She said, 'Ah, yes. Right. I'm the dumbass. Let's stop and get me some alcohol, so I can deal better with my dumbassed-ness.'

We pulled into the first liquor store we could find. I said, 'Chill here. I'll get you some pinot,' and I put on my disguise.

Jenn said, 'Wait a sec. No wine. Only clear.' That meant vodka.

**JENN BRADFORD** A couple swigs of Grey Goose, and I was set, ready to get nekkid. My only concern was that I didn't want to run into the Stiffie Twins. But if I did, it wouldn't have been as bad as the day before, because I'd be standing up for this shot, which meant at least there would be no chance of getting bashed in the forehead.

**NAOMI BRAVER** The second day of shooting was as easy as the first – easier even. I've said it before, and I'll say it again: Jenn Bradford was the biggest rock star in the entire world. It's just that the entire world didn't realize it yet.

It all went so smoothly that they were able to put together a rough cut of the video only seven days later, and I have to give Jenn credit. It worked. It totally worked. Yeah, it was still exploitative, but it was also funny, and well shot and, in its own tasteless way, kind of classy.

**JENN BRADFORD** See? Even when The Girls are out there for the world to see, I'm still a classy broad.

**BILLIE HOLIDAY'S GHOST** Does my Jennifer have balls, or does my Jennifer have balls? Made me wish that we had videos back in my day. I'd have gotten naked and done some freaky things to that camera that would've made even Miles Davis blush, and Miles was the biggest freak *ever*. Just ask him.

**MILES DAVIS'S GHOST** Hell yes, I was the biggest freak ever.

**BILLIE HOLIDAYS'S GHOST** Ah, Miles. We loved you madly.

Anyway, I talk a good game, but after seeing what happened to Jennifer, I wouldn't have wanted a video of me like that out there. As you probably know, I had plenty of other problems. If the world had had the opportunity to see my breasts anytime they wanted, well, that just would've caused more trouble than it was worth.

# Entertainment
## WEEKLY

**December 13, 2009**

## JENN BRADFORD, VERSION 3.0
### *Addition, Subtraction and Resurrection*

## by Jessica Reid

She's tearing up the charts. *And* she's naked. *And* she doesn't give a damn. Just listen: 'I've said it before, and I'll say it again: They're just boobs.'

So claims Jenn Bradford, the most downloaded video vixen in recent memory. Ever since the saucy singer/songwriter/keyboardist decided to share her privates with MTV's, and VH-1's, and iTunes', and You Tube's collective viewing audience, music journos have been trying to figure out whether her monster hit single, 'Addition by Subtraction', would've become a monster hit sans skin. The boys up in our office answer that question with a 'Damn straight', while the girls are slightly less enthusiastic about the whole thing. But virtually all of us agree: 'Addition' is a killer track, nipples or no nipples.

The tune flows so easily from Bradford that one has to wonder why it took her so long to flat-out rock out. Her previous recordings, while often transcendent and memorable, are at times esoteric enough to drive away even the hardest of the hardcore Bradford fan. 'It was an effortless experience,' Bradford says of writing and recording the platinum-selling single. '[The song] fell out of me. It was like I gave birth to it. Or vomited it up, one or the other.'

In terms of international visibility, Bradford now finds herself in the same rarified air as her former foil, Naomi. She's evolved from respected sidewoman, to critically appreciated bandleader, to musical lost soul, to undeniable rock goddess.

And oh, yeah – the boys up in the office heartily disagree with Ms Bradford's assertion that her boobs are just boobs. *Heartily.*

NAOMI BRAVER See? *EW* agrees with me about Jenn's rock goddess-ness, although I have to emphasize once again how less than thrilled I was by the way she went about reaching this particular plateau of goddess-ness. Okay, I don't feel like she sold out *completely*. I mean, it's not like she hired Kenny G., and recorded some lame Celine Dion kind of crap, and opened a theater in Branson, Missouri right next to Dolly Parton's Dixie Stampede Dinner & Show. It's just that up until then, she was kinda like eighty-five per cent music and fifteen per cent image. Then it got sorta reversed.

But Jenn's Jenn, and I love her, and I'll support her, even if I think what she's doing sucks. She'd do the same for me. Like according to the bajillion casting agents who haven't called me back, my acting sucks, and Jenn's still got my back. Besides, when she gets an idea for a song or a video or whatever, it's getting executed, no matter what I say or do. Especially after she gets a few gallons of Grey Goose in her.

MASUHARA JONES I was the assistant tour manager on the Naomi tour right before Jenn went off to start her solo career. That's where we got to be buds. But we weren't buds like my buds from back home in San Fran, because there was always that employer/employee thing happening. Jenn never talked down to me or anything, but there was that distance.

Still, over the last few years, whenever I had any kind of problem, Jenn was there for me. That's the way she is. Like she always brings people chicken soup when they're sick, or buys them random little presents, and she's never stopped doing that. She's a great girl. She's *my* girl. Even when she was in the midst of her 'Addition by Subtraction' madness, she still managed to be the true Jenn once in a while. Like she took me out to a killer birthday dinner that year, and she gave my stepbrother a couple of piano lessons for free. She's good like that.

But everybody who was close to Jenn knew that things with her weren't exactly the same, and they probably never would be. Her life changed, and she had to change with it. It was inevitable. Shit, she handled it better than I would've.

**JENN BRADFORD** Every once in a while, I wonder how I would've turned out as a person if I hadn't have, quote, *made it* as a musician. Would I still be living with Naomi in the East Village? Would I even still be playing music, or would I have gotten tired of the grind and the hustle? Would I be all married? Would I be a mommy?

I don't dwell on it too much, because the thought of not making a living playing music is frightening beyond words, and to me, being scared is counterproductive, and professional musicians can't be counterproductive. And I define myself as a professional musician. No, check that: I define myself as a *successful* professional musician.

Again, I'll tell you it's all about that validation.

Again I'll ask you, why do I need to be validated?

I mean, I know that I'm a good person. Or at least I aim to be. I always try to be decent to my friends and family, and sorta-boyfriends, and next-door neighbors. It doesn't always work out as well as I might've hoped – since sometimes my idea of being nice doesn't jibe with that of the cosmos – but at least I try. That should be enough. Knowing that you're trying to do the right thing, and sometimes actually managing to do the right thing – well, that should be enough validation for anybody. I shouldn't need validation from a stadium full of paying customers. If my parents, or my brother, or Naomi, or Masu, or even The Teej tells me they love me, or if a Zach Bingham or a Porter Ellis smiles at me and says, 'Jenn, thanks for buying me that Decembrists bootleg', or 'Jenn, thanks for bringing over that pound of delicious Brillat Savarin, it's the best cheese I've ever tasted', what more do I need?

Apparently, right then, I needed a lot.

**PORTER ELLIS** One day, things in my building were normal, and the next, I couldn't get to my front door without fighting through a flock of camera-toting cretins. They took pictures of me, and shoved miniature tape recorders in my face, and generally made the trip from the sidewalk to the lobby absolutely miserable. And this was all hours of the day and night.

The timing couldn't have been worse, because things were moving quickly with the club and I didn't need any distractions. I'd even come up with a solid opening date for the place, which I'd decided to name Beep. No reason, really – I just thought it sounded interesting and evocative. Our first show would be Valentine's Day, just five weeks away. It was to be a black tie only affair, with performances by a trio of acts who recorded for Blue Note Records, and catered by Mario Batali.

It was going to be an Event. With a capital E.

You see, I hired a PR firm who came up with a marketing plan that we agreed would launch the place strongly enough that we'd pack the house each night for six or so months. After that, Beep would be made or broken based on its own momentum, and quality, and consistency.

The PR firm decided that I should be the public face of the club. My account representative said that since I was an attractive, dignified, thriving businessman – who had a bit of public notoriety thanks to *Billionaire.com* – I could create some buzz just by making myself accessible to the press and the public. She believed that since jazz has such a limited audience, the music alone couldn't sell the place. But she also believed that jazz has an affluent audience, and she thought I could appeal to it. She insisted I get myself a new wardrobe. She said I needed to 'hip myself up'. So I went out and bought some trendier Hugo Boss suits to replace the more sedate Hugo Boss suits hanging in my closet. I'm not a fashion plate by any means, but I'm happy with Boss, and when I'm happy with something, I stick with it.

Over the previous several weeks, profiles of me ran in *New York* and the *New Yorker*, in the *Village Voice* and *The New York Times*. It felt like my picture was everywhere, and at times, it got to be embarrassing, but I knew I had to get used to it, because that was the way it was going to be for the next few months.

The paparazzi issue came to a head on a cold, gray, sleety Wednesday afternoon in January.

JENN BRADFORD Porter Ellis seemed to be MIA for all of December. I was wondering what the hell was going on with the guy, so a few times I banged on his door after midnight, but he didn't answer. I figured he was wrapped up in doing stuff for his jazz club, or traveling, or sleeping with earplugs. Or maybe he was ignoring me, who knows.

So I was glad when I ran into him that Wednesday, because I kind of missed bullshitting with the stuffy old fart. But it was some seriously bad timing.

**PORTER ELLIS** Jenn was asking you where I was during those few weeks before the *New York Post* fiasco? I guess I never did tell her, did I?

Well, I was out and about. Cavorting. Tomcatting around. After months and months and months of avoiding women, I decided enough was enough, and I got proactive. I went to every party or social gathering I was invited to, and I hit every jazz club in town on the pretense of doing market research, and I even signed up for an online dating site. It had been a long time since I'd been 'out there'. And I was very 'out there'. My PR firm was pleased.

I won't deny that sometimes being 'out there' was nice. One lady I met at Sweet Rhythm was simply lovely on every level, a charmer, an intellect and a beauty. She managed a women's boutique store on the Upper West Side, and was stable and poised, much calmer and saner than somebody like, for instance, my overly bubbly neighbor. I could've let myself fall for this boutique owner, and we probably would've worked as a couple for a good long while, but my gut told me that something wasn't right with us, that something was missing. My gut has always been good to me, and when it speaks, I listen. She'd also dropped the M word several times, and as you are well aware, at that point marriage was not a subject I was interested in discussing.

There were also some rough, awkward dates. One woman tried to put her hand down my pants at a restaurant in between the entrée and dessert. Some men were into that sort of thing, but I'd been down that road before, and wasn't anxious to go there again. Another woman was so blatantly gold-digging that I ended our date after the appetizer. The final woman I met was the definition of jaded, unbelievably depressed and depressing. At that point, I decided enough was enough.

If I may be blunt for a moment, I have to tell you that I wasn't proud of my own behavior during those couple of months. I slept with four different women in the span, only one of whom – the boutique owner – meant anything to me. I was thirty-nine years old, and there was no reason for that sort of behavior.

Well, in retrospect, maybe there *was* a reason. If nothing else, I most certainly learned what I *didn't* want in a mate.

**JENN BRADFORD** I was coming out of the building, and Porter Ellis was coming in. He was trying to fight his way through the photography pool, and not doing a very good job of it. I think he was afraid he'd ruin his nice suit. And it *was* a nice suit. He always wore nice suits. Still does.

**PORTER ELLIS** I'd almost gotten used to having those cretins on our sidewalk. Okay, I exaggerate – they weren't *all* cretins. A couple of them were actually somewhat friendly. But friendly or not, they were always snapping, snapping, snapping. I asked one why they bothered taking shots of me each and every day. Didn't it get repetitive? Wasn't it pointless? Why would some random newspaper reader care about my face? I'm really not that interesting.

He said, 'You're a public figure, and you live in the same building as Jenn Bradford. They pay me to document shit like that.' The irony is that whenever one of these pictures popped up in some newspaper or magazine, my PR rep loved it.

So that day, Jenn poked her head out the front door and yelled, 'Porter Ellis! Where've you been? I've missed you, honey!' Then she literally shoved her way past four or five of the photographers – she even knocked one of them on to the ground – and then jumped me.

**JENN BRADFORD** Yeah, I jumped him all right, but the guy didn't make it easy. He wouldn't open his arms, so I was forced to put my hands on his shoulders, raise myself up and wrap my legs around his waist.

After a second or two, he put his arms around me, if only to keep me from falling on my ass. That's when I stuck my tongue in his ear.

**PORTER ELLIS** I saw fireworks.

And no, I'm not talking figurative fireworks in the sense that the woman captured my heart, but rather literal fireworks to the tune of a dozen digital cameras flashing in my face.

**JENN BRADFORD** He can deny it all he wants, but he was, you know, aroused. I felt it. I'm sensitive to that kind of thing.

**PORTER ELLIS** I was this close to letting go of her, letting her fall on to the sidewalk, but I couldn't do it – partly because I didn't want a shot of me letting a big star crashing on to the hard concrete to show up on page 6 of the *New York Post*. The other reason was because dropping her on her backside wouldn't have been a nice thing to do.

**JENN BRADFORD** He told you he was gonna dump me on my ass on *purpose*? *Seriously*? That jerk.

**PORTER ELLIS** She then gave me a brief, hard, wet kiss on the mouth and said loudly enough for everybody within a two-block radius to hear, 'Porter Ellis, take me here and now, you rock-hard stud!'

**JENN BRADFORD** Pretty much each of the photographers stopped taking pictures and grabbed their cell phones, I'm assuming to call their editors. That's when I unwrapped myself from Porter Ellis, gave him a tiny smooch on the cheek, and said, 'Okay, gotta run. Take me another day, sexy. See ya around the ranch.' Then I sprinted to the grocery store.

Doing something as simple as grocery shopping had become an ordeal. I always dressed down when I was out and about, usually wearing a baseball hat and some shades, a tactic I learned from Naomi. It seemed to work for her, but I almost always got recognized. Most of the time it was somebody wanting an autograph, nothing more. But once in a while, it was some guy invading my personal space, telling me the awesome things he'd do to me if he ever got me in bed, and trying to touch my hair, or my arm, or my thigh.

I wondered if nude, *Playboy*-type models went through this kind of crap, whether they got macked on whenever they were in a public place. Do the general public think they have license to fondle somebody who'd disrobed on-screen or in magazines? Is this something I'd have to deal with until the 'Addition by Subtraction' video ran its course, or would the boys of the world continue being all grabby until I gained fifty pounds?

Coincidentally, right when I had that thought about getting fat, I was standing directly in front of the ice cream aisle. Needless to say, I indulged. Cherry Garcia. Good stuff.

**PORTER ELLIS** Sure enough, the next day, there it was, the whole thing, right there on page 6 of the *New York Post*. There were three pictures. One showed Jenn practically eating the side of my face, one showed her pulling my hair, and the last one showed her running away. I remember that damn article by heart:

*Richie-rich dotcom entrepreneur Porter Ellis here has his hands full with his new beau, notorious nudist and singer Jenn Bradford. Neither party would comment about their burgeoning relationship, but while these steamy photos were being taken, Bradford allegedly told Ellis to, '. . . [expletive deleted] me here and now, you big stud,' to which Ellis replied, 'I'm going to [expletive deleted] your [expletive deleted] for so long that you'll never [expletive deleted] with your [expletive deleted] [expletive deleted] [expletive deleted] again.'*

*Phone calls to both parties went unreturned, but we can assume that Bradford will be seen at the grand opening of Ellis's soon-to-be-the-trendiest-jazz-joint-in-town – Beep. Stay tuned . . .*

**JENN BRADFORD** I personally thought the article was pretty hilarious. Masu didn't.

**MASUHARA JONES** You think that article had a lot of expletive deleteds? I dropped so many F-bombs on Jenn that her cellie blew up.

**PORTER ELLIS** Almost immediately after the paper hit the stands, I got an email from the boutique owner. She wrote, *I guess I can see why you dumped me. I hope you and the naked girl are very happy together.* I wrote back to her with a truncated version of the real story, but she never responded. Can you blame her?

Even today, I'm still embarrassed by the whole episode. Unsurprisingly, the PR firm loved it.

**JENN BRADFORD** Zach called me that morning and said, 'Are you fucking your neighbor? I'm not jealous. I'm curious.'

I said, 'No, Weenie Boy, I am not fucking my neighbor. I was fucking with the paparazzi.'

He said, 'And that was the best way you could think of to fuck with the paparazzi? To make out with that uptight freak right in front of your building?'

I said, 'I wasn't making out with him, Zach. It was like a stage kiss.' He grunted, then I kidded, 'You know, for a tough indie rock dude, sometimes you're kind of a nancy-boy.'

Then he hung up on me. Somebody was in a mood.

**ZACH BINGHAM** *Rolling Stone* was given a pass for the grand opening of Beep, and I jump on it, partly because I want to see what the great Porter Ellis has to offer the music world, and partly because I have nothing else to do that night. And it's not like anybody else at the magazine particularly wants the pass anyhow. The good thing is that I like jazz as much as the next guy, so no matter how lame and snotty the vibe might be, at least I'll enjoy the music.

I end up flying there solo. This is when Jenn's afraid to leave the house, so I don't even bother asking her.

**PORTER ELLIS** Jenn slid a note under my door at some point during the evening before Beep's opening night:

### Good day, Porter Ellis

*If you leave my manager's name (Masuhara Jones)
at the door with a plus-one tonight, I promise I'll
never call you a rock-hard stud in public again.
And if you don't hate me too much, maybe you can
also stick me on the list, and maybe I'll come. But
maybe I won't. Aren't I intriguing?*
*xox,*
*Jenn*

How could I *possibly* say no to that? And please make a
note to your readers that I said that in an exceedingly
sarcastic tone.

**MASUHARA JONES** Jenn called me up on Valentine's Day
afternoon and asked if I wanted to take T.J. to this hoity-
toity jazz gig that night. I think jazz sucks, but I knew
The Teej would like it, so I said fine. But then Jenn was
all like, 'I'll probably see you there. But you have to do
me a favor.'

I go, 'Yeah?'

She was like, 'If I don't show up, you have to tell me
everything that happens.'

I go, 'Why?'

She was like, 'Well, I have a hunch that Zach's gonna
be there, and I'd love to find out how Indie Boy gets
along with a roomful of people who don't have any facial
piercings. I also wanna see how things go for Porter
Ellis—'

I was like, 'Who's Porter Ellis?'

She goes, 'Just some guy.'

After we hung up, I remembered that Porter Ellis was the dude she kissed in the newspaper. I almost called her back to ask what was up with him, which I never asked her in the first place, because I was so pissed off about the article, because it made her come off like a skeezer. But instead I called T.J. to invite him to the show, and we talked for a long time, and while we were talking, he remembered how much he likes me, then he came over and we did it two times in five hours, which is like a record for him.

**T.J. STEWART** Nah, man, The Teej's record is six times in four hours, which averages out to 1.25 times an hour. I didn't pay attention to shit in high school, but I learned my basic math, yo. I guess Masu don't know how to add, an' divide, an' multiply, an' shit. All she can do is hate on a brother.

Well, she can do some other shit too, but I ain't telling you what. I'm saving it for my own book.

**PORTER ELLIS** It was Valentine's Day, opening day, *my* day. I got to Beep just before noon, and it was empty, save for my bar manager. By that point, she'd been with me for a few months, and she had some emotional investment in the club herself, so she was almost as nervous and as excited as I was.

I ordered us some lunch from the diner across the street and we ate at the bar, not saying much. We chewed our chicken Caesar salads, and stared at the freshly painted and decorated walls, and the sleek tables and chairs, and the state-of-the-art sound system. I don't know what she was thinking, but I was as happy as I'd ever been.

The room was in pristine condition, and there was nothing I needed to do – no phone calls, no rearranging the tables, no nothing – and the doors weren't opening until eight, which gave me about seven hours to kill. I pulled out my BlackBerry and almost called the boutique owner, but I didn't. Then I almost called my first ex-wife. Again, I didn't. I didn't have a date for that evening, and while that wasn't a tragedy, it would've been nice to have somebody to share the night with. But after a bit, I realized that maybe it would be better if I was on my own. I'd be busy working the room anyhow, and wouldn't be properly attentive. It was for the best. I needed to be alone.

ZACH BINGHAM I bust out my tuxedo, which hasn't seen the light of day since, I dunno, my senior prom, or maybe my sister's wedding. I try it on, and it's loose on me. I'm not surprised I'd lost weight since high school. After all, I've been on the freelance writer's diet since my junior year at NYU.

I get to the club at eight fifteen – which is fifteen minutes after the doors were supposed to open – and there's a line halfway down the block. It's all screamingly expensive tuxedos and smoking-hot cocktail dresses as far as the eye can see, and I feel out of place and weird, but fuck it, I'm gonna hang.

Finally they start letting us in, and who's greeting people at the door? The man himself.

**PORTER ELLIS** I couldn't tell you exactly what it is about Zach Bingham that rubs me up the wrong way. If I'm being honest, I'll admit that he's not evil. Nor is he stupid. Most of the time, he's perfectly civilized. I suppose that in some other lifetime or parallel universe, we could have been friends, or at least friendly acquaintances. But in this one, we annoy the hell out of each other. At least we're polite about it though. More or less.

He was the thirty-sixth person in line. With an ironic, cheese-eating grin on his face, he sticks out his hand and says, 'Zach Bingham, features writer, *Rolling Stone*. I'm on the list.'

**ZACH BINGHAM** Porter gives me a look like, *What're you doing here?* I could tell he loses his cool for a second – but only a second. He's a polished guy, no doubt.

He shakes my hand, and smiles, and says, 'Will *Rolling Stone* be featuring Beep in its next issue?'

I say, 'Doubtful. I'm here for the free food.'

He still looks unfazed. 'Is Jenn here with you?'

I say, 'No. Is she here with you?'

He says, 'Why would she be with me?' He looks sincerely confused.

I say, 'Dude, you practically slept with her on page six.'

He says all sarcastically, '*Duuude*, you sleep with her every night.'

I think, *Not every night*, but whatever.

**PORTER ELLIS** I didn't have time for Zach. Not then. I had patrons to greet.

There was only one couple who ignored the dress code. The guy was about six foot two with dreadlocks halfway down his back. The girl was about five-two, and that's including her platform shoes. The guy, who was wearing a New York Knicks jersey that hung down to his thighs and jeans that hung down past his butt, was mauling the girl, who was wearing a tight red scoop-neck T-shirt and a very short skirt. The girl kept smacking the guy's hands away, but she had a huge smile on her face. She was obviously very happy and very much in love.

**MASUHARA JONES** For the first time in our semi-dating history, T.J. was being affectionate in public. Unfortunately, his version of public affection meant a whole lot of butt-grabbing, and very little hand-holding.

**T.J. STEWART** Come on, now. Asses are for grabbing. Hands are for bass playing and handjobs. Asses come first. It's all about priorities, baby. And Shorty's ass is *foine*.

**PORTER ELLIS** When they reached the door, this girl stood on her tiptoes, gave me a hug and said grandly, 'Porter Ellis, it's an honor to meet you.' I pulled away from her, then she said, 'I'm on the list. When's Jenn gonna be here?'

I said, 'Ah, you're the manager. I don't know when she's coming. I don't even know *if* she's coming.'

The girl said, 'Oh, she's coming.' Then she walked

past me and patted me on my behind. What is it about Jenn Bradford and her friends that makes them think it's okay to touch virtual strangers in what many would consider to be an inappropriate fashion? I don't appreciate it. Some people probably do. Maybe I'm too old.

But I didn't spend too much time thinking about it, because there were people to greet and seat. And I was having a ball doing it. Everybody was thrilled to be there, and it turns out it's fun to deal with the general public when they're in a good mood. It was considerably more fun than overseeing a website. I probably could've been happy doing it for years.

**ZACH BINGHAM** Masu shows up with Stewart, and they plunk right down at my table. She says, 'Where's Jenn?'

I say, 'Don't know. I could ask you the same question.'

She shrugs, then pulls out her cell. 'Let's text her.'

**JENN BRADFORD** That's why I sent Masu in the first place – I wanted her to be my eyes and ears in case I decided to skip it. When she texted me that Zach was there, well, that was a mark in the 'stay home' column. Zach had slid back into his clingy and possessive persona, and when he was in that mode, he could be very territorial, and very no fun. Also, he and Porter Ellis seemed to get into a pissing contest whenever I was around, and I didn't want to help create any unnecessary drama on Porter Ellis's big night.

On the other hand, the club was kind of my idea, and I really wanted to see if Porter Ellis nailed it. Finally, after downing a huge bowl of Cherry Garcia, I decided I'd go, but that I'd have to go in disguise. However, I couldn't go in my usual disguises, because (a) they were all lame, and (b) this was a black tie affair. All of which meant I had to get creative.

First off, I pulled my hair into a tight bun, something I'd literally never done in my life. It took me about four cracks before I got it to look presentable, but that's all it was, presentable. Really, it looked stupid as hell. But it was a start.

Then I threw on a pair of disposable jeans, and an Adidas hoodie – the very hoodie I wore during my first interview with Zach, as a matter of fact – and a simple pair of black Manolo flats. I called down to our doorman and asked him to hail me a taxi, but have it pull around the back of the building, near the Dumpsters. Going out the back was a pain in the ass, because it meant walking through the loose garbage in the alley, but tiptoeing around banana peels and leftover Chinese food was better than bulling my way through the photography pool.

I had the cabbie take me to the Ann Taylor in Soho, where I picked out the most conservative, bland, non-Jenn-like black power suit in the place. It more or less fit, so I told the salesperson I'd take it and wear it, and that she could go ahead and ring me up while I chucked my jeans and hoodie.

While she was running my credit card, I noticed a display of incredibly ugly spectacle frames in the case underneath the cash register. I snatched up a pair, threw them on, and checked myself out in the nearest mirror.

Somebody might have been able to peg me in broad daylight if they were standing about two feet away, but in a dark club, no way.

**PORTER ELLIS** Once the music started, I turned the doorman duties over to my bar manager so I could enjoy the scene. And I don't feel it's an overstatement to call that night magical.

The music was brilliant. There was some acoustic jazz, some electric jazz and some vocal jazz, and all of it sounded phenomenal, partly I believe because the musicians were inspired by their surroundings, and partly because the sound system was the best I'd ever heard in a club the size of Beep. It was the only system of its kind in the world, brand new, and brilliant. The food and drink were also wonderful, and the décor was a hit, especially that collage behind the bar. Some folks specifically went out of their way to tell me how much they liked it.

I knew that every night at Beep wouldn't be like this, but we were off to a terrific start. I felt confident that word of mouth, along with the continued PR blitz, would cement Beep's place in the New York music world.

I kind of wished Jenn had made it over that night so she could see what her casual little comment had begat.

**JENN BRADFORD** Porter Ellis never knew I was there. Nor did Masu or Zach. And if the three of them didn't recognize me, nobody would. I decided that the next day, I'd sign up for an Ann Taylor charge card. It'd be way better than a baseball hat.

**ZACH BINGHAM** Halfway through the first set, Jenn shows up in the crappiest disguise imaginable. The only reason nobody else recognizes her is because most of them are jazz geeks, and probably don't watch much MTV.

**MASUHARA JONES** Halfway through the first set, Zach elbowed me, then pointed at the back of the club, and there's Jenn, leaning against the wall, all decked out in a black suit that made her look like a marketing executive. I go to T.J., 'Jenn's here,' and I stood up and waved at her.

T.J. pulled me down, and goes, 'Girlfriend, don't be all creating a commotion, an' shit.'

I stared at him for a second, then I was like, 'Did you say girlfriend?'

He took one of his dreads and started chewing on it, and then he goes, 'Um, did I?'

I was like, 'Yeah, you did. I'm your girlfriend. And you're my bitch. So happy Valentine's Day, bitch.' Then I gave him the biggest, sexiest, hottest kiss ever.

After I was done, he goes, 'Aight, I'll be your beeyatch. Let's get the fuck out of here, yo.'

We knocked over about six people's drinks running to the door. When we got back to my place, he tried to break his record, but didn't even come close.

**T.J. STEWART** What can I say, man? I already busted my nut twice in the afternoon, plus I'd gotten my drink on at the club. So once we hit the sack, I was one and done. But it was a goddamn good one. Ask Shorty. She'll tell you.

**MASUHARA JONES** He's right. It *was* a goddamn good one.

**ZACH BINGHAM** I motion Jenn over, and she shakes her head, little shakes, and I'm pissed. She's the queen of mixed signals. One week she's all over me, making me breakfast, buying me shirts, licking my neck like I'm a candy cane, giving me one of her patented Brazilian Tiger Fist blow jobs. The next week, I get little shakes from the back of the club – a club, it so happens, that's owned by a guy she made out with on the street. After that time we kissed in Prospect Park on our first date, she barely ever kissed me outside.

Yeah, I know I'm sounding insecure, but it's Valentine's Day, and my sorta-Valentine's about ten yards away, and won't sit with me. I'm not saying I was being rational that night – Jenn's transgression didn't justify my annoyance level – but that's the way I felt.

I'm just speaking the truth. I've been honest with you during this whole interview process, so why stop? I've made myself look like a complete fool in *Rolling Stone* twice now, so at this point, what's the difference?

**JENN BRADFORD** I didn't sit down because from my spot in the back, I had a great view of everything. I could see that Porter Ellis smile – that rare, rare, shiny, shiny Porter Ellis smile – from across the room. Hells, I could've probably seen Porter Ellis's smile from across the street.

I could also see that Zach was annoyed I wouldn't sit with him. I knew I wasn't being fair to the guy. I would've been happy with keeping our relationship at the same sorta-level we'd been at since we got back together. Him, not so much. Even though he'd never out and out said anything about it to me, I knew he wanted more from me – his possessiveness, and clinginess, and burgeoning jealousy were making that quite obvious. That being the case, the right thing to do would've been to tell him that he'd be much happier with a woman who wasn't as busy, and besieged, and distracted as I was.

But I didn't.

Why? I was hesitant to cut the cord, because Zach had a whole heap of nice qualities, ones aside from his cute neck, and the most important one was that he was true blue. I knew he wouldn't mess around with anybody while we were together, even if our togetherness wasn't as together as, say, Masu and T.J.'s. Also, underneath all of Zach's indie dude cool guy posing, there was a pretty mushy guy. Sometimes he treated me like Kevin did when we first hooked up: flowers, and mix CDs, and silly little 'just because' gifts. But he still couldn't bring himself to call me 'baby' or 'sweetie'. You can't have everything.

All this was zipping through my head, and I couldn't turn my brain off and enjoy the music, or the club's vibe, or even the sweet collage behind the bar, so I went home, uncorked a nice bottle of Chardonnay, and took a one-hour bath.

I love my bathtub.

**ZACH BINGHAM** I can't lie, Porter's joint is smashing. I'm into it – more into it than I could've imagined – but after

Jenn bails without coming over and saying either hello or goodbye, I lose my groove, so I split and go over to the Mercury Lounge to check out a handful of bands I'd never heard of. They all suck. I go home, put on a Neutral Milk Hotel record, and feel much better.

Oh, and I also come up with a great idea about how I can win Jenn back. Or pay Jenn back, one or the other. So I email my *Rolling Stone* editor with a story pitch.

**PORTER ELLIS** My life has been the dictionary definition of a roller-coaster ride. I grew up poor, and ended up with money. I found, then lost love on four separate occasions. I created a company that I was quite proud of, then I sold it because I would've been an idiot not to. Then I built up a club, and for one night, it was both the best business and the best personal move I'd ever made.

But that only lasted one night.

**BILLIE HOLIDAY'S GHOST** I knew exactly what was going to happen to Beep. I couldn't stop it. It's against the rules of our afterworld. We can only interfere to a point. The only thing I could do was try and make sure that nobody got hurt.

I did my job. Nobody got hurt. At least physically.

# NEW YORK DAILY NEWS

## February 16, 2010

### FIRE CLAIMS NEWLY OPENED GREENWICH VILLAGE JAZZ CLUB
*No Injuries, Possible Arson*

### by Gregory Hernandez

A five-alarm fire ripped through the club Beep on 41 W. Greenwich St in Greenwich Village at approximately 4.15 a.m. yesterday.

Fire Chief Richard Clifton said there were no injuries, but then added that the building's infrastructure was '. . . compromised beyond repair'. Investigators have little clue as to the cause of the fire, but an unnamed source said that arson is not being ruled out.

Beep owner Porter Ellis, 39, could not be reached for comment, but his PR representative, Wendy Reese of Christopher & Associates, issued the following statement: 'While devastated by the loss of Beep, Mr Ellis's initial primary concern was the safety of his employees and clientèle. He is relieved that nobody was harmed, and will address the issue of rebuilding the venue at the appropriate time.'

Ellis is the creator of *Billionaire.com*, which he sold four years ago for a reported eight figures. Reese said, 'Beep was Mr Ellis's first foray into the field of entertainment. We do not expect it to be his last.'

The latest entry into New York City's floundering jazz scene, Beep opened its doors only two days ago with a gala, star-studded affair. Among the guests were New York stalwart directors Woody Allen and Spike Lee, actor Robert DeNiro and singer Jenn Bradford.

**JENN BRADFORD** The 'Addition by Subtraction' tour kicked off at the end of March, and it was a biggie: twenty-five cities in thirty-three days. Éclat was hoping that the shows, combined with the continued success of 'Addition by Subtraction' could move a few copies of *Reality Check*. I could get behind that strategy, so I put on my metaphorical helmet and got ready for the busiest, most elaborate, most expensive tour of my life.

But I was fried before we even left, because at the end of February, immediately before we hit the road, the fine folks at Éclat Records ran me ragged in the form of a whirlwind New York City schmooze-a-thon. I did six meet 'n' greets, two in-store autograph sessions and ten – count 'em, *ten* – dinners with a variety of music industry muckity-mucks. And this was all over a two-week period.

When I wasn't schmoozing, I was rehearsing with our new expanded band. You see, the fine folks at Éclat Records wanted The JB's live shows to be extravaganzas – we're talking horns, and strings, and background vocalists galore – and if they were paying for the extra ear- and eye-candy, who was I to say no? Problem was, I was running around so much that I knew I wouldn't have time to bring a new drummer properly up to speed, and that was vital, because my music would suffer without a drummer who knew the material inside and out. So I called Kevin. He said yes. Me and Kevin, together again.

Before I blew town, I barely saw my own apartment, let alone any of my neighbors. But whenever I made it home for an hour or three, there was no sign of Porter Ellis. Nothing. Like I never saw a light under his door, or heard any noise coming from his place. Our doorman claimed to have seen him a few times, and said he looked awful – unshaven and disheveled and, as he put it, 'generally messed up'. I couldn't picture Porter Ellis generally messed up, but I sure as hell could understand why he might be. Having your business burn down – and a business you love madly, at that – will do that to you.

But honestly, I didn't have time to worry about it. I had a tour to do.

**KEVIN MCALLISTER** Jenn asked me to go out on the road with her and T.J. . . . *and* a horn section . . . *and* a string section . . . *and* three background vocalists . . . *and* like 4,000 roadies . . . *and* a partridge in a pear tree. Not exactly my scene in terms of music – I liked more intimate situations – but the money was good, and as I wasn't working much and needed the bread, I said okay.

No, the tour wasn't about spending time with Jenn. It was about playing drums and getting paid. End of story, man.

After it was clear that Jenn and I would never exist as a couple again, I decided I should at least *try* and get my shit together, figure out how to properly love myself so maybe someday I'd be able to properly love somebody else. One of the things I did was to go out and buy this book about divorce, which is how I know about all that 'properly loving yourself' jive.

I know, Jenn and I weren't married, but like this book said, you have to allow yourself to grieve the loss of *any* long-term love affair, whether it's a marriage, or an engagement, or just dating, or whatever. It said that in every relationship – platonic friendship included – one of the parties at any given time has more power over the other one. The book also said that isn't a bad thing, it's just the way it is. Sometimes one person is in a needier position, and there's nothing you can do to change it. You just gotta roll with it.

When Jenn and I first got together, I guess I was in the power position. She was doing okay with Naomi, but everybody knew that she wanted to do her own thing.

But me, I was getting hired for studio gigs by cats I never imagined I'd ever play with. I had honeys all up in my face, all the time. I was feeling healthy and looking good. I was cocky and untouchable. However, it wasn't long before Jenn slipped into the power position, and once that happened, we never went back. It was probably why I ho'ed around on Jenn, you know, as a way to show the world that I was still The Man. And that's The Man with a capital T and a capital M.

But on the 'Addition by Subtraction' tour, Jenn *really* had the upper hand – not on me, necessarily, but on *everybody*. She was able to write her own ticket. Which she did.

**JENN BRADFORD** I hired two personal assistants and a scary-looking bodyguard named Louie. I *had* to bring them into the fold, especially Louie. I mean, at all the venues we gigged at, I couldn't get to or from the tour bus without being mobbed, and it got to be scary as hell.

When I'd push my way through the crowds, there was almost always lots of touching involved. *Lots*. Sometimes the touches would be innocuous – a pat on the back, a rushed handshake, an attempted hug – but sometimes I'd get straight-up groped.

Also, there were photographers *everywhere*, and they made my life a living hell. Like this one night, some dude tried to grab The Girls backstage after a show and I swatted his hand away; the next week, there was a picture of this little scene in *Us* magazine, with a caption that read, *Jenn Bradford gets physical with a loyal fan*. Brutal. Just brutal.

That said, most of the fans were okay, but they were always around. *Always*. Like they'd be waiting for me in the lobbies of all the hotels we stayed at, all armed with autograph books and CDs and posters – and body parts. Yeah, that's right – body parts. One classy gentleman asked me to sign his excited, um, manhood, right outside of the Four Seasons in Dallas. If it wasn't broad daylight, good ol' Louie would've happily snapped it off. That's why he got paid the big bucks.

I probably could've lived without the two personal assistants, but it got to the point where Masu couldn't handle the business end of my life by herself, and I figured that if she had two little slaves, she could delegate to them all the stuff she didn't want to do.

A typical afternoon for me meant two or three radio station interviews, a solo performance and/or an autograph session at a local record store, and an appearance on one of the local news/entertainment television shows, plus three phone interviews with random newspapers or magazines. I can't even imagine how many phone calls it took to arrange all of that. I figured she'd appreciate the help.

**MASUHARA JONES** I was handling all the business stuff fine. She didn't need to hire anybody else. She didn't even ask me if I wanted any help! She was like, 'These are your new helpers Mandy and Candy' – or whatever their names were – 'and they'll do anything you tell 'em to do.'

I go, 'I'm fine. I can handle it by myself.'

Then she was like, 'Okay, great, I'll see you later.'

She wasn't even listening. She wasn't being evil. She was off in the ozone, all by herself. And sometimes I wanted her to stay there. Because Jenn Bradford had lost the plot.

**JENN BRADFORD** Masu wanted me to cut back on the promotional events. She said I looked exhausted, and my skin was awful, and my performances were suffering, all of which I totally disagreed with, except for maybe the skin thing. I will admit to acquiring a zit or two. Masu also said she was concerned for my overall mental and physical health. I kept telling her, 'I'm fine, I'm fine, I'm fine,' but she kept insisting I chill out.

I told her, 'No. No. Nonononono. I have to capitalize. I have to keep moving forward. I have to get the numbers up. I can't stop. I *can't.*' Zach's words kept ringing in my head: *use all the weapons at your disposal while you still have them.*

Okay, maybe I was getting a little obsessive. And admittedly kind of weird. Like I-want-a-bowl-of-M&M's-in-my-dressing-room-except-only-red-and-yellow-ones weird. But I say that only in retrospect. At the time, I felt great, like I was always doing the right thing.

I was never wrong. *Never.*

**T.J. STEWART** Jenny-Jenn lost her shit, big time, and it happened *fast*, yo. Like one day, she was normal old Jenny-Jenn, doing her usual stupid crap, telling her usual stupid jokes. Then the next day, we have a sucky show, and our cool-ass beeyatch becomes a straight-up bitch.

**MASUHARA JONES** T.J.'s wrong. It didn't happen overnight; it was a gradual thing. He didn't notice it because Jenn had been isolating herself from the rest of the band since the beginning of the tour, so there's no way he could've known. I was with her more than anybody, but even I didn't know the full extent of her nuttiness until a little later. She was hanging out in Jennland, and nobody else was invited.

She wasn't being rude about it or anything. She just faded. She stopped talking to me. Okay, she was talking, but she wasn't saying anything. Until San Antonio. Then she talked for real. And it made me wish she'd shut the hell up again.

**JENN BRADFORD** I could try to explain to you for hours what goes on inside your head when you get famous, like *really* famous, like Madonna or Jack Nicholson famous, but you'd never get it. You have to go through it yourself to understand, and it's horrible, and I wouldn't wish it on anybody. Okay, maybe there's a couple of people I'd wish it on, but I won't say their names into your little tape recorder.

**MASUHARA JONES** Jenn's rider was ridiculous. What's a rider? Oh, it's the list of shit you need the concert promoters to provide for the band, like what kind of food they should serve your people, and how many mouths altogether they have to feed, and how many towels they need to provide you with onstage, stuff like that. Most riders are like, *Give us the best local food you can get,* *and make sure there are six vegetarian dishes*. The rest of the crap – bottled water, towels, yadda yadda yadda – almost always takes care of itself.

Jenn started in about the rider after this one night in San Antonio. It was a lame show. It sounded and looked to me that Jenn was phoning it in. T.J. played great though. At least I thought so. But I suppose I was biased.

Anyhow, when we got back to the hotel, Jenn knocked on T.J.'s and my door really loudly. Me and The Teej'd just finished doing it, and having her summon me was a massive buzzkill, but she was the boss. When I answered the door, she pulled me out into the hallway, and was all like, 'We need to rework the rider. The conditions tonight were unacceptable. That can't happen again. I want a dozen clementines waiting for me in the dressing room before every show. And I need a proper-sized area in the dressing room set aside where I can do my makeup. And nobody is allowed to fry any food within, like sixty yards of me, because I'm sure that's what's making my face break out. And there should be mellow lighting in the dressing room, like seventy-five watts tops, because it was too bright in there tonight, and that's why we sucked.' She was yelling. People were poking their heads out of their rooms.

I waited a bit after she finished, then I was like, 'Um, okay. Anything else?'

She goes, 'That's it for now. Shouldn't you be writing this down?'

I was like, 'Can we do this in the morning?'

She looked me up and down – did I mention I was

still naked? – and she goes, 'No. Put on some clothes. I'll meet you in my room.'

After Jenn left, T.J. was like, 'Yo, what the fuck was that?'

I go, 'I dunno, baby, but I gotta go.'

T.J. pulled the covers over his face and goes, 'Jenny-Jenn needs some serious boning. Call K-Mac. Get him on the stick. Or get his stick on the stick.' Then he started cracking up.

I was like, 'You're an idiot. You're lucky I already fucked you.'

I grabbed one of the hotel's fluffy white robes from the closet, threw it on and walked over to Jenn's room. I tapped on the door really lightly, and it flew open fast, like she'd been standing right behind there, waiting for me to show up. She pulled me into her room and started going off about everything that'd happened on the tour she didn't dig.

She goes all hysterically, 'That viola player is a bitch, and my monitor mix sucks, and we need to stop using the yellow spotlight because it makes my hair look Bozo orange, and we have to get a new piano bench, and no more Evian, just Poland Spring, and Kevin's making me nervous because he's being too nice and too normal.' If I didn't know she was anti-hard-drugs, I'd have thought she was coked up.

I was like, 'Are you done?'

She goes, 'Yeah. I'm going to sleep. Fix all this stuff. And don't forget to change the rider. And show me a copy of the new rider before you start faxing it all over the place. Good night.' Then she turned off the light, collapsed on to her bed and fell asleep immediately. I didn't know it was possible for somebody to fall asleep that fast. She went from spazzing to snoring in 2.2 seconds.

T.J. was crashed when I got back to the room – at least he was until I slammed the door and threw a pillow at his head.

He woke up and was like, 'Yo, what the fuck?!'

I go, 'I'm taking a vacation.'

He sat up and goes, 'You're leaving? S'up with that?'

I'm like, 'No, I'm not leaving, I'm taking a vacation from working. Jenn's got two little slaves with her. I'm delegating.'

T.J. goes, 'Whatever,' then he fell back asleep.

I was like, 'Thanks for the support, boyfriend.'

Anyhow, it turns out that delegating is fun, especially when your boss is going insane.

KEVIN MCALLISTER I didn't notice any of Jenn's freakouts, because I was all into my own thing, man. I pretty much *had* to do my own thing during this particular tour, because I didn't have anybody to hang out with. T.J. was all wrapped up with Masu, and Jenn was all wrapped up with Jenn. I had tons of time to myself, so I started reading a bunch, more than I ever had. Like I read this one amazing Jackie Robinson biography, which made me want to read this 500-page history of Negro League Baseball, which was also amazing. I also checked out Billie Holiday's autobiography. I'd never been much of a fan of hers, but at the bookstore, something compelled me to pick it up. I also skimmed through more self-help books, most of which were bullshit, but some of which had some interesting ideas.

But best of all, I was writing a lot of music. I splurged and got myself a keyboard/sampler, and Pro Tools for my laptop, so I could produce instrumental tracks while I was on the tour bus, or in the hotel room, or wherever. Sometimes T.J. offered to lay down a bass line for me, which was nice.

I didn't see Jenn much, except during soundchecks and gigs.

**JENN BRADFORD** I barely interacted with Kevin. Really, I barely interacted with anybody. I barely said three words to any of the extra musicians we hired.

When I did see Kevin, he was very polite which, for him, was . . . different. It's not that he was ever rude before. I guess the worst you could say was that he had a tendency to be inappropriate. Like he'd use his outside voice while we were inside, or he'd drop an 'F' bomb in an obvious no 'F' bomb zone, or he'd give a too-obvious look at some girl's tits. But on that tour, he was relaxed, I guess. Calm. Zen-like, even. That's the best way I could describe it. And I liked the new version of Kevin. I liked Kevin McAllister Mark 2 a lot.

All of which led to another Kevin Incident. But I really don't feel like talking about it.

**KEVIN MCALLISTER** No comment.

**MASUHARA JONES** Ah yes, the new Kevin Incident. I'll let Jenn field that one.

**JENN BRADFORD** Oh, come on, do I have to? Haven't you people heard enough about Kevin McAllister and my relationship already? No? Okay, fine, I'll spill, but after this whole book thing is over, you're totally taking me to that place on 51st and Seventh for some expensive sushi. It's called Masa. No, not Ma*su*, Ma*sa*.

We were playing the Arco Arena in Sacramento. It held over 17,000 people, and it was sold out, and logistically speaking, everything was on point. It was all perfect in every way – the sound, the lighting, the size, the vibe, the whole thing. The crowd was amazing. Sometimes a crowd just *gets* it. Those folks in Sacramento *got* it, and sometimes people *getting* it doesn't make a difference to us, but other times, it pushes us to places we didn't know we could go.

I was so hyped, so in that musical zone, that near the end of the show, I veered away from the set list, which isn't supposed to happen at mega-choreographed gigs like ours. Everything during those stadium concerts is set to a script in order to make sure that the lighting, and the projections on the screen behind us, and the dry ice, and all the bells and whistles synch with the music, so if you play a song that's not supposed to be played, everything goes to hell.

But we sounded so great that night. I felt good. I knew that I would. So I veered.

**MASUHARA JONES** What with all of Jenn's diva fits, I forgot what a brilliant musician she was. You know, each night I'd hear her plow through the same set of tunes over and over again, and it always sounded good, so I took it for granted. But that night in Sacramento, I remembered how she's gotten to where she is.

**KEVIN MCALLISTER** Man, she was good in Sacramento. Inspiring, even. And not to sound like I'm all on my own dick, but I was damn good that night too.

**JENN BRADFORD** Kevin was especially on fire, which was part of the reason that, right before the closing number – 'Addition by Subtraction', of course – I told the string section and the horn players to take a hike.

**MASUHARA JONES** I was standing at the sound board when she threw the auxiliary musicians off the stage. Our sound guy goes, 'Wonderful. Now Her Highness is gonna wig out during gigs. We're fucked.' I think he was talking to himself, but I heard it, and I have to admit I agreed with him.

I jumped off of the mixing board station, sprinted down the aisle and made my way backstage. By the time I got there, the horns and strings were standing in the wings, and this one trumpet player goes, 'Masuhara, your client is turning into quite the nutbag.'

I was about to tell him that I was gonna calm her down, and how she'd be fine by the time we got to Los Angeles, and besides, his paychecks cashed the same whether or not Jenn was in a straitjacket, but before I could do all that, this huge guy wearing a wife-beater T-shirt and ugly, tight black denim jeans shoved the trumpeter away, stuck a set list in my face, and then he goes, 'I'd like to remind you that if your little client over there isn't done by eleven, she's officially in breach of contract, and our union is gonna fine her ten thousand dollars for each minute extra she's onstage past eleven.'

I slapped his hand away, then I was like, 'Don't worry. I'll take care of it.'

And it totally got taken care of.

**JENN BRADFORD** I told the audience that I had to huddle up with my bass player and my drummer before we went into our next tune, because we were gonna try something we'd never tried before. The crowd was still right with me, and they clapped and whistled, and then when I started walking across the stage, it got really quiet, and this one girl screamed, 'Take as much time as you want, Jenn! We love you!' and everybody started clapping and whistling again.

**MASUHARA JONES** I was this close to running out into the crowd and smacking that loudmouth girl upside her head. The last thing I needed was somebody encouraging this sort of behavior.

**JENN BRADFORD** I wandered over to T.J., whose spot on stage was about ten feet from me, and asked him, 'Teej, do you remember when we used to do that Nat King Cole medley?'

He chewed on one of his dreads and said, 'I guess. We gonna jam on it?'

I said, 'No. Almost. We're doing a Billie Holiday medley. Grab your upright bass. We're starting with "God Bless the Child", medium tempo in B-flat, then we're going into "Lover Man", super slow in F-sharp, then we'll finish it off with "What Is This Thing Called Love?", super fast in C. Got it?'

He said, 'Bring it on, woman.'

The way our stage was plotted, Kevin was a good five yards past T.J., so while T.J. set up his acoustic bass, I slowly walked over, pulled myself up on to his drum riser – which is kind of hard when you're wearing thigh-high boots and a short skirt – and told him the plan. He said, 'Sounds great. I can't wait to hear it. And I'll be honored to play it.' Then he tapped me on the top of my head with a drumstick and gave me the kind of smile that'd made me fall in love with him in the first place.

I couldn't help what happened next.

MASUHARA JONES I was so shocked that I smacked the union guy on the arm and was like, 'Dude, can you believe you're seeing this?'

He didn't say anything for a minute, then he goes, 'No. No, I can't. But am I enjoying watching it? Yes. Yes, I am.'

**T.J. STEWART** Yo, I almost dropped my upright bass, and that shit's expensive. If it'd have broken, I probably would've made Jenny-Jenn pay for the repairs, because it would've been her damn fault. I mean, you can't blame Kevin. He was just sitting there.

**KEVIN MCALLISTER** No comment.

**JENN BRADFORD** All I meant to do was give him a little kiss on the cheek, but somehow my mouth found his mouth, and my tongue found his tongue, and my right hand found his chest, and my left hand found his right hand, and I put his right hand on my left breast and held it there, and I had no idea how long we were at it until after the show, when Masuhara told me that we'd made out for one full minute, which may not sound like much, but it is, it is.

We got a standing ovation, but I only found that out when I saw the whole thing on YouTube, because at the time – with my tongue in his ear, and my hand pinching his nipple – I couldn't hear a thing.

**KEVIN MCALLISTER** Seriously, no comment.

**JENN BRADFORD** When I finally let him go, he shot me a little smile and said, 'We have a gig to finish.' He pointed a drumstick at the piano and said, 'Go back to your piano and play us some Billie Holiday.'

Something was wrong. The Kevin McAllister I knew would never pass up a chance for an inappropriate public display of affection. I said to him, 'You didn't like that?'

He said more emphatically, 'Go back to your piano and play us some Billie Holiday.'

I said, 'You didn't feel *anything*?'

He sighed, then said, 'No. I didn't. Now go back to your piano and play us some Billie Holiday.'

I said, 'I don't believe you.' Then I reached down under his snare drum and did an inventory of his lap.

Nothing. He wasn't lying. I didn't feel anything down there, which meant that he didn't feel anything anywhere.

So I did what Kevin said. I went back to my piano and played everybody some Billie Holiday, at once broken and elated that Kevin McAllister had officially let me go.

MASUHARA JONES During the second time through 'Lover Man', when she sang the line about feeling sad and trying something she'd never had, I looked out into the audience, and I swear people were crying, it was so beautiful. Then somebody tapped my shoulder. It was the union guy. Tears were streaming down his cheeks. He goes, 'She can play as long as she wants to. She can stay on all night. I ain't telling the Teamsters a thing.'

JENN BRADFORD After we jammed on 'What Is This Thing Called Love?' for about five minutes, I was spent. I called the strings and horns back to work, then I counted off 'Addition by Subtraction' at a way-faster-than-normal tempo, probably because I wanted to get through the song and on to the bus as soon as possible.

Actually, I was so damn embarrassed about the latest Kevin Incident that given a choice between running to the bus or jumping off a bridge, I'd have gone with the bridge, but me being dead would've made it difficult to play our Los Angeles area shows, and they were gonna be some big gigs, so I went with the bus thing.

For the next two-plus weeks, all our concerts were within three hours of LA, so we decided to set up camp in the city instead of checking in and out of a hotel in San Diego, then one in Palm Springs, then one in San Jose, and so on. We had two days off before the barrage of shows started up, and the only people I spoke to during those forty-eight hours were the delivery boys.

**MASUHARA JONES** After the final Kevin Incident, Jenn withdrew from us even more. She wasn't eating hardly anything but pizza, she didn't leave the hotel except for shows, and she barely said two words to anybody, except for Louie, who'd become her BFF. Now Louie is a perfectly fine dude, but he's not too bright, and not too nurturing, and I don't care if he's reading this right now, because I'd say the same damn thing to his face. Jenn needed somebody to ground her, and Louie wasn't that person. She was totally rejecting my help, so I called in the bomb squad.

**NAOMI BRAVER** Masuhara texted me and begged me to, as she put it, 'Save Jenn from herself.' Nothing would've made me happier. Jenn had saved me plenty of times.

She was always the stronger one of us, and I was thrilled to be given the opportunity to help my almost-sister the same way she'd helped me so many times.

But I couldn't. Because I finally got a part in a movie. A good part. A supporting part, but a good part. The script was awesome, and the cast was stellar, and the director was getting all kinds of buzz, and the role was cool, and if I knocked it out of the park, it would definitely lead to more roles, and possibly even an Oscar nomination. The part came out of nowhere, and it was exactly what I'd been waiting for, the reason I left Brooklyn in the first place.

I was on the set for sixteen hours a day, every day, and on call constantly. I literally couldn't get away for even a hot minute. Jenn would understand. I hoped.

**JENN BRADFORD** I have an excellent memory – can't you tell? – but that first week in California was mostly a blank. I know we performed, and I know we performed well, because I've listened to the recordings. I know the paparazzi were still hovering around me, because there was an embarrassing picture of me in *Star* magazine. I think it was taken in the hotel lobby while I was waiting for the bus, and I looked like I was stoned.

Despite my more-than-periodic bitchiness, everybody in the band was being extra nice to me, even Kevin – *especially* Kevin – but I was such a zombie that I couldn't accept their help. Most days, there wasn't time to be helped. It was a busy life: wake up, then eat, then nap, then eat, then soundcheck, then eat, then perform, then sleep. Repeat. Repeat. Repeat.

What fun.

**MASUHARA JONES** Say what you will about Jenn Bradford, but my girl is a *professional*. A boulder could fall on her and she'd still make it to the gig, and still kick ass. I mean, she was practically catatonic, but she was still kicking it, and the crowds were going nuts, and the reviewers were freaking, and 'Addition by Subtraction' kept selling, and *Reality Check* even started moving again. Seriously, Jenn's a badass.

**NAOMI BRAVER** According to all the important people associated with my movie – like the director, the producers and the studio executives – I was performing well. Personally, based on the dailies, I thought I looked dorky and ugly, but the director was happy, so I was happy.

Masuhara kept after me about meeting up with Jenn. She called, texted and emailed, then called, texted and emailed, and so it went on – and on and on – and I kept telling her, *I can't, I can't, I can't.*

Then one day, she sent me an email with a weblink to somebody's video of the latest Kevin Incident.

Ouch.

**JENN BRADFORD** I was crashed out in our hotel in Seattle, having the most messed-up dream. I'm in a ship, and we're moving along some vast, empty ocean, and the water's orange, like the shade of orange my hair looks like under that obnoxious yellow spotlight they always pointed at me during 'Water'. It's a Viking ship, and there're fifty guys down in the hull – that's the section in the guts of the ship where they do the rowing from, right? – and they're all naked, and sweaty, and they all have enormous boners. It was so gross. Fortunately, I wasn't touching any of those many, many boners. I think if I was, I'd have tried to track down a shrink right then and there.

So we land on this island, and there are three giants waiting for us on the beach. Their faces are, like, one hundred feet up in the air, and the only details I can make out are that two of the giants are white and one of them is black, and they're all wearing loincloths that're covering their junk – thank God – and they all have big feet. I want to get back on to the ship and get the hell out of there, but all the Boner Boys have disappeared, so there's nobody to row me away. I guess they were pissed off I wasn't touching them.

I decide that my best bet is to get off that island any way I can, so I run back on to the ship, and start searching for a lifeboat. I find it, and I'm trying to figure out how to get it unchained and into the ocean, but before I can do anything, one of the giants grabs me by the hair and yanks me off the ship. He lifts me right up in front of his face and starts swaying me back and forth like a pendulum.

It's Zach Bingham.

He doesn't say anything. He grunts once, then passes

me on to the next giant, who is none other than Kevin McAllister. He grunts a whole bunch – actually, he was hooting more than grunting – then he waves at me with his index finger, and passes me to the next giant, who gives me a gentle pat on the forehead.

And right then, I was awakened to the sight and sound of somebody jumping on my bed and yelling, 'Jenn! Jenn! Jenn! Jenn! Jenn!'

**NAOMI BRAVER** Me, I think the best way to wake somebody up is to jump on their bed really hard and really high, and scream their name over and over again. Don't you agree?

**JENN BRADFORD** The jumper-slash-yeller hit their head on the ceiling, then got their feet tangled up in the sheets, then fell ass-first on to my left arm. At that point it was obvious I had been awakened by none other than my good pal Naomi Braver, the world's klutziest rock star.

I shoved her away from me – naturally she crashed on to the floor, flat on her face – and said, 'You couldn't have called first, Nay-Nay?'

She said, 'Nope. Sneak attack. And don't call me Nay-Nay.' She stood up and then plopped back on to the bed, nary a scratch to be seen. I swear, the girl's like a cat. You could toss her out of a third-story window and most of the time she'd land on her feet, completely unharmed. God protects drunks, animals, small children and klutzy rock stars, I suppose.

Then she started talking to me. Or more like talking *at* me. One endless run-on sentence:

'So one day I'm sitting at home, playing Guitar Hero 3 on Travis's Xbox, and the phone rings, and it's my agent from Endeavor, and he says I have to be on the set first thing in the morning the next day, and I said, *What set*, and he said that some guy from Dreamworks called and asked for me specifically, and the role's great, and I'd be an idiot to turn it down, and then he asks if I'm prepared to do a topless scene, and I said no way, and he said it wasn't *topless* topless, like nobody would see anything, because I'd be under the sheets or blocked off from the camera the entire time—'

And right then, it dawned on me who the third giant in my dream was.

NAOMI BRAVER I was just about to tell Jenn how I thought *my* in-front-of-the-camera nudity was harder than *her* in-front-of-the-camera nudity because when she was naked, she didn't have to make out with an almost-stranger, but before I could get that thought out, she smacked me in the leg with the back of her hand and said, 'It was Porter Ellis. It was Porter Fucking Ellis. What the hell was he doing there, patting me on the head?'

I said, 'Um, I couldn't really tell you. Who's Porter Fucking Ellis?'

She said, 'Just some guy.' I gave her a look, then she said, 'He's my neighbor who I pissed off, then I tried to kiss him to make him feel better, but that just pissed him off more. Remember that – the most embarrassing moment of my life?'

I said, 'You still think that's the most embarrassing moment of your life? Let's be honest here. I'd say putting Kevin McAllister's hand on your boob in front of 17,000 people has now taken the lead.'

She rolled her eyes and said all sarcastically, 'Gee, thanks, Nay-Nay. So when do you need to be back to the set? Like maybe now?' And then she collapsed on to my lap and burst into hysterical tears. It lasted about twenty minutes, but it broke my heart so badly that it seemed like twenty years.

**JENN BRADFORD** There are, like, six thousand things I love about Naomi Braver, but one of my favorites is that she's never passed judgment on me. She's way more conservative than I am, but she's never ragged on me about my sex life – which used to be pretty insane – or my clothes, or my vulgar vocabulary, or my choice of men. Okay, maybe she's said a thing about one, or maybe two, or maybe three, or maybe more of my boyfriends, but it was only out of love.

That's probably the reason the dam broke. Naomi knew me better than anybody, and she didn't want anything from me, and I didn't have to put on any kind of guise in front of her. I could just be me, and right that moment, being me meant being as miserable as I'd ever been, and crying like a madwoman.

What was I crying about? What *wasn't* I crying about! I was unbelievably lonely, but there was nobody I even wanted to eat lunch with. I hated being stared at, and pointed at, and photographed, and posted on YouTube. I was tired of playing the same songs the same way over and over and over again. I was a piece of meat, a piece of burnt, overcooked meat.

The irony was that this tour was the ultimate in validation. I was well and truly validated. It should've been the highlight of my life, but you know what? Turns out validation is *way* overrated. Fuck validation. Give me a bathtub, some Pinot Grigio, some flannel jammies, seven or eight Beanie Babies, a Thelonious Monk CD, two or three good friends, and that's enough. I wouldn't even need a keyboard. Or a boy. Okay, a keyboard might be nice, but not essential. Same deal with a boy. Well, maybe not a boy. A man. Yeah, a man would be nice.

You'd think a cry like that would've been cathartic. And I did feel somewhat better afterward – Naomi being there guaranteed that – but I was still a wreck.

After I finally calmed down, Naomi and I kicked around ways to make my life situation more tolerable. Maybe I could fire Kevin and get a new drummer whose presence would have no emotional effect on me. Maybe I could axe the whole band except for T.J., and we could do all our shows as a duo, like we did at Upper East. Maybe I could blow off the tour bus and rent a private plane, and fly from city to city accompanied only by Louie, which would make it easier to avoid the paparazzi, and the scary fans, and anybody else who was contributing to my misery.

Or maybe I could pull the plug altogether.

**MASUHARA JONES** When I answered the door, the first thing I noticed about Jenn was her eyes. They were so red that my first thought was that she and Naomi had smoked a couple of bowls. My second thought was that she'd been on a twenty-minute crying jag. But considering the pissed-off look on her face, my third thought was that she was gonna fire me.

I pulled her into my room and said, 'What's up, girl?' I was all nervous.

Jenn was like, 'We're done, Masu. It's over.'

I'm like, 'You're firing me, aren't you? Don't. Seriously, don't. You can't blame me for any of the fuck ups. I was delegating. You *told* me to delegate. Anything that got fucked up wasn't my fault. It was those two little ditzes you hired. They're morons, Jenn—'

Jenn gave me a look like, *You're insane*, then goes, 'I'd never fire you. My life would be more of a disaster than it already is if you weren't around. But you're gonna be out of a job for a while.'

I was like, 'Say what?'

Then she goes, 'I'm retiring.'

**JENN BRADFORD** Can you believe how long it took me to realize that being anointed a rock goddess sucked? I didn't need it any more. I was done. Over it. I thought, *I'm a woman, listen to me roar, and I've been down on the floor, and now I'm getting the fuck back up and going the fuck back to Brooklyn.*

It was probably one of the two or three happiest days of my life.

**MASUHARA JONES** I was like, 'Honey, that's the best idea I've ever heard. Take a few months off to recover. Hell, take a year.'

She goes, 'No, you don't understand. I'm retiring. I'm done. I swear, as soon as the reporters start leaving me alone, I'm gonna apply for a job at Whole Foods, or a veterinarian's office or something. I'm outta here. Pretty please, book me on the first flight to LaGuardia, or JFK, or Newark, any goddamn airport that's within a cab ride of Brooklyn. I don't care how much it costs. I just wanna go home, get into a pair of flannel PJs, climb into bed, eat some healthy food and drink some good wine, and watch all the movies I've missed over the last three years, and not shave my legs, and not think for a long, long time.'

I was like, 'Girl, that sounds damn good to me. Except for the healthy food part. When I get home, I'll bring you some Cherry Garcia.'

**NAOMI BRAVER** Hey, don't blame me for Jenn's retirement. It was just a suggestion. I didn't think she'd go through with it.

But I'm glad she did.

**T.J. STEWART** I was psyched, yo, especially when Masu told me we'd still get our entire salary for the tour. That was when Jenny-Jenn in my mind stopped being a bitch, and went back to being a beeyatch.

**KEVIN MCALLISTER** Masuhara was the one who broke the news about the tour being over. I asked her why Jenn didn't tell me herself, and she said, 'Jenn's at the airport. Her flight's taking off in, like, a minute. Don't feel bad. She didn't say goodbye to anybody except me and Naomi.'

It's too bad she didn't say goodbye, because I haven't seen her since.

JENN BRADFORD Airports used to annoy the hell out of me, but after being cooped up in a tour bus for a long, long time, Sea-Tac felt like Mecca.

And can we talk about the magic of air transportation? I was in front of my condo in Brooklyn only nine hours after I'd decided to retire from the music biz. A tour bus would've taken, like, six years, and I would've been stuck in it with a bunch of boys who insulted each other constantly, watched their *Scarface* DVD over and over again, and couldn't – or wouldn't – stop farting and belching. That was another good thing about retirement: I wouldn't have to be around as many boys. I was tired of boys.

For a change, there wasn't a single reporter or photographer by the door of my building. I'm sure they all thought I was still in Seattle. Once the word got out about me walking away from the tour, I was sure the madness would start up again. But I didn't care, because I wasn't gonna leave the apartment, and I wasn't gonna answer the phone, and I wasn't gonna even stand by any of my windows. I wanted invisibility. Masu or my label could handle the press.

I said hey to our doorman, then I walked toward the elevator, and I got more tired with each step. My suitcase was getting heavier and heavier. Good thing I wasn't living in a walk-up like the one Naomi and I shared back in the day. I don't think I would've made it up even three stairs.

I stared out of our glass elevator, and the East River – the dirty, smelly East River – looked good enough to swim in or drink from. That's how out of it I was.

We got to my floor, and the door opened, and there's Porter Ellis, sitting on the floor, leaning against his door, hair unkempt, scraggly beard, major sunburn, wearing a T-shirt, shorts and sunglasses, staring at the ceiling, looking – as our doorman had put it weeks ago – generally messed up.

I let my suitcase fall to the floor and all but collapsed down right next to him. 'Hey there, Porter Ellis.'

He said, 'Hey there, Jenn Bradford.' He didn't look at me, just at the ceiling.

I said, 'What're you doing out here? Personally I think your seating system is way more comfortable than this floor.'

He said, 'I left a couple things in the apartment, and I guess I gave back my key. I thought I kept a spare, but clearly I didn't, so I'm waiting for the superintendent to get here and let me in. He should've been here about an hour ago.'

I said, 'Wait, what do you mean, *gave back your key?*'

He said, 'You've been out of town?'

I said, 'Yeah. Just got back this second.'

He said, 'So you weren't around for the commotion yesterday.'

I said, 'What commotion?'

He finally looked at me and said, 'My movers. I'm leaving. Actually, I already left.'

Wow. I didn't think Porter Ellis would ever go anywhere. That apartment was so *him*, that I expected he'd stay there forever. Plus even though I didn't know him all that well, I never pegged him for the kind of guy that makes sudden moves. I always thought of him as a planner. But I guess having your dream burn down will make you rethink things.

I examined his sunburned face for a bit. He was a handsome guy. I couldn't believe he hadn't been scooped up by some gorgeous heiress, or an exotic princess from some small country in the Middle East. I sat down on the floor beside him and said, 'I'm gonna miss you, Porter Ellis. Who'da thunk *that*?' Then I put my head on his shoulder, and he put his arm around me, and the next thing I remember was the superintendent showing up about half an hour later.

**BILLIE HOLIDAY'S GHOST** Probably one of the favorite songs I ever recorded was called 'Detour Ahead'. If you'd like to hear it, I'd recommend going to your local music store or your favorite online retailer and ordering up yourself a copy of *The Ultimate Billie Holiday* on the Hip-O record label. I don't get any royalties up where I'm at, but my estate does, and I'd like my great-great-great-granddaughter to have a college education, so you should not only buy copies for yourself, but also for your friends and family. And there's this box set called *The*

*Complete Decca Recordings* that I'm sure you'll enjoy. It's expensive, but I know you'll dig it.

At any rate, 'Detour Ahead' may as well have been written for Jennifer. I'd sing the song for you right now, but as I mentioned, those afterworld copyright laws are tough. But you know what? Once you find out what happened next, you'll know exactly what the song is all about. Confused? Don't worry. You'll see what I mean soon enough.

# Rolling Stone

## August 1, 2010

### OOPS, I DID IT AGAIN
*The Heartwarming Tale of a Journalist, a Princess, and a Huge Bottle of Lotion*

### by Zach Bingham

There's a picture of me over on page 15. Go on, take a look. As you can see, in it I have my arm around the waist of my interview subject. In general, touching an interview subject in a semi-intimate fashion is a journalistic no-no. But what're you gonna do?

Most who look at the picture will think something along the lines of, 'Who does this disgustingly underfed, unbelievably pale, insanely over-pierced, pseudo-indie-rocking, Hunter S. Thompson wanna-be think he is, wrapping his hand around the toned waist of arguably the smokin'-est singer on the planet? Not only that, but he forced his editor's hand by mentioning the shot in the lead paragraph, which meant those *Rolling Stone* chumps *had* to run the photo. How badly does this dude need to be validated? He must really loathe himself.'

Sadly, you're pretty much on target.

Just over a year ago, I wrote an article for this very magazine called 'Road Rage'. In it, I documented the beginning of my frustrating on-again-off-again affair with the now-apparently-retired singer/songwriter/pianist Jenn Bradford. The article pissed off Jenn, mortified my parents, and lost me virtually every ounce of street cred I'd garnered over the past six years. (The lack of street cred is why I knew my editor would bite on my pitch of this very article. You don't need street cred to write about *American Idol*-ized royalty.) In retrospect, I believe 'Road Rage' should never've seen the light of day, even though my heart was in the right place when I wrote it. It was a love letter, albeit a shitty one. I vowed never to do anything like that ever again. No more putting myself into the story. I'm a music reporter. I should report the music. Period. No, *exclamation mark*.

And I kept my word. For about 12 whole months. Then I met Princess.

Lindsey Prince became Princess at 19, when, a couple days before her initial *American Idol* audition, her mother decided that 'Lindsey' was far too plain a name for the likes of her über-breathtaking, über-talented daughter. 'At first I thought "Princess" was totally lame,' Lindsey explains, 'but when Simon Cowell gave it the thumbs up, I thought, *Okay, maybe this wasn't such a bad idea. Mom gets props.* And besides, I can go back to being Lindsey when I'm 30 and decide to record, I dunno, a tribute to Tony Bennett or something. *Lindsey Does Tony.*' She laughs, then adds, 'That'll be a slam dunk, because I did a guy named Tony at a party during my sophomore year at Brown, so I've had practice.' Then she elbows me and says, 'Get it?'

I get it. I also get that I'm on a slippery slope. This is only my first conversation with Her Highness, and I'm thinking, *Shit, this chick is funny, and charming, and she's got a brain, and she's smokin', even more smokin' than Jenn Bradford, and Jenn Bradford is super smokin'. This could be trouble.*

I was right.

*continued on page 35*

**PORTER ELLIS** You want to know about the fire? Long version or short version? Long version? Fine.

Beep's opening night was a triumph for me on every level, more fulfilling than any aspect of *Billionaire.com* ever was. As I said, I liked the hands-on, personal aspect of the entire venture. This may sound corny or clichéd to you, but there was something about the patrons' smiles that made the event more moving than any of my weddings even. Then again, the manner in which I look back at my weddings is probably tainted by the eventual dissolution of my marriages, so that may not be the most apt comparison. Point being, it was an exquisite evening.

I got back to my condo around four in the morning and knew from experience that, no matter how late it was, and no matter how tired I was, I wouldn't be able to sleep. I didn't sleep the night that *Billionaire.com* went public, nor did I sleep the night after I sold it. When my life takes a sharp turn, my brain races, and I have no ability whatsoever to shut it off, so rather than lie in bed and stare at the ceiling, I try to be productive. To me, cooking and eating is productive, so I took a quick shower, then went into the kitchen and made myself some apple pancakes. The phone rang only a few seconds after I sat down. I screened the call, thinking it was my second ex-wife, who still has an annoying tendency to call at inappropriate hours. It wasn't her. It was my alarm company, notifying me that there was something wrong at my club, that the police and fire department were on the way, and it might be a good idea if I got down there as soon as possible.

By the time I arrived fifteen minutes later, the fire seemed to be under control, but it was too late. Far too late. For all practical purposes, Beep was gone. I found a small group of police officers – two in uniform, two in suits – and introduced myself. One of the plainclothes detectives pulled me aside, and said, 'I'm sorry for your loss, Mr Ellis. I'm from the Bomb and Arson division, and I'm hoping you'll be able to come to the station at some point in the next twenty-four hours and answer a few questions.'

I said, 'You think this might be arson?'

He said, 'Yeah. This place went up too quick and too hot for some people's taste. Let's just say this thing wasn't started with a lit cigarette, you know what I mean?'

I said, 'No, detective. I don't know what you mean.'

He said, 'The pattern and speed of the fire makes us suspicious. Is there anybody you can think of who has a beef with you?'

As far as I knew, aside from my last ex-wife, the only person who had been noticeably angry or aggressive with me at any point in the last few months was Zach Bingham. I was so out of sorts that I almost gave the detective his name, but quickly realized that would be absurd. He was an insufferable young man, but I suspected he was harmless. I said, 'No, detective. As far as I know, I have no enemies.'

He nodded skeptically, then asked me, 'What kind of insurance do you have on this place?'

I said, 'I have a good policy.'

He said, 'How good?'

I said, 'Very good.'

He said again, 'How good?'

I said, '*Very* good.'

He took out a notepad, then said, 'Can you give me specifics, please?'

I said, 'Detective, do you know who I am?' He nodded. I said, 'Taking that into consideration, do you think I would have my own club burnt down to collect what to me is an unimportant sum of money?'

He said, 'Define unimportant.'

I said, 'Do I need to call my lawyer?'

He said, 'Would you be willing to take a polygraph test?'

I said, 'Absolutely. Let's go and do it now.' I was well aware my lawyer would be upset if he knew I'd offered to be strapped to a lie detector without asking him first, but I was angry and tired and miserable, and, above all, completely innocent. If the detective wanted to make a power move, I'd power move him right back.

He closed his notebook, gave me a tight little smile, and said, 'We'll be in touch. But I'm sure a polygraph won't be necessary.' He offered his hand and said, 'Again, I'm sorry for your loss, Mr Ellis. I'll be speaking with you soon.'

I stayed at the club – or what the club used to be, I suppose – for another hour or so. I watched it go from being a pile of ash to a crime scene.

It took them two weeks to determine that it was an electrical fire. The investigators decided it was something in the sound system, of all things. So much for the best sound money can buy. The insurance policy paid me off in full – I'm sure much to that detective's chagrin – and my lawsuit with the sound company is still pending.

Next? After about a week of wandering through Brooklyn and Manhattan like a zombie, I threw four or five days' worth of kick-around clothes – T-shirts, jeans, shorts, that sort of thing – and some books into a suitcase, threw the suitcase into my car, and drove. No map, no plan, no non-essential personal items, no nothing. Okay, I did take my BlackBerry and my laptop. Those *are* essential. I'm a dyed-in-the-wool businessman, and no matter how depressed I may be, I have to be at least somewhat accessible. You never know what might come up.

I don't recall the exact route I took across the country. Many of the specifics of the trip are a blank. I know I started out heading south. I spent a few days at a dilapidated beach house on the Outer Banks in North Carolina, staring either at the ocean or whatever book I happened to pick up. I grabbed a meal with one of my cousins in Atlanta. I wound my way back up north through Chicago, then Detroit, then I crossed into Canada and visited Toronto for a week. I'd never been there before, and it was a lovely city – good food, kind people, very clean, even a bit restorative. But I still wasn't ready to go back to Brooklyn and face my empty apartment, so I pushed on. I remember stopping in Denver for a day or two, another fine city, calm and low-key. Just for the heck of it, I stayed in Vegas for a night. I'd never seen the place before that, and if nothing else, it was good for a laugh, and I needed all the laughs I could get. By the time I got to Los Angeles – almost eight weeks after I left New York – I was ready to be home. But not my home. A new home.

I didn't want to move into another big condo unit. I wanted to downsize. I wanted to shrink my world. I wanted to make my Beep-less world disappear. But what I *didn't* want to do was spend weeks and weeks house-hunting, so I just grabbed the first place that I liked, which took a grand total of two phone calls, one realtor, and three hours. It was a big, but not too disgustingly big, one-bedroom loft in an old, old building in Greenwich Village. The loft layout was perfect: I'd sleep in the bedroom; the CDs, the stereo equipment, my seating system, and the furniture that made up my home office would go in the living room; and everything that wouldn't fit – or anything that reminded me of Beep – I'd donate the proceeds to charity, probably an epilepsy foundation, because my sister suffers from it.

Moving day was a disaster. I'd been planted in my condo – which was only the fourth place I'd lived as an adult – for almost ten years, and had either forgotten or blocked out how miserable a moving day can be. Nothing got broken or destroyed, but it seemed to me that the movers were always on the precipice of dropping anything electronic. I was so frazzled that I didn't remember to do a final check of my old place after the movers left, and didn't realize until much later that evening that I'd left the chargers for both my cell phone and my laptop in the bedroom. Aside from the cell and the laptop themselves, those were probably my two most important pieces of business equipment. Like I said, I have to be accessible.

The next morning, I went back to Redhook to rescue my chargers, but couldn't get into the unit because I'd already given the keys back to the building super-intendent. I called the Super and explained to him what had happened, and he said he'd be right over. I sat down on the floor in front of my door and stared at the ceiling, wondering if moving was the right move, still trying to figure out what the hell I was going to do for the next forty or fifty years.

A few minutes later, the elevator door opened, and there's Jenn Bradford, hauling an oversized suitcase, sweating, hair unkempt, no makeup, hiding under a baseball hat and sunglasses, wearing a T-shirt and jeans, looking – as our doorman might have put it – generally messed up.

She let her suitcase fall to the floor and all but collapsed down right next to me. 'Hey there, Porter Ellis.'

I said, 'Hey there, Jenn Bradford.' I gave her a quick once-over – I was shocked at how exhausted she looked – then I went back to looking at the ceiling.

She said, 'What're you doing out here? Personally I think your seating system is way more comfortable than this floor. But that's just me.'

I said, 'I left a couple things in the apartment, and I guess I gave back my key and I thought I kept a spare, but clearly I didn't, so I'm waiting for the superintendent to get here and let me in. He should've been here about an hour ago.'

She said, 'Wait, what do you mean, *gave back your key?*'

I said, 'You've been out of town?'

She said, 'Yeah. Just got back this second.'

I said, 'So you weren't around for the commotion yesterday.'

She said, 'What commotion?'

I finally looked at her and said, 'My movers. I'm leaving. Actually, I already left.'

She stared at me for a little bit, and I stared right back. Even as disheveled and tired as she was, Jenn was still a gorgeous woman. And the way she looked at me, the tone of voice with which she spoke to me, her clumsy efforts to befriend me over the last year or so, it all bespoke of a good heart. I decided she was an okay girl. A pain in the ass, yes, but basically a decent person. She said, 'I'm gonna miss you, Porter Ellis. Who'da thunk *that*?' Then she put her head on my shoulder, and I put my arm around her, and motioned to the suitcase, and asked, 'Where are you coming from?'

She told me what led up to her retirement, which I'm sure she's already discussed with you in great detail. I felt terrible for her. The majority of the factors that helped end that particular chapter of her life were beyond her control. I could relate.

After she finished her truly awful story, she asked me to tell her exactly what happened with Beep.

So I told her. And she listened. And after I finished, she said exactly one word: 'Rebuild.'

Right away, I said, 'Absolutely not.' Of course I'd thought about doing just that – I spent almost two months driving across the country, during which time I had nothing to do *but* think about *everything* – and I still couldn't envision myself getting enthused about a theoretical Beep Two.

She said, 'Why not? You already own the piece of real estate, and I'm sure once the ashes are gone, you'll be able to build on it again. You can start over. *Anybody* can start over.'

I said, 'I know I can. It's more a matter of desire, which right at this moment, I have none of.'

She put her arms around me and said, 'The desire will come, Porter Ellis.'

I gave her shoulder a squeeze and kissed her forehead. Then I leaned my head on to hers – I'm a few inches taller than she is, so it felt like a natural position for us – and we sat there for, I don't know, five or ten minutes until the Super showed up with my key.

**JENN BRADFORD** While Porter Ellis ran into his apartment and grabbed whatever it was he'd left in there, I went into my place, kicked my suitcase across the room – stubbing the shit out of my toe – then I walked over to my piano, plopped down on to the bench, and repeatedly banged my forehead on the keyboard.

A minute or two into my headbanging, Porter Ellis came in, closed the door and said, 'Jenn, if that's your next record, I'm dying to hear it.'

I gave the keyboard one more bang, then said, 'No, *this* is my next record.'

**PORTER ELLIS** Jenn then proceeded to play a jaunty, swinging version of Nat King Cole's 'Straighten Up and Fly Right'. Then she did a Duke Ellington song, 'Don't Get Around Much Any More'. She followed that up with a blues tune I didn't recognize – it might've been something by Muddy Waters – and then wrapped up her mini-concert with a slick rendition of the Miles Davis song 'Four'.

I had no idea.

**JENN BRADFORD** Porter Ellis gave me a standing ovation – actually, he was already standing, so it's not like he specifically got up to clap, but for the sake of argument, I'll call it a standing ovation – and then he said, 'I would buy *that* record in a heartbeat.'

I said, 'Don't hold your breath, Porter Ellis. Retired means retired. I'm done. No recording, no more gigging, no more nothing. Except for this piano, I'm giving every piece of my equipment to charity.'

He said, 'How about an epilepsy charity? My sister has it.'

I said, 'Epilepsy it is.'

He thanked me, then said, 'That's too bad you're done, Jenn. You're an excellent jazz vocalist. For about six months before Beep opened, I looked all over the city for a good female singer to book for our eighth week, and you're just as good as the majority of them. If not better.'

Him saying that meant a lot to me, because this was a man who had some pretty high standards. Plus in terms of jazz, he knew his stuff, even more than Zach with his indie rock. I said, 'Thank you, Porter Ellis. I know how much you hated my albums, so that's big of you to say.'

He snorted, then said, 'I don't *hate* your albums.'

I said, 'Do you like them?'

He looked at his watch, then smiled and said, 'No time to answer such a loaded question. Gotta run. Busy, busy, busy.'

And there was that Porter Ellis smile. It lit up his face. He didn't look generally messed up any more. I said, 'Porter Ellis, did you make a joke?'

He said, 'Yes, albeit a bad one.'

I said, 'It *was* a bad one. Sucky, even. We'll have to work on that.' Then I played him another song.

**PORTER ELLIS** It was an exquisite rendition of 'Lover Man'. Billie Holiday would've been proud.

**BILLIE HOLIDAY'S GHOST** I *was* proud.

**PORTER ELLIS** I said, 'Seriously, you should do this for a living.'

She said, 'Porter Ellis, I don't care about making a living. I am not leaving this apartment for a long, long time.' She stood up, opened her piano bench and pulled out a pen and some music paper. Then she wrote down her cell number and said, 'But I'll tell you what. Call me if you ever feel like bringing over one of your caramelized onion pizzas and a bottle of wine. If you do, I'll play you the entire Miles Davis songbook. Promise.'

I said, 'Maybe I'll take you up on it. But I still think you should consider doing this for real.'

She said, 'Yeah, well I think you should consider rebuilding your club.'

**JENN BRADFORD** He gave me an exaggerated eye roll, and I said, 'Don't you roll your eyes at me, Porter Ellis. I'm serious about this. Tell you what. If you ever reopen Beep, I'll help you promote. The club will be packed to the rafters every night. I'm a one-woman public relations dynamo.'

He rolled his eyes again – it was even more

exaggerated this time – and said, 'Tempting offer. And thank you. But don't hold your breath.' He kissed me again on the forehead and said, 'I really do have to leave. Maybe I'll call you about the pizza.'

I said, 'You should.'

He said, 'Maybe I will.'

He didn't. It was a long while before I saw Porter Ellis again.

MASUHARA JONES It wasn't even a month after Jenn retired before I started getting super bored. The only exciting thing in my life was T.J., and damn, was that boy getting consistently more exciting. He claims he's writing a book, and if he does, I'm sure you'll find out what his definition of 'exciting' is. It'd probably sell a lot of copies. T.J.'s a big pervert.

Anyhow, back to me being bored. Jenn hooked me up with some mad coin, so I was financially set for a while and wasn't gonna jump on to the first gig that came along. But there weren't any gigs coming along, so it turned out that wasn't a problem. I reached out to all my connections, posted ads on Craigslist and built a website, but nobody was looking for a tour manager, or a personal manager, or any kind of manager at all.

But I still wanted to stay on top of the music biz happenings, and that meant buying every magazine out there. And one of those magazines was *Rolling Stone*.

JENN BRADFORD Naomi was calling me every day to check in, and it seemed like every time she called, I was crashed. One day she said, 'Jenn, I read somewhere that one of the signs of depression is sleeping too much.'

I said, 'I read somewhere that one of the signs of being really tired is sleeping too much. I'm not depressed. I'm tired.' And I wasn't depressed. I was relieved. It had been practically nine years since I'd been that relaxed. Every day I became more positive that my decision to call it quits was the right one.

Masu also called me a lot, but she never asked how I was doing, and her lack of concern was refreshing. All I heard from everybody else in the world – parents, Travis, Naomi, record label people – was, 'Are you okay? How are you doing? Feeling good?' Masu and I barely even talked about my physical state, or my mental state, or the state of the entertainment industry. We talked about music plenty – yeah, I was retired from performing, but I'd never retire from listening, and there was this new Otis Redding reissue that neither of us could seem to get out of our CD players – but we didn't discuss anything about the music business. That is, until Zach's bullshit Princess story in *Rolling Stone* came out.

ZACH BINGHAM I'm kind of expecting Jenn to call immediately when the issue with my Princess article hits the stands at the end of July, but she's strangely silent. I'm pretty sure she's livid – there's no way she wouldn't be – although there's this small, perverse part of me that thinks there might be a chance she'll want to get back with me, if only out of a sense of irony. Regardless, I'll be shocked if she lets it go without any kind of confrontation.

Ironically, after what I consider to be the most passionate start to any of my relationships, things go sour with me and Princess almost immediately. I get one excellent month with her before she unceremoniously dumps me. And she does it the pussiest way imaginable – by a text message. Nine words and one symbol: WE'RE DONE. CHANGING MY CELL # SO DON'T BOTHER CALLING. And this is *before* the *Rolling Stone* comes out, but after it goes to press, so I can't change the article. Talk about mortifying.

I feel used by Princess, like the only reason she slept with me was so I'd write about it and make her seem more controversial, and less *American Idol*-y. She and her management must want to dirty up her image. Nonetheless, we had some interesting times together, most of which I plan to write about in my own book.

Anyhow, Jenn never calls – why would she; she probably thought I was using her to jumpstart my career – and at this point, I don't think I really care. I mean, walking away from her tour like that? She's a train wreck.

**JENN BRADFORD** After I read the article eight or nine times, I called both Naomi and Masu, and asked them what they thought I should do.

Naomi said, 'Let it go. Release that negativity into the ozone. He'll get paid back karmically.'

Masu said, 'I will happily kick his ass for you. I haven't kicked anybody in the balls since I kicked Kevin, and my Pumas are itchy, baby.'

So my choices were to listen to Naomi and handle it LA style, and let bygones be bygones, or listen to Masu and take an East Coast approach, and get violent.

I love Naomi, and she always gives me awesome advice, most of which I take, but I'm from Brooklyn, and this situation called for some East Coast action. And you can't imagine how badly Masu wanted in.

MASUHARA JONES When Jenn told me how she was going to pay our boy Zach back, I was like, 'Girl, you need backup. You're a lot of things, but you are not a fighter.'

Jenn goes, 'I'm not gonna beat him up, Masu. How stupid would it be for an interview subject to hit a writer? It'd be a public relations fiasco.'

I'm like, 'What do you care what other people think? You're retired.'

After a long pause, she goes, 'Hunh. You do have a point there.'

I'm like, 'If you do it right, violence solves everything. I'm gonna email you a link to some of my favorite stuff from *The Art of War*.'

She's like, 'Excuse me?'

I go, 'It's this philosophy book about fighting. Like *Zen and the Art of Motorcycle Maintenance*, except instead of being about fixing bikes, it's about kicking ass. Check it out. You'll be super bad.'

She's like, 'Masu, you're insane.'

I'm like, 'Yeah, but you still love me.'

JENN BRADFORD I didn't call Zach to tell him I was coming over. I skimmed through Masu's *The Art of War* webpage – it was interesting, but it was less about kicking ass and more about the philosophy of confrontation, which I don't think my pretty little hair-trigger ex-manager necessarily grasped – then headed to his apartment. Sneak attack, East Coast-style.

By the way, the paparazzi situation had improved immensely. There were sometimes a couple of them hanging out by the front door during the afternoon, but they were inconsistent, so about fifty per cent of the time, I was able to get in and out of the building without being bothered at all. Unfortunately, this wasn't one of those days. For some random reason, there were four snappers camped outside, which wouldn't do, because the last thing I needed was to have one of them follow me down to Zach's place. All of which meant I had to escape out the rear exit and wind my way through the piles of garbage. I guess it was a propos – walk through garbage to get to garbage.

Zach wasn't home when I showed up, so I got comfortable on his front porch, cranked up my iPod, and waited. And waited. And waited. I waited for over two hours. It was totally worth it.

ZACH BINGHAM I'm coming home from selling some promo CDs at the used record stores on St Mark's Place, and there's Jenn parked on the front steps of my building, cocooned in headphones, bopping to her music, looking cheerful and completely at ease. Like I said, it was inevitable she'd get in touch, but I didn't figure she'd ambush me. Most of the time, people of her stature don't just *show up*.

I'm not nervous or anything. The fact that she's here means there's a chance she finds the article kind of silly. Maybe she doesn't take it personally. Maybe she'll be civil.

Or maybe not.

**JENN BRADFORD** Zach walked up to me with a big, fat, phony smile plastered on his face and said, 'I swear I was gonna call you, Jenn. I can't believe you bailed on your tour. That is so cool. Unprecedented. Seriously, can I do another piece on you? You're, like, the most sought-after person in music. *Spin* will love it.'

I said, 'Yeah, well, how'll *Rolling Stone* feel about it?'

He said, 'I don't think *Rolling Stone* will be using my services any more.'

I said, 'Oh, gee, why not? Doesn't your editor want to hear about which female vocalist you're going to fuck next? I mean, that's the best way for you to make a splash, right? Interview a singer, then fuck the singer, then write about it? That's the Zach Bingham plan, right?'

He said, 'So you're saying you didn't dig the Princess article?'

**ZACH BINGHAM** Yeah, it's true, I haven't written anything for *Rolling Stone* since Princess, probably because the feedback on that article was unbelievably negative. One of the few staffers up there who I'm still friendly with tells me they got almost 3,000 emails about the piece, over 2,800 of which were negative. I don't ask my friend exactly what the emails say. I'm not that much of a masochist.

**JENN BRADFORD** I stayed calm, which is what *The Art of War* says you're supposed to do in these situations. Good stuff.

**ZACH BRADFORD** The weird thing is that she's got this beatific, almost sexy smile, like she's psyched to see me, like she wants to mess around, like she's still into me. So I say, 'You look great, Jenn. Calm, even.'

She says, 'The Princess thing was, um, quite the surprise, Zach. It must've taken a ton of courage to tread in the same water again, especially considering what happened with us.'

I say, 'What did happen with us?'

She says, 'Nothing. Absolutely nothing. We were nothing. *You* were nothing.'

And then the most childish, most idiotic thing I've ever said in my entire life jumps out of my mouth: 'Are you jealous that I fucked Princess, Jenn?'

**JENN BRADFORD** Was I jealous? My knee-jerk reaction was that he was the most arrogant delusionoid in New York City, and anybody who's lived in New York City for more than, like, six seconds, is well aware that we have more than our fair share of arrogant delusionoids.

But asking was I jealous is a totally legitimate question. At one time, I liked Zach, liked him quite a bit, and he knew that, because I told him time and again. He could be fun, he was smart, he helped me out of my dating funk, and he had that utterly lickable neck. So sure, there might've been a bit of jealousy hanging around.

But on the other hand, we'd been drifting apart – probably drifting since right after we got back together after our first post-*Rolling-Stone*-article break-up – and it was all but inevitable that we'd break up. Thing is, neither of us was ballsy enough to proactively pull the plug. We figured – or at least *I* figured – that a few weeks of no phone calls or emails would kill it. Considering what he did with Princess – and considering he felt compelled to tell the whole magazine-reading world about it – I guess he got it. And I guess he wanted to stick it to me.

That all being the case, jealousy was not an option. Anger was. Calmness went out the window. Sorry, Sun Tzu.

**ZACH BINGHAM** The sheer quantity and quality of curse words that Jenn drops on me is awe-inspiring. She calls me names that are rancid enough to make Lil' Kim blush. She tells me to do things to myself that are not only physically impossible, but are so disgusting that I actually get a little nauseous.

And then she lets loose with the shot heard around the world.

**BILLIE HOLIDAY'S GHOST** It wasn't only the shot heard around the *world*. It was the shot heard around the *afterworld*.

**JENN BRADFORD** All I can say is that it was a good thing I'd retired from performing when I punched Zach Bingham in the jaw. I jammed my right pinky but good, and it would've put me on the disabled list for a month.

**ZACH BINGHAM** All the magazines and newspapers get it wrong. They say Jenn broke my jaw, and that I had to get it wired shut, and that I lost two teeth in the process. Wrong, wrong, wrong. Nothing's broken and my natural teeth are all still in my mouth. The worst injury is to my cheek, which gets sliced open by one of Jenn's rings. There's a lot of blood, and it requires stitches, and I bruise up pretty badly, and the bruise and the stitches are what all the dudes from *The New York Times*, *Spin* and *Maxim* see – and that's what they write about. Nobody tries to interview me. Nobody tries to get my side of the story. It is all photos and innuendo.

So to set the record straight: Jenn Bradford did not break my jaw, nor did she knock out any of my teeth. I did *not* get beaten up by a girl.

**JENN BRADFORD** Zach can deny and deny all he wants, but I opened up a can of whup-ass on that Weenie Boy. Oh, did he tell you about that knee-shot to the balls I gave him? Brilliant. Masu was so proud.

**ZACH BINGHAM** Okay, yeah, that's right, she gets me in the jewels. But at that point, I'm not fighting back, so it's a gimme.

**BILLIE HOLIDAY'S GHOST** Now I'm not one to condone violence, but I definitely believe in exorcising demons, and if Jennifer had to put a hurtin' on Mr Bingham's face and privates to make the next step in her life, well, who am I to argue? A girl's gotta do what a girl's gotta do. That was always my philosophy when I had to deal with Duke Ellington.

Truth be told, Jennifer didn't need a man. She *thought* she did – to an extent, she almost always thinks she does – but that simply wasn't the case. All she needed was herself and her music. But it so happened that right at that moment, she needed something else, some positive feminine energy, and I knew Naomi and Masuhara would provide that.

Plus she also needed to stop reading *The Art of War*. I've met Sun Tzu, and he is a freak. And not in a good way, like Miles Davis.

Anyhow, she needed to purge all men from her life. *All* men.

Deep down, Jennifer knew that solitude and abstinence would help enable her to go forward with her life, to move to the next chapter. And it was an important chapter at that.

But I wasn't worried, because as far as I could tell, there were no men in the picture to nudge Jennifer off of her preordained path.

# Time Out
## New York

### February 6–13, 2011

**CLUBS**
***BEEP BEEP 'N' BEEP BEEP . . . YEAH!***
**The Village jazz scene gets a much-needed shot in the arm – again.**

### by Benjamin Weissman

One year ago this week, Beep opened.

One year ago this week. Beep closed.

The allegedly hip jazz joint – and I say 'allegedly' because we can't find a single person who was actually in attendance on the club's sole evening of existence – will reopen exactly one year after it burnt to the ground in a spectacular fire that left nobody hurt except for Beep's owner and mastermind, *Billionaire.com* billionaire Porter Ellis.

Fortunately, Ellis's pain was of the emotional variety. 'You will not believe the amount of fireproofing we've done,' he sighs. 'We were one hundred per cent up to code last year. Now we're two hundred per cent up to code, if not more. You could come in there with a flamethrower, and nothing would happen.' He chuckles, then adds, 'But hopefully nobody's going to test that.'

We were told that opening night the first time around was a star-studded affair, but Beep Version 2.0 will be a mellower evening. 'This time around, we're going to cater to *everybody*,' Ellis says. 'The reason I opened the club in the first place was because I love jazz, and it took me months to realize that my paradigm last year was geared toward the upscale demographic. It's sad that it took a fire to make me see that wasn't what I wanted. The fire might well have been the best thing to happen for the Greenwich Village jazz consumer since John Coltrane burned up the Village Vanguard back in 1962. Of course, Trane's fire was figurative.'

Ellis notes that in contrast to last year's high-end décor, Beep's new interior is spartan and welcoming, a patent reflection of Ellis's vision. 'The seating is comfortable,' he explains. 'Nothing fancy, nothing trendy, just chairs you can sit in for three sets without your hindquarters falling asleep. All you'll see when you walk in are the comfortable chairs, and the stage, and the bar. That's it. Less is more. The only thing that's similar to what we had last year is the big music-themed collage on the back wall.'

'How did you replace the sound system that apparently caused the fire in the first place?' I ask.

'On the advice of my lawyer. I'm going to refrain from commenting on that.'

As for the bookings, well, let's say Ellis is taking the altruistic route. 'We're bringing in top-notch international talent, but our cover charges will be only between $7.50 and $15.00, with only a one-drink minimum. So the most anybody will ever have to spend at Beep is $20.00.' (Ellis tactfully doesn't mention that you can't walk out of the Vanguard, or the Blue Note, or Birdland for less than fifty bucks a head.) 'I'm well aware this won't be a profitable venture, but as long as I don't start completely hemorrhaging cash – which, based on my account-ant's projections seems like an impossibility – I'm in for the long haul.'

Ellis says that the club's first performer is a surprise, and a big one at that. How about a hint? 'Nope. But trust me. You'll like it.'

Porter Ellis is a convincing guy. We trust him. We'll be there.

**Beep reopens its doors on February 14th. Artist(s) T.B.A.**

PORTER ELLIS Yes, I did it. I Beeped again. Why? Simple. I had nothing else to do.

I received some intriguing offers in the interim, the majority of which would probably have been quite profitable, but I chose not to accept. For instance, an investment group in California wanted me to help them put together a proposal to buy the Los Angeles Dodgers. That was an interesting proposition, and their presentation was outstanding, but I don't care for sports, especially baseball. Then there was another group who claimed they had devised a search engine that was more powerful than Google. Again, a phenomenal presentation, but again, no interest.

If I may be honest for a moment, when I launched *Billionaire.com*, I didn't find it particularly interesting . . . but I was very interested in making money to help my family, so I stuck with it, and look what happened. Only five years later, I was in a position where I could pick and choose from a myriad of business models. Unfortunately, in my mind, the pickings were slim.

So after weeks and weeks of contemplating my navel, I called, and text messaged, and emailed my Beep team and told them all that I wanted to reopen our doors on February 14 – about four months from then – and if they wanted in, they should say yes now, or forever withhold their piece.

Each and every one of them said yes. I was thrilled, more thrilled than I could have ever imagined. It was a new beginning, and as a bored, just-turned-forty-year-old, a new beginning was exactly what I needed.

**JENN BRADFORD** Yes, I did it. I sold each and every piece of my music gear and gave the money to charity. The only thing I kept was my acoustic piano. Just because I was retired didn't mean I was dead, and the only way anybody could ever get me to stop making music would be to kill me.

As usual, Masu thought I was nuts. She said, 'Girl, you're gonna wake up one day and be like, *Where's my Fender Rhodes? Where's my jillion-dollar mixing board? Oh yeah – it's at the Salvation Army!* And you're gonna be sooo pissed.'

I said, 'I told you, I'm gonna get a job at Whole Foods, and if I want to buy some equipment, I'll ask my manager for more hours.' Actually, a retail gig wouldn't have been necessary, because my accountant set me up so that if I lived smart and invested wisely, my royalties would most likely cover my bills for the rest of my life. And living smart meant downsizing my living quarters again.

Unlike when I bought my condo in, like, six seconds, I had to be a bit more careful about how I handled this particular purchase, because I was tired of moving, and I wanted to plant some roots. So believe it or not, after weeks and weeks of research, and phone calls, and legwork, I decided to move out to the suburbs of New Jersey. And I say 'believe it or not' because my new place – a small two-bedroom house with a backyard that has plenty of room for an infrared grill – is a good forty-five-minute car ride from Manhattan, and an hour from Brooklyn.

I'd been a city chick for my whole life, and it was time to give the country a shot. Not that New Jersey was the country, but you get the point.

**NAOMI BRAVER** At first I was pissed at Jenn when she told me she was moving to Jersey. If she was gonna move anywhere, it should've been to LA. She would've been close to me, and to her brother, and to the ocean. So I totally went off on her.

**JENN BRADFORD** Naomi's Cali cool went right out the window.

She said, 'Everybody out here is fake. I mean, there are plenty of nice people, but I don't have a Jenn, and there aren't any Jenns out here, and even if there are, I can't find them, but I can't come home because I love acting, and I'm getting good, and I'm getting parts, but I'm getting lonely, not that Travis isn't awesome, but it would be nice to have a girl around—'

I finally interrupted her, because when Naomi got on one of her rolls, it could go on for hours. I said, 'Listen, I'm okay with leaving the City, but I'm not okay leaving the East Coast.'

She finally calmed down and said, 'Okay, but you have to give me your word that since you've decided to be a lazy-ass non-worker for the rest of your life, you have to spend at least four weeks of the year out here.'

I said, 'Word given.' And I've kept my word. Matter of fact, soon as you're done grilling me here, I'm hopping on a plane and going to Los Angeles to see my girl.

**PORTER ELLIS** The music press was hounding me practically non-stop about which artist would be the first to grace Beep's new stage. My mantra to them was, 'Trust me, you'll want to be there.'

The problem was, I wasn't sure if the *artist* would want to be there.

**JENN BRADFORD** I hate packing so much that I ended up giving away even more of my stuff. I mean, let's be honest here: were 216 pairs of André Courrèges go-go boots really necessary? And did I really need to haul 6,164 CDs out to Jersey? I thought of that John Lennon quote, imagining life with no possessions. Yes, I believed it would be easy if I tried.

I donated all but five pairs of the go-go boots to the Rock and Roll Hall of Fame, which sold most of them in a silent auction that raised money for music education. The CD purge, however, was much, much tougher. I spent hours deciding which ones to keep, and which ones to give to Masu, to T.J., to Naomi, to my brother, to my parents, and which ones to give to the garbage can. By the way, a goodly number of the ones that went to the garbage can were ones that otherwise would've gone to Zach. Not that I'm vindictive or anything.

At first, I divided everything into a dozen piles, which got subdivided so many times that I ran out of floor space, so I had to expand into the hallway and out to the elevator, which meant I had to leave my front door open, which probably wasn't the best idea, because you never know who'll wander in.

**PORTER ELLIS** The elevator door opened, and there's Jenn, sitting on the floor Indian-style in the hallway, back facing me, surrounded by hundreds and hundreds of compact discs. She was so wrapped up in doing whatever she was doing with the CDs that she didn't even notice my arrival. I watched her for a bit – she was fun to watch, it turned out – then cleared my throat and said, 'Hello.'

She spun around and hurled a Herbie Hancock CD at my head.

**JENN BRADFORD** Hey, I didn't know it was Porter Ellis. It could've been one of those paparazzi jerks.

**PORTER ELLIS** I ducked. The disc missed me and hit my old front door, and the box shattered. Plastic shrapnel everywhere.

I said, 'Nice to see you too, Jenn.'

She jumped up and ran over to me – knocking down about ten tall piles of CDs in the process – and wrapped me up in a hug. She said my name three times – 'Porter Ellis! Porter Ellis! Porter Ellis!' – then gave me a warm kiss, half-cheek and half-mouth. 'What brings you back to Redhook? Did you leave another useless piece of electronic gear in your bathroom or something?'

I said, 'None of my electronic gear is useless. Unlike your battalion of equipment.' I peeked inside her apartment, and save for the mountains of CDs, everything was boxed up. 'Moving, I see. The building turnover continues.'

She said, 'Yeah, it's the end of an era. Seriously, what're you doing here?'

I stepped inside her apartment, and was surprised at how few boxes there were. The last time I was by Jenn's place, there was barely any empty floor space, and I would've expected to see more boxes. A *lot* more boxes. I asked her, 'Have you already moved some stuff to your new place?'

She said, 'No, I got rid of a lot of things. Some clothes, some shoes, some books. But mostly, as you so aptly put it, my battalion of equipment.'

I know she said she was going to do it, but I had thought she was kidding. I was shocked. This was not good news. I said, 'Does this mean you've given up music altogether? I know you retired, but I figured you'd still keep playing. It always struck me that the only way anybody could ever get you to stop making music would be to kill you.'

She nodded and said, 'I couldn't have put it better myself. But I still have my baby grand, which I still play every day.'

I said, 'Good thing. Because, well, read this.'

**JENN BRADFORD** He handed me this flyer:

## BEEP PRESENTS
# JENN BRADFORD

Join vocalist and keyboardist Jenn Bradford in this intimate setting, and see the platinum-selling rock star make her debut as a solo jazz artist. Bradford will take on the music of Billie Holiday, Duke Ellington and Miles Davis, among many others. This is a once-in-a-lifetime event that is not to be missed.

- February 13 – February 21
- Three sets per night: 7.30, 9.00 & 10.30 p.m.
- Cover charge: $7.50 + one drink minimum

**BEEP**
**41 W. Greenwich St**
**New York City**

*For more information or reservations,*
*please call the Beep hotline:*
*(212) 415-BEEP*

It's not easy to shock me, but damn, was I shocked. I stared at it for a good two minutes, then I said, 'Porter Ellis, what the hell?' I think I kind of yelled it at him.

He took a step away from me and said, 'You won't do it?'

I said, 'Has anybody seen this?' Yes, it's true, I was yelling.

He said, 'Only my graphic designer.'

I read it again, then I said in a much quieter voice, 'You know I quit, Porter Ellis. I'm done. Retired means retired. How could you assume that I'd do a gig at your little club just because you waltz in here and hand me a piece of paper that says I will? And even if I did say yes, how could you assume I'd be able to slap together three sets' worth of material in three weeks? This sort of bull-in-a-china-shop technique may work in one of your high-powered business thingies, but I am not a business. This isn't the way I work.'

He took a deep, sad breath, and said, 'So you're not going to do it.'

He reached to take the flyer from me, but I snatched it back. 'Hells, yeah, I'm gonna do it. What time's sound-check?'

Man, that Porter Ellis has a killer smile.

**PORTER ELLIS** I didn't really send out the flyer. I printed up a single copy, and that one was for her eyes only. We didn't want to promote the show too much, because we didn't want it to be a zoo on opening night. We knew the press and the public would hear about the shows via word of mouth soon enough, so we'd have plenty of zoo to deal with the rest of the week. But I wanted that first night to be intimate.

**JENN BRADFORD** The next three weeks were hell. Why? Well, try learning the music and lyrics for about fifty songs while relocating from one state to another, and let me know how it works out for you.

Okay, it wasn't really that bad. I mean, how awful is it listening to your favorite records by Ella Fitzgerald and Sarah Vaughan, and by Dinah Washington and June Christy, along with Cassandra Wilson over and over again? Truthfully, once I chose and transcribed my repertoire, it was a breeze.

I ended up spending more time working on my presentation than the music. I couldn't rely on licking the piano and telling sex jokes any more. I had to be a big girl, and let the music speak for itself. I had to balance being a true artist and an entertainer, all while staying true to myself. I also realized I could no longer wear my baby-doll shirts, or my short skirts, or my fuck-me pumps. Everything had to change: my sound, my attitude, my look. I had to be the classiest broad I could be. I had to grow up. As recently as one year ago, I would've kicked and screamed about it. Now I was ready.

Was I nervous? Suffice it to say that the week before opening night, I slept a grand total of, like, six seconds. If that.

**PORTER ELLIS** The week before opening night, I slept a grand total of six seconds. If that. It felt like I spent the entire week staring at the clock, willing it to move faster.

Finally, February 13th.

It was a typical New York winter night. Bitter cold, but no wind or snow to keep anybody holed up in their apartment. Anybody who needed to be at Beep had no excuse not to be at Beep.

I told Jenn that the first set was scheduled for seven thirty, and she didn't have to show up until seven unless she felt compelled to bond with the piano for a while, so I got there at five o'clock, just in case she decided to arrive early. It turned out she didn't arrive early, which meant I was forced to stew in my own juices for almost two hours.

Jenn showed up right on time, right at seven o'clock, and let me tell you, that woman cleans up nicely.

**JENN BRADFORD** What did I wear? A Carmen Marc Valvo black velvet cocktail dress with matching gloves, a pair of Amina slingbacks with three-inch heels, and I brought along a cute white pashmina from Bloomie's in case Porter Ellis's heating system sucked.

The hair? I had it done in an up-do, so I could show off my 1.2-carat bling earrings, and my four-carat super-bling necklace.

**PORTER ELLIS** I don't like to curse. I think it's undignified, and say what you will about me, I always try to carry myself with dignity.

Also, I'm not a religious man.

But all I could say when Jenn Bradford floated into my club was, 'Jesus God, holy fucking shit.'

**JENN BRADFORD** I guess Porter Ellis thought I looked pretty okay.

He jumped up from the bar, ran over and offered to take my coat. I gave him a careful kiss on the cheek – it had taken me about an hour to put on my makeup, and nothing on my face was gonna get smudged on my watch – and looked around the club.

It was nice. More than nice. Gorgeous. Blacks, and silvers, and mellow lighting, and comfy-looking chairs, and an astounding Bosendorfer piano, and a fully stocked bar. It was sleek and modern, but timeless and unpretentious. And, unlike virtually every other jazz club in New York – unlike virtually every other jazz club in the world, for that matter – it was *pristine*.

But something was wrong. Massively wrong.

Nobody was there.

The place was empty. Apart from me, and Porter Ellis, and a piano, and that collage on the wall that looked like my old apartment's floor on a good day. That was it.

I said, 'Where the hell is everybody, Porter Ellis?'

**PORTER ELLIS** I'd been trying to decide how to handle this moment since I came up with the idea two months prior. I considered actually writing something out, but that might have seemed contrived, and the scenario was contrived enough to start with, so I thought it would be more prudent to speak off-the-cuff, from my heart. Off-the-cuff isn't my default mode, but this was a special situation. Very special.

**JENN BRADFORD** He took a deep breath, then looked at me, but only saying 'looked at me' takes away from his intensity and warmth, his confidence and assuredness. I'd never been looked at with that particular combination before, and I have to admit, it kind of turned me on.

And the fact that he looked super hot in his Hugo Boss suit didn't hurt.

**PORTER ELLIS** She told you I looked confident and assured? Well, I wasn't. Not even close.

**JENN BRADFORD** He said, 'Remember the day we ran into each other in the hallway? The day you told me you retired?' I nodded. 'Remember how you played a few songs for me? Nat King Cole, and Duke Ellington and such?' I nodded again. 'It touched me, Jenn. It moved me. It everything-ed me. And I wanted to feel that again, but in a proper setting, with a proper piano, and both of us in a proper emotional state. We were both pretty out of it that day, remember?' I nodded again. All I could do was nod. I sure as hell couldn't speak.

He ran his hand through his hair. It got all messed up, but neither of us really cared. He said, 'Also, I know that after this week, you're going to be in the public eye again. You're going to love playing this music, and people are going to love listening to you play it, and you're going to make a record that will put you on a career path that I think will make you happy and fulfilled, and you're going to travel the world, and barely be home ... and I decided that before that happens, for one night, I wanted you all to myself.'

Damn, he was good. I said, 'Porter Ellis, if you're saying what I think you're saying, you can have me to yourself for more than one night.'

There was that smile again. He said, 'Really?'

I said, 'Yeah. Two nights. Maybe three, if you're really nice.'

**PORTER ELLIS** Then she glided over to me and kissed me on the neck. It was only a tiny kiss – almost as if a warm, wet butterfly had landed on my shoulder – and it was highly appropriate.

And then she kissed me on the mouth.

**JENN BRADFORD** For a guy who I'd always thought was totally stuffy, he was an amazing kisser – so amazing that I stopped worrying about ruining my makeup.

**PORTER ELLIS** I have no idea how long we kissed for. After a while, Jenn pulled away, looked at her watch, and said, 'It's almost seven thirty, Porter Ellis. Just about time for the first set.'

I said, 'Be sure and save your energy. You have two more sets to do tonight. Plus you have to be ready for the real opening night tomorrow.'

She said, 'Honey, for you, I have enough energy for, like, six zillion sets.'

Then the gifted, the beautiful, the brilliant, the astounding Jennifer Marie Bradford played me the finest concert I'd ever heard, or ever will hear. And she hasn't stopped playing for me since.

**BILLIE HOLIDAY'S GHOST** The only thing that was missing on stage – the only thing that would've made it entirely flawless – was a sexy, curvaceous black background vocalist with a gardenia in her hair. But that's only my opinion. I think both Mr Ellis and Jennifer were plenty happy without me.

For that matter, Jennifer didn't need me at all any more. She had found what she was looking for – and what she deserved – which enabled her to follow her preordained musical path, which was why I was there in the first place. It saddened me to leave her, but what made it okay was that I knew that, in terms of her music, she was set for life.

So all of a sudden, I found myself with a little bit of extra time on my hands – which meant I could go to work on Mr Stewart.

**T.J. STEWART** Say *what*? Woman, I am perfect just the way I am . . .

# The New York Times

## February 17, 2011

### A NEW BEGINNING
*Jenn Bradford Turns Over a New Leaf at Beep*

## by Carole Anne Rudolph

As a musician, if you stylistically reinvent yourself on a regular basis, you stand to lose a good chunk of your fan base, also on a regular basis. For example, look at Elvis Costello. He's been through several guises – punker, New Waver, jazzer, soulster, lounger – and despite the consistently high level of his recordings, his sales figures have been trending downward since the mid-1980s.

As demonstrated by her performance at the Greenwich Village jazz venue Beep, Jenn Bradford isn't the least bit concerned about what her core listeners think of her. Ms Bradford's musical approach has undergone several Costello-like permutations, but she seems to have found one that will stick, and the million-plus people who bought her smash hit song 'Addition by Subtraction' won't be happy about it.

Ms Bradford is now a jazz singer. A real one. And one to watch out for.

During Thursday night's late show, Ms Bradford – who is returning to the public eye after a year-plus hiatus from live concerts and recording – reworked and personalized such diverse selections as the chestnut 'On the Sunny Side of the Street', Joni Mitchell's esoteric 'The Dry Cleaner from Des Moines', and James Brown's 'It's a Man's World'. And it was all voice and piano, but Ms Bradford didn't need anybody else. Addition by subtraction, indeed.

A winning performer, Ms Bradford's revamped stage presence is elegant, yet she has not sacrificed her innate sincerity and keen sense of humor. She joked with the enthusiastic audience, she cheerfully plugged Beep's upcoming schedule, and she charmingly flirted with club owner Porter Ellis. Hardcore jazz listeners might think of Ms Bradford's populist patter as pandering. I call it entertainment.

If Ms Bradford continues down this path, she'll undoubtedly alienate a whole bunch of record buyers. But those who stick with Jenn Bradford will be purchasing her work for years to come.

**BILLIE HOLIDAY'S GHOST** The remainder of Jennifer's week-long tenure at Beep was simply lovely. Naomi and Jennifer's brother Mr Bradford surprised Jennifer when they flew in from California to take in the shows. Jennifer's immediate family, and extended family, and extended *extended* family all came by to show their support. Masuhara and Mr Stewart were there each and every night, each and every set, holding hands and, as they used to say in the gossip columns, canoodling.

Beep was packed to the rafters, and the vibe was terrific. Nobody gave anybody any attitude, nobody was being elitist, nobody hassled anybody else. It was all about the music, which is exactly how it should always be.

You may be asking right now, *What about that club owner of ours?* Well, the entire week, Mr Ellis didn't miss a single one of Jennifer's songs, oftentimes shirking his duties as the boss. To him, watching and listening to Jennifer sing the works of his favorite artists was more important than being a businessman, and anybody who knows Mr Ellis knows that that's saying something. During Jennifer's sets, he ignored his staff, and his cell phone, and, well, *everything*. He merely sat at the end of the bar and watched her, just watched. And in between each tune, Jennifer would watch him watching her, and to my eyes, it couldn't have been more beautiful.

For Jennifer Bradford and Mr Porter Ellis, it went on like that for a long, long time.

# Acknowledgments

Massive props to my eternally patient, always giving, and mad cool editrix Catherine Cobain, who always pushes me to be the best A.M. I can be, and who made certain that Jenn didn't actually turn into a slutty bitchface. Also, a shout-out to her fellow LBD and Headline hotties Claire Baldwin, Sara Porter, Sam Combes, Lucy Henshaw, Sarah Thomson, Joanna Kaliszewska, Jo Liddiard and Emily Furniss.

And as always, much love to my mega-hot, mega-supportive, mega-*everything* partner, Natty Boo.